Death in Hamburg

A Barry and Rebecca Forester adventure

By John Barnes

Copyright 2012
By John Barnes

To granddaughters Sophia and Milla

Other Barry and Rebecca Forester adventure books available on Amazon.com and Kindle:
    Death in Sentari
    Death in Montevideo
    Death in LA (available January, 2013)

Other books by John Barnes available on Amazon.com....
    Connie and Russ
    Retirement: One man's adventures
     exploring life's final frontier

Prologue

Sandy Springs, Georgia
November 30, 2009
Reflections

Rebecca drove Barry to the hospital in their black Honda Accord, staying under the speed limit because she'd gotten a speeding ticket the week before. She moved west along Atlanta, Georgia's sunny ring road, glancing occasionally at her husband, who seemed unusually silent.

"How you feeling, Bear?" she asked as she turned off the freeway.

"Knee continues to hurt like hell," Barry said. He'd torn a tendon playing tennis, and was about to undergo outpatient arthroscopic surgery.

"Aw. Did you get the Vail reservations?" she asked.

"I did, but I'm having second thoughts. Shouldn't we be at home while the house is being shown?"

"No, it's better to be away," Rebecca said. "We get so little time together as a family. The kids love Vail and Beth's getting to be a really good skier."

Their children, Jason, 16, and Beth, 14, would return from their Michigan boarding school in three weeks. Then the family would head west to ski.

Yesterday, their Sandy Springs house had its first showing for local realtors. Several attendees told Rebecca that their place should sell quickly. She and Barry hoped so. In the past two weeks they'd spent almost $9,000 on repairs and touch-ups, the bulk of that to stage their house's interior and exterior.

Since moving to Sandy Springs three years ago, they'd deliberately left their four-bedroom house's bland exterior as is, fixing only what needed fixing, updating kitchens and bathrooms, repainting and re-carpeting, but leaving the outside unchanged so as not to attract attention.

They always bought in the best subdivisions, paying cash. They also paid cash for food and almost everything else. The credit cards they used often had fake names and addresses.

"I'm going to need new glasses and contact lenses soon," Barry said. He saw the hospital in the distance and pointed it out to Rebecca, which irritated her. He knew she knew its location.

"Didn't you just have your eyes checked?"

"Yes, but my last new glasses were five years ago. Also, our dentist said I need two new teeth. I'm going to an orthodontist next week. He'll tell me if I need implants or a bridge."

"I'd go with implants," Rebecca said as she pulled into the hospital parking lot.

"You already told me that," Barry said.

Only their trust lawyer and their CIA contact, Chester Field knew and used their business phone numbers. Individually and as a couple, they remained unknown to any of the world's Intelligence agencies, their anonymity making them attractive to clients and allowing them to charge a premium for their services.

When traveling, they employed disguises and false identities, often using more than one in a given day. They seldom appeared together when working. If possible, they left behind no fingerprints, DNA or other evidence.

"I turn fifty on July Fourth, Becs. I'm starting to fall apart."

"You still look pretty good to me, Bear," Rebecca said. This was true. Barry had barely an ounce of fat on him, stood six feet tall and had all his hair. By anybody's standard, he remained a physically attractive man; but she understood the unspoken context of his complaint about aging.

He'd screwed up their last assignment in Uruguay, uncharacteristically letting his guard down. He'd been captured by enemies. She'd had to rescue him, which hurt his pride.

She drove around almost five minutes, becoming increasingly irritated, finally finding a parking place. Barry let her hold his arm and help him hobble slowly between cars through the parking lot to the hospital.

He was slowing down, she thought. He'd started napping occasionally in early afternoon, probably because he was bored. This worried her. Each relied on the other. Their lives depended on this.

As they approached the hospital's front door, Barry stopped.

What?" Rebecca said.

"If they discover that the Pole is still alive, would

you go after him?"

Rebecca hadn't thought about the Pole since leaving Uruguay in early November. Hidden by shadows across a cobblestone street from the Montevideo pier and 50 yards away, she'd shot him. He'd toppled into the sea. The next day he was declared missing and most probably dead, but the body had never been recovered.

"What made you think about the Pole now, Bear?"

"I don't know. Hateful man. Would you go after him again?"

"If it can be proven incontrovertibly that he survived, then maybe. What do you think?"

"I don't know."

"If it happens, we can talk about it, okay?"

"Okay," Rebecca said. She opened the hospital entrance door and helped Barry in. "Let's get you well first. Then we can talk more about the Pole."

Escape

Tykocin, Poland
September 8, 2009
Stolen

Blond eighteen-year-old Ania Olinska, 5' 4" and 105 pounds, headed briskly towards the barn through five a.m. darkness.

She planned to milk the cows, return to the house, drink a glass of milk, eat a piece of toast with jam, get organized for school and board the school bus.

She was her class's best student, her IQ 146, or genius level. She'd been accepted by Krakow's Jagiellonian University, Poland's oldest and most prestigious.

Monday through Friday, from late August to late May, her bus stopped punctually for her at seven a.m. on the main road a mile away. Miss it and she missed school.

Tykocin, a small rural place of slightly more than 2,000 in Poland's northeast, had no high school. Most of the town's teenagers quit school by the time they turned 16.

During World War II, hardscrabble Tykocin developed a bad reputation. In 1941, Nazis, in collaboration with townspeople, rounded up the town's Jews, marched and trucked them to nearby Lopuchowo Forest, shot and left them dead and dying in freshly dug open pits.

Ania and many friends her age shared a vague shame growing up in such a notorious, drab and impoverished environment.

She felt vaguely uncomfortable around the town's few remaining silent or guilt-denying octogenarians, but this morning she was not thinking about any of that.

Born when her mother was 40 and her father 52, her parents were getting too old to run their small farm. Her father had heart trouble and no longer did much. He and his wife were desperate to sell their land, but so far there'd been no takers.

Ania worked long hours outside class helping her parents. Unlike most teenagers, she never complained. She eagerly moved through her days, anticipating the moment when she'd leave impoverished northeastern Poland and enter a bright new world.

****

Two masked men grabbed her as she reached the barn. They chloroformed, bound, gagged, blindfolded and threw her in the back of a panel truck.

For three days, she traveled inside various vehicles, only occasionally glimpsing daylight. Her captors gave her water and stale bread. She had to defecate in a pail. The windowless vans' corrugated steel floors made sleeping impossible.

At various stops, young girls, the majority blond like herself, joined her, many hysterical, some drugged and so spiritually lost they couldn't speak. Six hours or so later, a girl would be dropped off and another climb in back.

The girls who did speak Polish told of abductions similar to hers. Others mentioned phony job offers, or love affairs turned ugly. One girl said her family sold her for the equivalent of five hundred dollars U.S. so they could buy pigs.

For two nights and three days, various foreign men kissed, fingered, slapped, beat and raped her vaginally and anally, the same treatment others with her received.

Once Ania reached Hamburg, Germany, her captors confined her to a small room almost 24 hours a day for the first six weeks. There she slept, sponge-bathed herself, went to the bathroom and handled as many as 15 customers a day, not to include the brothel manager and his employees.

Every Friday morning, a doctor checked her for disease. Every Sunday morning, a woman came to cut her hair, check her teeth and clip her toe and fingernails. Her captors offered her drugs but she refused.

Weeks after arriving in Hamburg, she was moved to a brothel in another part of the city, but her life and routines did not change.

She lost track of days. Later, she realized it had been slightly less than 13 weeks from her abduction to the day her fortunes dramatically changed.

Montevideo, Uruguay
November 11, 2009
Survival

Thousands of miles southwest of Tykocin, the Pole struggled to avoid what others had already concluded was certain death.

His body tormented him with every move. He'd been shot through the shoulder earlier that day. Just ten minutes ago, a medic had given him a cortisone shot in this shoulder and another under his ribs, where he'd been shot earlier. The cortisone helped but could not completely mask the pain.

He'd been walking along the pier with a man helping him escape, and failed to spot a sniper in the shadows.

The shot grazed his neck and sent him into near panic. The sniper fired high twice more, the bullets whizzing past where his head had been. By then he'd started his fall into the murky, oily water and sunk from sight.

He allowed himself to sink deeper than he wished before struggling to stop his plunge and move upward. He'd always been a good swimmer, but his clothes, heavy shoes, bandaged shoulder and the rib cage wound made swimming almost impossible.

He started back up, holding his breath, staying under water as long as he could. He surfaced far under the pier where he couldn't be seen. That was the good news.

Coming up for air, he realized with horror that the water came to within four inches of the pier's floor, meaning he could not get his nose or mouth clear to breathe.

He sunk again and this time, when the top of his head hit the bottom of the pier, he tipped his head back as far as he could, scratching his forehead in the process. The first few times he tried this he swallowed water and feared he'd drown.

It took two more tries before he learned how to take in enough oxygen. If he relaxed and lay on his back when surfacing, he could inhale the needed air; but there were other problems.

The darkness, coupled with a pervasive claustrophobia caused by at most three to four inches of available air space, kept him frantic and almost overcome by claustrophobia.

He considered breaking for clear water, but knew that if he did, he'd be seen and dead soon after.

He forced himself through pain, boredom and terror to remain beneath the pier until the first hint of dawn, confident that by now the sniper and anyone else who'd watched him drown would be home asleep.

Quietly, tediously, he edged forward, hugging the pier, edging laboriously to where the big cargo ships moored.

Using his good arm, he climbed the first ladder he saw, one slow, painful rung at a time, exposed skin wrinkled, clothes and shoes soaked. He glanced at his Rolex, which remarkably still kept time. He'd been underneath the pier almost five hours!

Climbing out of the water exposed him. He expected someone to yell or shoot at him, so he stayed in shadows, concerned that the sniper or the police might return.

He stood over six-feet three inches, was heavily

muscled and bald-headed, meaning he stood out and would easily be remembered.

The Montevideo police and Uruguayan Intelligence had circulated bulletins on him. They'll still be seeking him, unaware that he'd fallen into the sea. He needed to get out of town now.

He tried his cell phone. Waterlogged, it no longer worked. He checked what he had. His fake passports and ID's had vanished during his time under the pier. His wallet contained a few hundred dollars in Uruguayan money, two U.S. twenty-dollar bills, Visa and MasterCards with a different surnames, plus Polish and German drivers licenses.

He found a slip of paper with the necessary phone numbers. Water had gotten to them and the ink had run. He could discern enough to make a reasonable guess as to what each number had been.

Fortunately, he'd earlier committed one number to memory. Best of all: He had the flash drive! He stared at it sealed safely inside the sandwich bag. Its data was worth millions if he survived the next few hours.

He calculated that he'd been awake almost 24 hours. He should sleep. His body wanted that; but he forced himself to stay awake. He must get away from the docks and out of the city.

Careful to keep in the shadows, he limped back towards Constitution Plaza, normally a ten-minute walk. In his present condition, it took longer. No buses ran. He'd looked for but had not seen any cabs.

One police car leisurely passed, the policeman eating a donut. He flattened himself against the side of an alley. The policeman looked in his direction but appeared to miss him.

Three hotels faced the Plaza. He could not enter any of them. His clothes had almost dried but were wrinkled and smelled of oil and brine. His flimsy cotton shirt hung in tatters. He'd be reported immediately. He must steal a car, but where?

The Hotel Pisa garage entrance was unguarded! He stayed in the shadows and limped in and up the ramp, praying that no one had seen him.

On the first level, he counted 16 cars but avoided them. There was a direct entrance into the hotel and a light on inside. Someone might be awake there.

He silently tiptoed up a second ramp to the next level and saw four cars. He tried their doors. All were locked. He heard footsteps He crouched between a Fiat and ancient Mercedes and held his breath.

A night watchman emerged from the ramp leading to the third level, paused, shone his flashlight carelessly around and continued down the ramp to the first level, footsteps echoing.

He took off his shirt. Pain shot through his shoulder and under his ribs, causing him to stop. Sweat appeared on his forehead.

He wrapped his shirt around his right hand. Thirty-nine years old, he still could press 400 pounds. So it was no surprise that with one blow he broke the Fiat's driver's-side window.

Fearing he'd be stopped if seen driving a car with a broken driver's window, he slowly and carefully, using his shirt to protect against cuts, removed as much glass as he could, gathered it in his shirt and gently placed the shards in a barrel half filled with old newspapers and cigarette butts.

Through the garage windows, he realized that it

was almost morning. A glance at his watch said five: fifty-five a.m.

Hot-wiring the car was easy. He coasted down the ramp with the engine off, then started the car as it entered Constitution Plaza. It quickly turned over and roared to life. He was free!

With relief bordering on euphoria, he headed along the coastline on an almost empty highway towards Punte del este, a two-hour drive. He checked the gas gauge. He had a quarter of a tank, enough to get him out of town. He'd worry about getting more gas once clear of the city.

Montevideo, Uruguay
November 12, 2009
Questions

Uruguay's Deputy Intelligence Chief, Alvarez Conrado, 62, and 48-year-old Blanca had a problem, which each appeared reluctant to solve.

In 1977, then special agent Alvarez rescued 16-year-old Blanca from a hostage situation. On each year's anniversary of that rescue, Blanca sent Alfredo a thank-you card. A year after both their spouses died in 2008, they met again and fell in love.

Since living together, Alvarez was beginning to resemble a penguin. He even walked like one. Blanca was putting on weight as well. They were shortening their lives, Alvarez believed, but would die well fed and happy. There was no way he could diet. Her cooking was that good.

This cool November evening, Alvarez stood on the pier where the night before he'd witnessed an unknown, unseen sniper shoot a psychopath named Wojciech Krzysztofski, causing him to drop like a stone into the sea.

Krzysztofski, nicknamed 'the Pole,' did not resurface, which was not surprising. Within the past 16 hours, he'd been shot in the shoulder, then hours later shot again, this time just below his rib cage, and now, apparently, he'd taken a bullet in the neck. No one suffering such wounds could survive a plunge into the cold, oily Atlantic Ocean.

Nevertheless, the harbor police sent divers under the pier to see if the Pole's body might have lodged there. Boats with wide nets dredged the close-in open sea and nearby inlets where detritus washed up. The Pole's body had not been found.

"We'll have one final go at it tomorrow," a detective named Jaws said. He got the nickname because his protruding jaw resembled that of Beavis in the TV cartoon series Beavis and Butthead, which had experienced brief popularity in Uruguay.

"Wouldn't the body have resurfaced by now?" Alvarez said. He glanced at his watch. It was almost Noon.

"You'd think so," Jaws said. "The current may have taken the body west. Sometimes bodies wash up miles from here. We had one like that just last year."

"The Latvian sailor. I remember," Alvarez said.

"There've been several, so we may not find the Pole's body for awhile."

"Be good to finally close the book on him," Alvarez said.

"A nasty man," Jaws said.

"The worst," Alvarez said. "Well, time to get home. Blanca's preparing pot roast."

"Lucky you. That'll put some more meat on your bones."

"I've already got the meat, Jaws," Alvarez said. "What's added will be fat. We'll have you and your wife over one of these nights."

"I'd like that," Jaws said. "I'm retiring soon. Wife and I are going to move in with an aunt in Argentina."

"I'm retiring in September," Alvarez said. "But you know that. Tell me when you find the Pole's body."

"Will do," Jaws said. "It should surface soon."

Hamburg, Germany
November 12, 2009
Escape

Because Ania acted meek, passively complicit and never complained, after several weeks, she was no longer the flavor of the month. Her captors ignored her.

Three men supervised the prostitutes in her brothel and lived separately from them in the back rooms. A third man was added on busy weekend evenings.

These supervisors tended to be large and muscular enough to keep order with the girls and handle rowdy guests, drunks and druggies.

During each 24-hour shift, a backroom supervisor was not permitted to leave. Each man got off every other day. While on the premises, they had food brought in and could sample any of the girls not with customers.

A fourth man stayed in or near his office adjacent to the building entrance. He handled rudimentary bookkeeping, maid service, house payroll, bill paying and other administrative details.

His shift lasted from ten a.m. until six p.m. He wore a suit, was considered 'management,' and answered to an upward chain-of-command located elsewhere.

Several times, Ania got glimpses of her brothel's outside management. A paymaster named Karl dropped by every Saturday morning to collect proceeds from the previous week.

Karl's boss, Fritz, usually showed up Wednesday afternoons. Fritz held meetings with the manager and backroom supervisors. These confabs usually lasted no more than an hour.

Fritz's presence intimidated both the house manager and backroom supervisors, who at times cowered in his presence and spoke disparagingly about him during his absence.

This morning at seven a.m., three months after Ania's Hamburg arrival, a backroom supervisor called in sick, meaning one of the two existing supervisors had to pull a 48-hour shift.

Anxious to get some air before the front room manager arrived and the day's shift began, the supervisor told his companion, Turku, that he was going out for coffee. He promised to bring back pizza.

Bored, Turku, a hairy monstrosity in his late 20's, six feet and close to 250 pounds, immediately headed for the room of the newest girl, a tiny Lithuanian blond carrying a teddy bear who'd arrived no more than ten hours ago.

While he busied himself beating and having sex with her, Ania, already fully dressed, quickly and quietly moved down the hall and entered Turku's unlocked room.

She took his cell phone, gun and 200 euros from his wallet. She checked to see if the gun was loaded, grabbed a handful of extra bullets and left.

From five doors away, she could hear Turku's victim's pitiful screams and moans. Standing silently in the open doorway, Ania stared at the emaciated young girl cowered naked in a fetal position, trembling in a corner.

Turku had not heard Ania's approach. He stood with his back to her, naked except for the gaudy gold chain around his neck. She smelled his sweat mixed with stale cigarettes and even more disagreeable odors coming through the open door of his victim's pitifully small adjoining toilet.

"Hey, Scheissekopf!" Ania said.

Turku turned, a smirk on his face. Seeing the gun, his smirk vanished. Wild with fear, his eyes frantically searched the barren room for a weapon.

Ania shot him in the stomach. He roared in anger and clutched the area where the bullet entered, as if this futile action would hold back the blood and negate the damage.

Her second shot hit him in the testicles. He doubled over, head still up, eyes again frantically searching, and collapsed face first into his already gathering blood.

Ania hurried to the manager's office and rifled through correspondence, keeping an eye out the front window for the second supervisor's return.

With the butt of her revolver, she broke the flimsy look on the manager's desk. In a lower drawer, she found a plastic bag filled with female driver licenses. She pawed around in the bag until she found a license with a photograph that resembled her.

The name on the license said Agnieszka Albin, hometown, Radosz, Poland. Good. For the time being, she'd be Agnieszka Albin, a fellow Pole an inch taller and two years older but otherwise a close enough match.

In a lower drawer, she found almost a thousand euros, which she pocketed. Done, she looked up and saw two girls standing in the hallway watching her.

"Please, go back to your rooms. I'll be gone soon," she said. All but one of the women sullenly shuffled off.

"They'll get you, you know," a tall, emaciated woman with stringy black hair said. She had big, drooping breasts, their huge dark nipples visible through her nightgown.

"Not if I get them first," Ania said.

The woman shrugged, not buying the bravado. Ania walked back to check on the supervisor. His dull eyes seemed unable to focus.

She considered shooting him again but ignored the impulse and left.

Outside, she saw she'd been living in an industrial neighborhood near the docks. Smoke stacks of big container vessels loomed over a series of dirty brick buildings and empty streets.

Cool morning airbrushed her skin. As she turned the corner, she saw the other backroom supervisor carrying a pizza, whistling and walking towards the building she'd just left.

Unaware of her, he put the pizza down and took

out keys to open the door. Too late, he sensed her presence behind him.

She shot him in the back of the head. While he lay dying, she went through his pockets, found 75 more Euros and change, wiped off the gun she'd use to kill Turku and him, left it beside the body, took his gun and ammo clip from the holster under his left arm, grabbed a slice of pizza, and this time left for good.

Los Angeles, California
November 12, 2009
Rogue

The Baron, birth name Walter Stolz-von-Neubach, 52, gazed uncomfortably across the table at his unprepossessing lunch companion. They sat alone in a private back room of a Korean restaurant on Wilshire Avenue, a half mile from Beverly Hills.

"Good food," the Baron said. The Baron's spicy marinated pork and steamed vegetables tasted okay but he did not feel comfortable with his guest, who called himself Rolph, an odd alias for an Asian.

"This is one of my favorite places when stopping in LA," Rolph said. His unhealthy looking pale white skin suggested life in a cold climate without much sun.

Random strands of wispy black hair covered part of his shiny, pink forehead. His cheap blue suit's shoulder seams puckered, the lapels unfashionably large. The heavy rough fabric looked synthetic.

"I'm glad we could have this meeting unobserved, and I apologize for holding it so far from Hamburg, but I'm sure, once you hear what I propose, that you'll understand," Rolph said.

"Don't mind at all," the Baron said. "I like LA. I welcomed an excuse to get away."

Thin-lipped, with sandy blond hair and of average height, the Baron had skin so pink and fresh it looked as if he never shaved. Well educated and urbane, he spoke fluent French, English and German, He was nobody's idea of an arms broker, which was to his advantage.

"You can talk freely in here. It's been swept," Rolph said.

"Good," the Baron said, not believing this. He presumed that Rolph was a general or other high-ranking North Korean official. North Korean private businessmen, if such people actually existed, did not roam the world. The country had nothing to sell other than nuclear assistance.

"So what do you have in mind?" the Baron said.

"I've assumed you're set up to deal with the Iranians?" Rolph said.

"Of course," the Baron said. "They haven't been buying much lately, parts and equipment, that's about it. I've helped some with that."

"Good," Rolph said. He'd ordered short ribs with cucumber kimchee basted with a spicy marinade that smelled good, making the Baron wish he'd ordered the same. He watched Rolph cut into his short ribs with knife and fork. Didn't Koreans use chopsticks?

When first entering the arms business, two men tried to jump the Baron inside a nondescript midtown office. The Baron buzzed a secret friend who handled the problem brutally and unequivocally.

Word got around. Despite his effete looks and manner, the Baron had no-nonsense outside muscle.

Since that one test, he'd not had problems, but you never knew.

Rolph put down his silverware. "I have something the Iranians want and I'm hoping you can deliver," he said.

"What is it?" the Baron said, believing he already knew. He waited eagerly. He'd taught German in a private school, sold insurance, then stocks and mutual funds, jobs he distained. Arms brokering paid considerably better, which today's meeting was about to demonstrate.

After a chance introduction while visiting friends in Slovenia, weeks later he closed his first arms contract, with the CIA as his first client.

Like other contractors who dealt with the CIA, every year he had to submit to a lie detector test, and every year he passed.

He didn't tell the CIA he also dealt with its enemies and the CIA did not ask, which he presumed meant they knew and didn't care.

"We have enriched uranium," Rolph said almost in a whisper. He did not say who 'we' was.

The Baron wondered if his lunch guest was rogue or a legitimate North Korean official, then decided it made no difference.

"We have a problem. There's no way we can get isotopic metals through the straits of Hormuz. The Americans have highly sophisticated new ways of detecting such shipments, no matter how miniscule. We're going to park the shipment near Hamburg. We need somebody reliable to handle the ground exchange, to include dealing with the Iranians, end-user certificates, everything."

"No problem."

"If you can do this," Rolph said, "you'll likely have the merchandise in your possession no more than a half hour to an hour. You'll move it to a private airfield, where it will be loaded and flown to Iran."

"Okay," the Baron said, still somewhat puzzled. He wondered where Rolph learned English. The man's accent was neither American nor British, the consonants frequently mangled and cadences off, but fluent it was.

"Okay," the Baron said. "Details can be worked out. Same codes going forward?"

"Yes and No. Same codes but advance everything three spaces."

The Baron smiled. "That's not all that sophisticated, but if you're confident…"

"I'm confident," Rolph said testily. "I'm here to get things started. Others in Hamburg will contact you."

"How much money are we talking?" the Baron said.

"$35 million," Rolph said. "With $1,000,000 to you. For that fee you must make covert arrangements with the Iranians, get their agreement on price, manage delivery, authentication and handle everything else."

"What if the Iranians want to negotiate on price?"

Rolph smiled. "They won't," he said. "That's been settled."

"Time line?"

"There isn't one," Rolph said. "Getting the cargo to you will take time. It's going by a circuitous route."

The Baron walked to his car, thinking that his commission would allow him to leave the arms business permanently.

He could disappear. Pockets of expatriate

Germans could be found everywhere in South and Central America. He'd start giving that some thought.

Punte del este, Uruguay
November 12, 2009
Connection

The city reminded him of Miami and Cancun, built on a peninsula lined with tall, pastel-colored hotels facing a sea filled with yachts and small pleasure boats.

Getting there from Montevideo took slightly more than two hours. He stopped and paid cash for gas a half hour out. He drove with windows down, the sea air invigorating him.

After rubbing down the car to remove his prints, he left it in a parking lot behind the bus station. While waiting for shops to open, he walked bare-chested up and down the beach in the cool morning air, attracting no attention. He did not stand out. Others in the vicinity moved about looking similarly scruffy.

Hungry, he watched early-morning surfers, mothers with young children and dogs playing on the sand. At seven a.m., he enjoyed black coffee, scrambled eggs and bacon at small restaurant a block from the beach.

At eight-thirty a.m., he found an open drugstore and bought a bottle of Aleve. Two pills and 20 minutes later his pain slowed to a series of dull aches.

He also purchased a cell phone with a prepaid card but later realized it didn't contain enough credits to call Poland. He solved that problem an hour-and-a-half later.

At a swank men's store's ten a.m. opening, in the space of 15 minutes, he spent almost 1,600 dollars buying linen shirts, Bermuda shorts, underwear, two pairs of cotton slacks, a new belt, loafers, flip-flops, silk-blend socks that extended to his calf, toiletries, a wool, fitted brass-buttoned blazer, and a fancy leather bag to hold it all.

He paid extra to have alterations done immediately. They took an hour. The sports coat fit him reasonably well but he was so big in the chest that he couldn't button it.

Informed that the tailor would have to take the coat apart and that this would cost the equivalent of $60 more, he said that was okay. He'd wait.

He asked the clerk if he could borrow his cell phone, promising to pay him back for the call on the spot. The clerk looked unhappy but agreed.

"Is it a world phone?" the Pole asked

"I call relatives in Italy with it," the clerk said.

The Pole took the phone. went to a far corner, punched in Poland's international code, and then a number. He got an answer on the third ring.

"Yeah," a rough voice answered in Polish, "who the fuck's calling me from fucking Uruguay?"

"My, such refined sentiments, old friend," the Pole said. This was followed by much laughter on both ends. "I need transportation," the Pole said.

"Where from?"

"Punte del este, Uruguay."

"To where?"

"Anywhere but here."

"Do you need documentation?"

"Yes, to include a couple of different passports

with German names.

"Are you safe where you are?"

"Hard to say. Nothing lasts forever, my friend, especially freedom."

"True. Just a second. I've got people in Buenos Aires, so that's good; but I need a day to put this together. That's not far from you, is it?"

"No more than an hour by commercial air, less by private plane, I suspect."

"This shouldn't be difficult, although you never know. There's always risk." He paused. "I'm looking up hotels on the Internet."

More silence, then, "Okay. A guy named Carlos will enter the Puerto Las Palmas Hotel tomorrow at ten a.m. I picked it because it's close to your city center. Can I call you back at this number?"

"Who the hell is Carlos?"

"Who cares? It's not his real name. He'll take care of getting you out of there. Can I call you back?"

"No. I'm using a salesman's cell phone. Don't think it'd be wise to impose on him again. Plus, none of the pre-paid cell phones for sale here will let me call Poland."

"Pity."

"Yes, it's an inconvenience."

"What happened to the four Corsicans I sent you last week?"

"Dead."

"All of them?"

"Yes, I think so. I'll explain later."

Silence. "Jesus Christ! Those were good men."

"They were. I'll be looking for Carlos tomorrow at ten a.m. at the Puerto Las Palmas, right?"

"Better make that two p.m."

"Got it."

"This is going to cost."

"How much?"

"Won't know for sure, but you're looking at $10,000 to get you to Buenos Aries, another ten for new identities. You can take the photos when you arrive. I have your measurements, eye color and all that, so they can get started. From Argentina, you can make your own air arrangements back to wherever, am I right?"

"You are."

"So, give me your codes and I'll get started here."

The Pole provided two private bank access codes and a third code authorizing payment without question for up to twenty-five thousand dollars, but he did not tell his Polish contact this. "If anyone asks, I'm dead, okay?"

"All right."

"Officially, early this morning I drowned at the Montevideo docks, shot by an unknown sniper."

"Legit?"

"Very much so. If I can get my ass out of here, I have a chance to shed my past and start clean."

"Ready to begin a new life filled with as much treachery, rash behavior and debauchery as the old one?"

"No. This time I hope to be legit. My attorney will sell my condo and furniture in Warsaw and declare me deceased as soon as legally permitted. Have no idea how long that'll take. I could care less. I'm moving on."

"Intelligence services throughout the world will cheer your demise."

"That they will."

The Pole hung up and returned to the salesmen,

who'd positioned himself between the shop's entrance and exit, worried he might lose his cell phone.

Looking relieved to get it back, he checked the charges. They amounted to approximately fifteen dollars U.S.

"Will a U.S. twenty cover it?" the Pole said.

The salesman nodded, delighted and asked if change was needed.

"No, keep it. And thanks for your help."

Hamburg, Germany
November 12, 2009
Shelter

Ania felt dirty, unkempt and in need of new clothes. Most big department stores in Hamburg closed Sundays, but she eventually found a small shop open on Monckebergstrasse near the central railroad station. She bought two pairs of Levis, some colorful tee shirts, a jacket, blouses, new socks and tennis shoes.

At a nearby store on the same street, she purchased half a dozen cotton underpants, several pairs of white socks, and two A-cup bras.

Her final treat was to get a haircut, manicure and massage from two Filipino women whom she suspected also offered sexual services.

She stayed the night at a church mission sleeping on a cot in a large room with dozens of other women of various ages, most homeless like her but none, as far as she knew, who spoke Polish.

While showering, two girls next to her embraced and languidly fingered each other from behind, their heads tilted backwards, eyes closed, mouths open.

She ignored them, unwilling to delay the pleasure she felt standing free under hot water that she believed cleansed her spiritually as well as physically.

The mission's nuns were nice and asked no questions. She wanted to stay longer but was told she must leave at seven a.m. the next morning because the space was needed for other purposes during the day.

****

At eight a.m. the next morning, Ania bought a hard roll and coffee at a tiny shop and walked the streets to familiarize herself. Several turns later, she realized she'd slept the previous night no more than three blocks from the brothel where she'd been imprisoned.

The mission would be an obvious place to look. She told herself that she'd been lucky and must be more careful.

She took a streetcar to the dock area and walked around looking for Polish signs or people speaking her language. Several hours later she had success.

The sign outside the restaurant said 'Ognisko domowane gotowanie' (Home Cooking). Inside, five stools faced a counter. Behind it, a waitress shouted customer orders through a small passageway into the kitchen. The cook heated pre-cooked pierogis, bigos, mushroom soup and other Polish standards and passed them through.

Ania entered and asked an old, stooped Polish man with coke bottle glasses if he needed workers. He hired her immediately as a dishwasher paying four Euros per hour for an eight-hour shift.

She did not know that the minimum wage across Germany ranged from five to eight Euros per hour. Had she known, she wouldn't have cared. She was undocumented and lucky to secure work so quickly.

For the moment, she had no money worries. After clothes shopping, she still had more than one thousand Euros and hoped to save them for as long as she could.

Her second night away from the brothel, she stayed in a youth hostel five blocks from the waterfront. Walking home late from her dishwashing job, she spotted a burly man she recognized hovering nearby, the one who'd called in sick at the brothel the day she'd escaped.

He stood casually at a corner eating a bratwurst he'd just bought from a sidewalk vendor. Was he looking for her, or did he just happen to be there? She had no idea but left quickly, hoping that he'd not seen her.

She slept nervously that night in an alley behind some trashcans without being disturbed, waking up the next morning resolute and full of purpose.

She'd been an innocent. Now she was damaged goods. So be it. She'd spent enough time as a victim. Right then she made up her mind. She decided that she'd kill those responsible for her degradation. If she avoided capture or death, she'd return to Poland and resume her life.

Hamburg, Germany
November 12, 2009
Discovery

Fritz Engel, 34, listened with growing frustration to his paymaster, Karl Kleinholtz, 28, describing the scene at Brothel Number Two.

"Okay, let's take it from the beginning," Fritz said. Of average height, his impeccable grooming, at least in his own mind, compensated for the fact he was fat, which he accepted as no big deal. Fritz hated exercise and loved food. Simple as that.

He lived in an expensive apartment in the Hamburg suburb of Altona overlooking the Elbe, his wife a high school classmate he'd knocked up his senior year. They had three children still under the age of five.

Most days, Fritz took the S-bahn to work, a ride of about 20 minutes through the densely populated city. With caveats, Fritz felt satisfied with his situation.

He'd passed tough State exams to become a tax manager, but making professional headway had been difficult. The best firms rejected him. Fritz's lower class mannerisms, bad grammar and defensive attitude hurt him with job interviewers.

A friend who also played the horses at Trabrennbahn referred him to a job paying considerably more than what he'd found on Internet job sites. The caveat: Fritz would be working for a criminal enterprise. Tired of the job search, he signed on.

He kept the criminal aspect of his work from his wife, who loved being a stay-at-home mom, and he took care, lecturing himself constantly.

'You must always disassociate yourself from

anything obviously criminal, Fritz. Do the accounting, the oversight and all the rest as professionally as you can, leave the dirty work to others, stop playing the horses and go home to your wife and family every night.'

The lecturing worked, sort of, although staying clear of the dirtier aspects of his job had proven impossible, his present chat with paymaster Karl Kleinholtz a good example.

Karl, 32, seemed to enjoy dealing with the Turks, Ukrainians and other scum hired to run and supervise the brothels.

Frequently smelling of too much cologne, Karl liked to leave his shirt unbuttoned almost to the navel. Thin and possibly consumptive, he fancied himself a lady's man. In reality, he resembled a garishly dressed, drowning rat.

His past included drug problems and a short prison sentence. He'd now been clean two years. Not only did he demonstrate street smarts, to Fritz's surprise, Karl wrote carefully researched and reasonably grammatical reports.

"I showed up on time for my weekly inspection and to collect the week's receipts," Karl said in his rasping voice.

Fritz nodded. Every Saturday, Karl visited all five brothels between nine and Noon. Early Monday morning, Karl presented his written report. Fritz would check and log in the receipts, then discuss Karl's summaries.

Typical problems could include a girl's drug overdose or suicide, supervisors not showing up, altercations with customers, and police bribes.

Such situations required discrete solutions.

Otherwise, you got fired, or worse. Karl's precursor had 'disappeared' after 'indiscretions' upper management found but never revealed, although the presumption was that this previous paymaster had lied about money collected, keeping some for himself.

To Karl's credit, he didn't let problems linger. If the on-site manager said a back-room toilet had been repaired, Karl demanded a receipt.

He'd tour the premises. If he found a girl with visible marks of brutality, he'd report it. Damaged women were not good for business.

Each brothel was assigned revenue targets. In any calendar year, a brothel averaged eight to 12 girls in residence. Turnover was high. Twenty to 30 girls might pass through a brothel in a year, most coming from Thailand, the Philippines, Eastern Europe, and the Balkans.

The average girl serviced approximately ten customers a day, or approximately $1,000. Ten girls working six days a week generated $60,000.

The syndicate's five Hamburg houses were expected to gross $300,000 weekly, but few months saw that much come in.

Girls got sick and could not work. Supply lines to the Philippines or Eastern Europe momentarily dried up due to local or international police interdiction. Procurers quit, girls got too heavily into drugs, died, escaped on their own, or disappeared.

Local managers and back-room supervisors stole when they could. Business volume for unknown reasons would slacken one week at one house while the other houses easily met their financial targets.

Expenses stayed high. Most houses sat in badly

lit, run-down industrial areas and carried low rents; but protection money paid to police and other authorities often siphoned as much as 20% from the gross. Administrative expenses took another 20 percent. Then there were the intangibles.

A customer's bad experience at one house could ruin business there as word surreptitiously made the rounds of places where johns congregated and told stories.

When this happened, the girls had to be dispersed to other places, often to other German cities, France or Belgium, and fresh young girls brought in. Quick action was paramount. Delay more than a week and your business might suffer months before recovering.

Having five brothels in one city meant that individual houses competed against each other. This was encouraged. Each front-room manager was free to run his own 'specials.'

Frequent customers got free drinks and 'special opportunities,' which included parties after locally important events such as horse races and soccer games. The best customers got free time with girls if they brought in new customers.

"Okay, so you showed up at your regular time," Fritz said. He leaned forward in his chair, clearly worried.

"Right. And there was Max dead on the doorstep."
"What time was this?"
"A little before nine a.m."
"Had anyone reported his death to the police?"
"No. I got him inside in time, I'm quite sure. I've kept my eyes and ears open, but sources tell me there haven't been any phone calls to the police, so I believe

we're in the clear."

"Good work, Karl, and good that you arrived when you did! I'm pleased with how you've handled this," Fritz said. "I'll let Serge know of your quick thinking."

"Thanks," Karl said. The education gulf separating him from Fritz made him feel uneasy and at a disadvantage, which he resented. Nevertheless, Fritz's compliments made him blush with pleasure.

"Once I got inside, one of the girls took me to Turkuo," Karl said. "He'd been shot in the stomach and nuts. He was dead before I got to him."

"Do we know who shot him?"

"A Polish girl. She arrived several months ago. Her particulars are in the file I just gave you," Karl said.

"Do we know where she is now?"

"No, Sir." Karl stared a moment at Fritz's suit. The material had what looked like gold threads woven in. Fritz's soft blue shirt had cuffs with the initials FE sewed in big, loopy, ornate letters. Karl wondered how much such a shirt cost.

"Did any of the girls escape with her?"

"No. They all stayed, frightened and docile as mice."

"So what did you do with the bodies?"

"I called the cleanup squad and they arrived a few hours later. We held off opening the house until two p.m. By then everything had been spiffed up, to include Max's blood removed from the outside steps."

Fritz frowned. 'The cleanup squad' was code for Hector and Hugo, who reported to his boss, a Russian named Serge whom he'd not heard from in two weeks, making Fritz feel isolated, which was more to worry about.

Hugo and Hector, two overweight, homely brothers close in age, both early 40's, did a little of everything no one else wanted to do. They killed, cleaned up and disposed of bodies, usually by incineration. When they arrived, it was best to leave.

"So everything's back to normal?" Fritz said.

"Yes," Karl said. "Client access wasn't interrupted. The girls seem settled back into their routines."

"Replacement for the Polish girl?

"Arrives the middle of next week," Karl said.

"So we can expect some slippage in revenues for a week or two."

"Yes, sir."

"Anybody trying to find the Polish girl?"

"Yes. Hugo and Hector said they're pursuing her."

"How do they know that the girl killed both men?"

"Because she wanted us to know."

"How?"

"She killed Turku with his own weapon. Then she killed Max with Turku's weapon and left it near Max's body."

"And then she took Max's weapon?"

"Yes, that's right," Karl said.

"Wonder where she'll leave Max's weapon?" Fritz said.

"Hopefully not with either of us," Karl said.

Punte del Este, Uruguay
November 13, 2009
Loose

The Pole treated himself to lunch al fresco at a combination bar/restaurant just off Avenida del Cabildo. From where he sat, he could see the cabstand outside the bus station.

Two or three taxis at a time lingered there, their owners smoking cigarettes and chatting, picking up fares and leaving, quickly replaced by new cabs.

Beyond the cab stand lay beaches filled with colorful umbrellas, chairs, ice cases and women and men wearing almost nothing.

He stayed away from bars. He turned down the occasional street prostitute. He warily watched any police. To his relief, the few times he saw them, they paid him no attention.

His injuries, he realized, would heal in time. The bullets had been removed, the areas treated. He needed to get his dressings changed but would wait until he got to Buenos Aries.

Contacts there could point him to doctors trusted not to talk. Every six hours, he took another two Aleve to keep the pain down.

He discarded his old clothes in a trash bin behind a bank. That night, fearing that the two fake ID's he carried might already be compromised, instead of using them to get a room, he slept on an embankment behind a bush, wearing his Bermuda shorts and a cheap tee shirt purchased the afternoon before, using the bag that held his new clothes as a pillow. The night got cool but he managed a decent and restful sleep.

The next day, at approximately ten minutes before two p.m., a tall, youngish man wearing Bermuda shorts and flip-flops walked towards the front of the Puerto Las Palmas Hotel, looked around and stopped.

"Are you looking for a ride?" he said.

"Who are you?" The Pole said.

"Carlos."

"Good. Let's go."

Carlos removed a cigarette pack from his shirt pocket, tapped it on his open palm, extracted a cigarette, offered one to the Pole, shrugged when the offer was refused, lit the cigarette and took a deep puff.

He'd not bothered to tuck in his shirt, which was wrinkled, nor had he combed his hair, appearing as if he'd just wakened from a long sleep.

About 40, something in the way he moved, the dead-eyed way he looked at you, as if didn't care if you lived another second, plus his seemingly fragile sense of his own importance, told you he was a thug stuck in some hierarchy's lower rungs who yearned for more respect but wasn't getting it.

Carlos punched numbers into his cell phone, waited to connect, mumbled something incomprehensible in Spanish, shut the phone and off they went.

Carrying everything he currently owned in his expensive leather bag, The Pole followed Carlos, who'd parked his car six blocks from the hotel. The long walk caused renewed pain he hoped he concealed. Carlos seemed not to notice and did not say three words during the journey.

At the private airfield a ten-minute drive outside the city, maintenance people serviced several expensive looking private jets parked at the field's the far end.

"Rich tourists from Argentina," Carlos said. "They fly here with their families and other times with their mistresses for the weekend."

A female clerk and an older man who might have been a flight instructor, office manager or both, sat inside a small, neat office. Carlos did not enter.

He made another phone call, pocketed his phone and when the Pole asked how much longer, Carlos grunted "Soon," which became 45 minutes. In the interim, one private jet landed.

A happy looking mother and father with two teenage daughters got off one plane. An S Class Mercedes drove on to the tarmac, picked everybody up and sped off.

Then a small Cessna dropped through the clouds, its wing tips swaying awkwardly in the wind. It landed unevenly, first one wheel and then the other.

"Jesus Christ!" the Pole said.

"Don't worry. He's makes this flight often," Carlos said.

A swarthy, squat Italian-looking maintenance man with longish hair employed a series of deft hand gestures to move the Cessna into position, then watched as the Pole, carrying his new leather bag, climbed into the cockpit next to the pilot.

"Aren't you coming?" the Pole asked Carlos.

"No. Have a good trip."

The Pole nodded to the pilot, a young man with long black hair to his shoulders wearing Khaki Bermuda shorts, orange, cracked-leather work boots and a tee shirt. He looked like a beach bum.

"Okay, let's go!" the Pole said irritably. He felt

uneasy with the pilot and not sure about Carlos. He was still without a weapon, his wounds hurting.

The Cessna taxied to the end of the runway, paused, the pilot exchanged brief conversation with the tower, and the light plane, slowly at first, moved down the runway, quickly picked up speed, rose high above Punte del este and headed west.

Frankfurt am Main, Germany
November 14, 2009
Iran

Mahmoud Karimi, 56, a pleasant, always-smiling man with a receding hairline and a growing pot belly, owned a Middle Eastern restaurant in Altona that served the usual shish kabobs, hummus, pita sandwiches and other middle eastern fare.

He drew patronage not just from a small expatriate Iranian community but from the German public and a large Turkish community. He served well prepared comfort food, while keeping a stern eye on the kitchen and cash register, while taking time to chat with customers.

Admired in the broader Shiite and Sunni Islamic communities for his wife's and his charitable gifts, Mahmoud was careful never to speak out politically for fear of offending Iran's Mullahs or nativist Germans.

Nevertheless, American and German Intelligence suspected that Mahmoud worked for the Iranian state. His restaurant was watched. If you were seen with Mahmoud more than once, a dossier would be opened in your name and agents would comb through your past.

Thus, illegal or 'gray area' business with Mahmoud required complicated rituals involving cut-outs, lots of conversational innuendo, and hurried meetings in odd places.

Six years ago, the Baron brokered with Mahmoud the sale to Hezbollah of armor-piercing rockets, crates of C-4 plastic explosives, mortars and fragmentation grenades, the connection made by a Moldavian friend using Air Cess, an airfreight company owned by the Russian, Viktor Bout, allegedly the world's most successful arms dealer.

Afterwards, the Baron frequently mentioned his Bout connection, until Bout, lured into a trap by American agents in Thailand, was transported to an American prison to spend the rest of his life.

This time, the Baron and Mahmoud met through the auspices of a Hamburg University physics grad student from Tehran, who showed up at an art opening where codes were exchanged and a meeting arranged.

****

Two weeks passed before the Baron worked his way through another labyrinth of 'chance' meetings, and exchange of codes that led finally to Mahmoud.

In the back office of a crowded combination antique emporium and furniture store, Mahmoud served the Baron tall glasses of sugary tea and did most of the talking.

"Don't want yellow cake. Enough of that already around," he said. Cesium, Radium, Palladium, Wolfram, Cobalt 60...not interested. However, I'll pay $25,000 per kg for any uranium tetrachloride you can get your hands on."

The Baron had no idea of what any of names mentioned were, whether they were raw, processed or enhanced, or how they figured in the manufacture of a bomb, so he kept his mouth shut and tried to look knowledgeable and receptive.

"We can use Plutonium 239 and Uranium 233 and 235. If you've got Weapons Grade or Super Grade, we can do business."

The Baron smiled. "I can get Weapons Grade."

"No Super Grade?"

"Unfortunately not."

"Then Weapons Grade it is," Mahmoud said. He stirred his tea but did not drink.

"How soon can you deliver?" he said.

"Can't give you specifics," the Baron said.

Mahmoud nodded. Nuclear materials were carefully guarded from their mining in, say, the Congo's Lubumbashi Mines, to the time they entered an industrial plant in the Urals, the Institute of Physics and Power Engineering in Russia, or the Ignalina nuclear power plant in Lithuania.

Nuclear thefts from mines, labs, industrial plants, and storage were opportunity gambles. The thief waited, sometimes years, for a security breach. A warning sensor goes dark. A guard calls in sick and is not replaced. Some one or many are bribed to look away.

More nuclear material got interdicted than got through, although actual statistics authenticating this assertion did not exist.

Even when carefully cover-wrapped in lead, new detectors at customs stops, airports and ports could detect the most minute radiation.

"Have you considered how you're going to transport the material from wherever you're getting it?" Mahmoud said.

"Yes, that's been discussed. We have a plan."

"Good, although I can't tell you how many of these conversations I've had. Three-quarters of the time, nothing comes of them. Half the men who've sat where you're sitting are now either dead or in jail, so I'd be careful."

Mahmoud watched the Baron's face. Not a flicker of fear. Either he's a fool or incredibly sanguine, Mahmoud thought.

"There's the matter of authentication," Mahmoud said. "The stuff has to be tested. That will require that some of it is given to me by you of your own free will."

"You'll need to have somebody in Hamburg ready at a moment's notice to do the authentication."

Mahmoud nodded and added a warning.

"If, after authentication, you try then to pass off lower-grade, you'll have a drawn out, unpleasant experience. You understand that?"

"I don't like my integrity challenged," the Baron said. "Trust me, I can take care of myself."

"Good," Mahmoud said. "Clean deals benefit everyone. What you're attempting is considerably more sophisticated and difficult that peddling arms. Be careful."

The two men shook hands, the Baron leaving quickly.

Around the corner from the furniture store and out of sight, he threw up in an alley, which helped but did not solve his ill ease.

Still sick, he returned home to nervously await what came next.

Hide and Seek

Punte del este, Uruguay
November 23, 2009
Success

From a seat in a diner across the street, Sammy Kan watched the gated police car pound. Surveillance was not difficult. The constant movement of customers constantly entering and leaving the diner gave him cover.

Other than his obvious Asian ancestry, nothing much distinguished Sammy. To blend with the resort community, he wore shorts, sandals and a short-sleeved Hawaiian shirt. He spoke American English without an accent. He could have been a tourist from Michigan or Nevada.

He sat in a corner with a paperback book, smoking a cigarette and nursing a cup of coffee. Small, in his early fifties with facial skin like parchment, he'd leave one cigarette burning while he lit another.

Sammy had been coming to this same restaurant for several days between interviews, waiting for an opportunity. He even ate dinner there occasionally. Whether ordering a meal or just coffee, he always tipped liberally. If the restaurant got busy, he'd leave his seat so that the waitress would not be denied a customer. The restaurant manager and staff noted and appreciated this, and left him alone.

The trail that led Sammy and the other Hong Kong detectives to this Uruguayan resort town emerged after a few random observations.

On the 12th of November, a policeman driving the early-morning Montevideo streets thought he might have seen a large, disheveled man in the shadows.

A few blocks closer to Constitution Square, an old Fiat was reported stolen from the third floor of a hotel parking garage. The car's passenger window had been broken.

Detectives found the window's glass shards wrapped in a torn tee shirt stuffed in a trash container. They also found microscopic shards in the area where the car had sat. The shirt smelled of brine and sweat.

They searched the shirt and the area for prints but found nothing usable. Could the Pole have somehow escaped drowning, made his way to Constitution Square, stolen a car and escaped? If so, where would he go?

Police officials continued to doubt that the Pole remained alive. He'd been shot three times, the last time in the neck. He had only one good arm, the other supposedly bandaged in such a way to restrict its movement.

He'd been seen falling into the water, which was cold and contaminated with engine oil and who knew what else. The police as much as said the case was closed.

Sammy reported each day's findings or their lack to a Hong-Kong-based English- and Chinese-speaking intermediary who admitted to fronting for someone else but would not reveal the person's name.

Sammy and his fellow detectives assumed that the mainland Chinese government was the secret employer. This did not sit well. As Hong Kong natives, they distrusted mainland officials. Being paid double what they could earn for similar assignments helped assuage such misgivings.

Their search quickly led to Punte del Este. A stolen Fiat with a broken drivers side window was found abandoned behind a bus station there.

During almost a week of 16-hour days, the detectives talked with more than 200 people in retail stores, rental car agencies, gas stations, hotel registration desks and other businesses without generating a single lead. Then came success.

A men's store salesman recalled selling a lot of expensive clothes to a large, bald man who used a phone to call Poland long distance. His credit card led to a numbered offshore account, where the search stalled.

Sammy was told that getting names associated with unnumbered accounts was nearly impossible.

Equally unfortunate, this same bald man had erased the phone number he'd called and the clothing salesman refused to give up the phone so that its contents could be mined.

Another problem: The local Police, for whatever reason, refused to let the group search the impounded Fiat for fingerprints. They were told that whoever stole the car had wiped it clean.

A high fence topped with barbwire surrounded the police car pound. Cops came and went all day through its wide gate to drop off or drive away with impounded vehicles. Owners arrived, paid fines and left with their cars or trucks.

Sammy had been watching the lot for three days off and on, and every day, it seemed, a new officer drew duty there. In late afternoon, just before closing, Sammy finally got into the police impound without being detected.

The officer-in-charge and a fellow officer had turned their backs and were walking to a car at the lot's west end. Once they were out of sight, Sammy walked in, darted to his left and disappeared behind several trucks, one of them jacked up and missing tires.

The two policemen returned minutes later, chatted, the car pound officer said goodbye and returned to the shack where keys and records were kept.

Punctually at five p.m., the officer-in-charge locked up and left. Darkness was coming quickly, so Sammy hurried.

The Fiat's passenger door was unlocked. Inside, Sammy saw that techs had dusted in the usual places, to include steering wheel, windows, floor shift, arm rests, center stack and other metal and seating surfaces plus the trunk.

The glove compartment door had been dusted as well, but when Sammy opened the glove compartment he noted the interior was clean.

From his brief case he removed a small can and sprayed the glove-box interior with a light-colored mix of silver and graphite dust. Then he lit the newly dusted area with a small ultra-violet penlight. There was a print!

He pressed a tape carefully over the print. Carefully, he slowly removed the tape, checking to see that the print had adhered, did one more inspection, and left!

To avoid observation from the diner, he picked the lock on a side gate and disappeared.

That evening, he sent a photocopy of the print to Deputy Intelligence Director Alvarez Conrado in Montevideo.

****

An hour later, one of Sammy's fellow detectives, a small bald Chinese man in his 50's with big horn-rimmed glasses stood outside the manager's office at the local air field and interviewed a maintenance man who recalled watching a man climb up into a small Cessna and leave Punte del este six afternoons ago.

"Big dude. Well dressed, bald," the man said. "His suitcase had shiny thick leather and looked expensive."

"Did he leave on a commercial flight?"

"No, no, a Cessna, a private plane. You get very little commercial flying out of here other than UPS," the maintenance man said. "The plane had no markings. That usually means smugglers in this part of the world."

"And elsewhere," Sammy's detective friend said. "So there won't be any flight records?"

"Nope. The manager is paid to make sure that doesn't happen. Sometimes I'm also paid to keep quiet."

"Then why are you talking with me?"

"Because you're paying me," the man said. "The flights go back and forth between here and off-the-grid airfields in Argentina. They come at odd times, not just at night, as you'd expect. The plane that left with the bald dude could have landed anywhere, most likely somewhere in close-by Argentina."

****

With this news and the fingerprint, Sammy and his companions returned to Montevideo in two cars. They stayed at the Carlton Hotel to write their report and await fingerprint analysis, which Deputy Director Alvarez Conrado promised to expedite.

Alvarez phoned Sammy Kan the next day. They had a hit! The print belonged to the Pole!

That night, after calling their Hong Kong intermediary with the news, they celebrated at the restaurant at the top of the Carlton Hotel, spending with tip almost $1000 on food and booze.

At nine a.m. the next morning, Alvarez notified Interpol, which issued a Red Notice.

The Pole had been responsible for the deaths of law enforcement people and civilians in Germany, Poland, Thailand, Japan, France, Uruguay, Canada and the United States.

Because he was universally loathed, news of his seeming impossible survival stirred interest across the globe.

In Langley, Virginia, CIA agent Chester Field was alerted by an analyst that afternoon and immediately began thinking about what to do next. The Pole had killed two of his agents. It infuriated him that his enemy remained alive.

In Shanghai, the intermediary dealing with Sammy Kan phoned Dragon Motors CEO Tama Wu on a secure line and told her the news. She clapped her hands. Vengeance, she told herself, would be hers!

At three p.m., Sammy Kan's mainland-China intermediary ordered Sammy and the other detectives to head for Argentina and continue their search there.

Hamburg
March 17, 2010
Improvising

For a month, Ania continued her dishwashing job. She kept a gun with her at all times, fearful that the sex traffickers would find her.

The Polish milk bar owner agreed to let her sleep on a cot in the kitchen as long as she took the late shift and cleaned up after closing.

She started work at six p.m. The milk bar stayed open until Midnight on Friday and Saturday nights and until ten p.m. weekdays.

After closing, an hour to two hours usually sufficed to clean, put everything away and prepare the small kitchen and dining area for the next day.

She quickly grew tired of the routine. With the old man's help, she found a fourth-floor single room for rent three blocks from her job, with shower, hot plate, water and electricity included for 800 Euros per month. That left her with 700 Euros for other needs. She could live on that.

A month later, she switched from the night to the day shift. She'd arrive at ten a.m. and work until six. At seven p.m. she began studying German.

A nice middle-aged, single man named Jürgen Hodel taught the course in the basement of a nearby Lutheran church.

The course ran five days a week and cost ten Euros for each two hours, but by signing up for the week in advance she paid forty-two Euros.

"It's smart marketing," Jürgen told her later.

"Most people don't come all five days. Most, in fact, don't last six weeks. Those students leave money on the table."

The course consisted of staring at a screen where stick figures pantomimed an interaction, supplemented by four- or five-page Xeroxed handouts detailing the conversation in German. You memorized the German and used it to carry on conversation with the person next to you.

Some days, Ania would be the only student. Other 'regulars' included a Pakistani who spoke Urdu, two young American girls, herself, a Czech and an older French lady who only came sporadically.

She quickly realized that she had a facility for language learning. Jurgen, who worked as a first-level administrator for a company that supplied parts to the local Airbus factory, noted this. She also sensed his romantic interest.

This suspicion was confirmed during the second month of the course. He asked her to stay after and then offered to buy her dinner. Ania accepted.

She'd been getting lunch free at the milk bar, a candy bar or raw carrots sufficing for dinner. Jürgen expanded her horizons. He took her in his old Volkswagen to a Chinese restaurant.

Conversation came with difficulty, but she liked him. He did not immediately try to have sex with her or kiss her goodnight.

She had him leave her a block from her apartment because she still entrusted her home address to no one, and continued to carry a loaded gun in her purse.

The dinners became a regular routine two and three times a week. By now, three months into the

German language course, she began to understand snippets of conversation.

The TV above the counter at the milk bar droned in German day and night. The familiar soap opera plots and actors with their differing speech rhythms and pronunciations helped.

She bought herself a cheap radio. The moment she got to her tiny room, she'd turn it on to some talk program and let it chatter endlessly in the background.

After four months, she was speaking colloquially, could read street signs and a map, ask directions, make small talk and was beginning to read newspapers.

Although she did not let down her guard, her fear of discovery lessened. The sex traffickers seemed to have forgotten her, although she'd not forgotten them.

Meanwhile, Jürgen taught her how to use his computer. One night, she returned home to find a second computer sitting on a small table in an alcove of Jurgen's apartment.

"It's for you," Jürgen said.

Overjoyed, she told him to lie on his back and she would perform sex on him! That night, she spent an hour bringing him almost to overload, backing off and starting again. When she finally brought him release, he cried with joy, tears wetting his face.

Within weeks, with Jürgen helping, she was using the computer to write rudimentary German essays, using Word Spell Check, Dictionary and Synonyms.

By now she'd told him about her past, which he took reasonably well, although she knew her story upset him.

One evening, she and Jürgen drove past the brothel where she'd been incarcerated. She saw customers walking in, one of whom she recognized.

She noted light shining through the window blinds in the front rooms, and shuddered. The smells, fear, sounds, and sights associated with that life returned.

She hated herself for her complicity and for her victimization. That night she could not sleep. She lay face up, staring at shadows playing on the ceiling while Jürgen slept soundly beside her.

Lucky him, she thought. He'll never feel the rage I feel. I know killing is wrong. I Know I should get help. I'm deranged. I'm a serial killer and even worse. I'm not done. I will kill again, and soon.

Buenos Aries
April 3, 2010
Launch

The Pole seriously considered staying in Argentina. For the first time in a long while. his anonymity made him feel relatively safe.

He might have remained had he picked up enough Spanish, but he had not and did not care to learn. Not enough literature and good philosophers writing in that Spanish, he told himself.

The physical repair work on him had been completed. If you'd seen him three months before in Punte del Este or Montevideo, you'd not recognize him now.

There'd been painful plastic surgery to alter his nose, ears and eyebrows. He'd grown a nice full beard.

He now had three beautifully fitted wigs, each different, to cover his baldness. He'd even lost the hitch in his gait following painful but successful surgery on his leg.

The best news was the grafting of a new thumb. He'd lost part of his old thumb in 1997 when tortured by Philippine rebels. The missing thumb had made him easy to identify. That would no longer be true.

About to turn 40 in two months, he'd stand naked in front of a full-length mirror and still like the way he looked. No sagging skin or other clues suggested that his body had begun its inevitable decline.

He worried regardless, thinking he likely had less than a decade as an enforcer before he'd have to yield to younger and stronger competitors. It was time to use his mind more and his strength less.

So far, he'd managed to keep his aggressive tendencies in control. He did slap a woman when she refused his advances, but did not break any of her teeth, apologized, gave her $500 U.S. and the matter remained unreported.

Not wanting to bring more attention to himself, he stopped going to that bar. For him, that was progress.

He'd decided that Europe would be his best place to begin a new life. He knew his way around.

He told himself that he no longer needed to strong-arm people. He could pay others to do that. He'd find something more 'elevated.' After all, he had a PhD.

But what could he do? He couldn't return to Poland, his first choice. He'd been declared dead there. His apartment and furnishings had been sold, his estate settled, the money placed in a trust and transferred off shore into a numbered account.

With Poland out, Germany seemed the best

option. He spoke the language. He didn't like the German temperament; but making anecdotal generalizations about nationalities was a waste of time. He'd adjust.

He had the luxury of time. He'd use it to find a kind of work that elevated rather than demeaned him. In the meanwhile, he missed the constancy of a good woman.

Through underworld contacts, he linked with his former lover, Beata. She'd been diagnosed with AIDs and almost died, but apparently was now disease-free.

They began talking long distance. She sounded excited to hear from him again.

He asked if she thought they had a future together and she said they should try. This overjoyed him.

He told her they must wait, that he did not know where he'd end up, but once knew, he'd call for her. She told him to take his time. When he decided, she'd come.

****

Since escaping Uruguay, while undergoing and recovering from operations, the Pole had not been idle. He'd saved the flash drive he'd stolen.

It contained code, which he sold for $7 million to Dream Industries, a regional Indian automotive company headquartered in Mumbai. The deal took less than a month.

The Pole's timing was fortuitous. A month later, Dream Industries CEO Sajan Singh, died of a heart attack. The new owners might not have done the deal.

Meanwhile, his search for work left him with a discouraging conclusion: Legitimate businesses were out.

Officials would want to know why they hadn't heard of him before?

He let it be known through underworld connections, to include his offshore bank, Caesar Enterprises, that he was looking for a 'good situation.'

Caesar Enterprises funneled criminally generated cash into legitimate businesses. He could operate comfortably with the help of such a bank.

The Bank found him two possibilities: The first involved re-organizing muscle along the Marseilles docks and inland. A coalition of unions and unidentified 'entrepreneurs' would pay him through the bank, meaning it would be impossible to connect his customers to him.

The Pole rejected the proposal. He wanted something more dignified, although he did not say this. Six weeks later came a second proposal, which he took.

Buenos Aries
May 9, 2010
Interested Parties

Sammy and an interpreter sat with the tall, severe looking middle-aged woman on her break at a nearby coffee shop. She was the 23rd plastic surgeon receptionist interviewed over a two-month period.

"Yes," she said, when shown several pictures of the Pole, "Our office did a lot of work on him and contracted out some to other surgeons. He also wanted a thumb attached and a limp in his right leg fixed. We only do the face but directed him to surgeons who could help him with his other requests."

Sammy asked if she could get before-and-after photos.

"No. I wouldn't feel comfortable doing that," she said. Sammy did not push. He thanked her and handed her $100 US.

That night, he and a compatriot broke into the plastic surgeon's office and found the Pole's file. It included before-and-after photos and the names of surgeons to whom he'd been referred.

Sammy was stunned at how radically different the Pole looked after three different surgeries conducted over a five-month period. He also noted that Maximillian Siegfried Schroeder was the alias used when contracting for the surgeries.

The detectives checked the Pole's address and phone number in the plastic surgeon's file. The phone number no longer worked and the address turned out to be an empty field.

Next, Sammy's compatriots procured flight manifests from the past five months for shipping lines and airlines flying out of Buenos Aires' Jorge Newberry and Ezeiza International Airports.

The tedious collection effort required more bribes plus innumerable hours checking hundreds of pages for any name they could link with any of the Pole's aliases. Each day, a new report would be added.

For all Sammy Kan and the other PI's knew, the Pole could have decided to stay in Buenos Aries. Or, assuming he'd left Argentina, he could have departed Buenos Aries by plane, ship, tramp steamer or private plane using an unknown alias.

He could have been smuggled by car or truck into another country and stayed or flown elsewhere from there using a variety of even another alias.

Nevertheless, they happily took their pay and continued their seemingly Quixotic search.

Wonsan, North Korea, May 15, 2010

Close Call

"Hurry!" the nervous pilot whispered. He tapped his earphones. "Boats approaching fast from the west. Estimated five minutes away, maybe less. Time to go!"

Frank Bishop, 34, nodded, motioning for the masked men to get back in their boat and leave.

He and his pilot worked days as mid-level managers for an American engineering company currently in a joint venture with a Japanese firm. They did their freelance smuggling nights.

A light rain raised obscuring mist across the Sea of Japan. Choppy waters made it hard to keep one's balance. The pilot sat hunched over the wheel, listening to voices inside his earphones.

Cockpit instruments cast a barely perceptible glow. The pilot held three fingers in the air, meaning the enemy was now just three minutes away.

Despite helpful cover provided by rain, mist and moonless dark, Bishop shared his pilot's tension. He'd experienced several close calls.

You'd hear the patrol boat engines approaching. Their sound would fool you, making you think they were far off. Suddenly, out of night and fog their silhouettes would appear f50 yards from you closing fast.

His boat, built in Long Beach, California, powered by two 500-horespower Pratt and Whitney aircraft engines, had a large cargo area that just 15 minutes ago held two thousand pounds of contraband rifles, ammunition, plastic explosive, eavesdropping equipment and specially designed radios that provide SOS and GPS support.

He'd been told only that an insurgent group inside North Korea planned to blow up several nuclear reactors, kill North Korean President Kim Jong-Il. Hopefully, the guns would help.

In return, Bishop received a box four-feet square so heavy that it had to be loaded with a winch. Inside this box's wood exterior, he knew, an inner container of four-inch-thick lead protected uranium Isotopes worth multi-millions of dollars.

Bishop was skeptical about the North Korean renegades' chances. Kim Jong-Il had agents everywhere. One mistake and the underground group would be rounded up quickly, brutally interrogated and shot.

He'd hand off the uranium to an unknown third party in open sea. He had no idea where the cargo would go from there.

He'd be paid $75,000 for the job, plus the cost of gas and other expenses, $25,000 of that he'd give to his pilot, assuming the North Korean patrol boats did not get them first.

Unmarked and painted a flat black, Bishop's boat looked like a naval architect's interpretation of a knitting needle or gar pike, its thin shape and plastic hull difficult to detect by radar, its only armament a machine gun, useless except at close range.

Two masked North Koreans, identifiable only by their aliases, Wolf and Sue, hurriedly placed the last of the munitions in the hold of their fishing boat.

They'd commandeered an odd mad-Max affair, an oversized-flat and almost square metal deck attached to an ancient wooden hull.

A winch, a six-foot-high signal mast topped by a single unlit bulb and a glass pilot's window at the rear of the boat were all that protruded from the flat, bare-bones hull.

The North Korean pilot fired their mad-Max boat's engine. It emitted a dull rumble beneath the sea.

One of the smugglers waved, the boat slowly turned and with its contraband quickly headed towards one of many small islands dotting the sea a half-hour speedboat ride from the North Korean port of Wonsan.

In the past month, Bishop had made two trips to these islands. They numbered 20 and included hundreds of hidden coves, which for centuries had served as pirate and smuggler destinations.

Bishop had never seen much of Wonsan. The city's over 300,000 electricity-deprived people had left on only a scattering of dullish lights.

To Bishop's left and not far behind, a flare lit the sky. For an instant, he saw two North Korean gun boats clear as day running parallel to each other coming towards him.

He also thought he heard a helicopter somewhere unseen above, but after checking realized, to his relief, that he was wrong.

He and the pilot headed into open sea, the sound of the boat's engines deafening, the islands of Wonsan quickly disappearing.

A second flare exploded. In its momentary illumination he saw the lights of two boats farther behind him now. The pilot made a motion and Bishop reacted.

He grabbed a long aluminum tube, pointed it skyward and rearward. There was a whooshing sound. A bomb launched, followed by a second to the right and a third to the left.

The bombs exploded in sequence upon water contact, throwing up a momentary barrier of incandescent metallic material designed to confuse radar and blank a half a square mile square with odiferous, muddy mist that clogged engines and obscured vision.

A third North Korean gunboat appeared from the right, its searchlight shinning. It fired off a missile that exploded twenty yards to Bishop's left, sending a swell that drenched him. More shells followed. Ten nerve-wracking minutes of this and the North Koreans gave up.

"That was close!" Butler said as the brilliant lights illuminating the coast of Japan appeared on the horizon.

The pilot shut off the engine and lit a cigarette. The silence felt wonderful after the angry roar of the engines, sea splash, explosions and adrenalin rush of the chase. Only the slapping of the waves against the metal hull disturbed the quiet.

"Whew!" the pilot said.

"Just another day at sea," Frank Bishop said.

The pilot laughed.

****

Angry seas and rain again tossed Frank Bishop's needle-nosed black boat. Sometimes the hull rose and slammed back down, rattling the cockpit area and keeping both pilot and Frank Bishop more nervous than usual; but the stormy sea and sudden appearance of fierce rain did have one advantage.

Visibility shrunk to almost zero. Fog hugged the water. Radar showed that no North Korean or Japanese patrol boats lurked in the area.

The pilot kept checking coordinates and then that became no longer necessary. As mist lifted temporarily from atop the sea, both men saw the Handymax freighter with Maltese registration, four cranes visible,

The freighter had dropped anchor. On deck, a European of undetermined nationality waved.

It took a nervous half hour to get the boats parallel-tied. The storm noise and sea turbulence made this task at times almost impossible.

Two parka-wearing men directed the winched box containing the uranium on to the deck.

"Heavy sonnofabitch," Frank yelled in English.

"Sure is, one of the men yelled back. "Three people died getting it this far." Then he added ominously, "Good luck."

****

Back on land later that night, Frank Bishop sent a coded message to the Baron telling him that 'the package' was on its way.

The next night, Frank went to the Agave, a high-end Mexican bar up some stairs in Tokyo's Ropongi district.

He sat in a rawhide chair, smoked an expensive cigar and slowly drank a chilled xalixco silver tequila.

The noise and heavy haze of cigar smoke irritated his ears and eyes. He left at ten p.m., not sure why he'd gone, taking the subway back to his apartment in nearby Shinbashi, looking forward to another job next week, next month, or whenever.

****

That same night, the Baron met briefly with Mahmoud in the back of a Somali restaurant and told him that the shipment was on its way. In return, Mahmoud assured the Baron that he'd have the money ready.

"This assumes you can get the material into the country," Mahmoud said.

"This is different," the Baron said. "We've gotten through the worst part, stealing the stuff and getting it out of the country. It's now on the high seas and for now immune to discovery."

"Maybe. We'll see. It's when it gets back on land that most interdictions occur," Mahmoud said.

"This will be different," the Baron said. "We have an innovative way to avoid Customs."

"Hope so," Mahmoud said.

****

Later, the Baron had second thoughts about Mahmoud. What if he didn't come up with the money? Then doubts about his own abilities intruded. Could he manage this?

He sipped a cognac and gazed through his condo's floor-to-ceiling living room window at Hamburg's dark, sinewy canals and brightly lit downtown skyscrapers

Should he call Lash?

Lash was the Baron's enforcer. An uneducated man of the streets and ten years younger than the Baron, Lash worked as a truck driver when he could. Mostly, he hung around bars wearing a tee shirt and picking up men. The Baron supported him financially.

Their relationship was not based on shared hobbies, lasting physical attraction or other common thread,

They'd been lovers only a few weeks but companions of a sort almost three years. They complimented each other, the Baron a planner but conflict averse, Lash an action seeker prone to violence.

The Baron would set up meetings with potential business partners. If they tried to harm him, Lash would leave the Baron's attackers maimed or dead. Early on, this happened enough to keep the game interesting for Lash.

Afterwards, the Baron would be horrified and repulsed by the carnage; but after the passage of a few months, satisfied that a form of justice had been exacted, he'd find himself eager to repeat the game.

He lacked the necessary cruel amorality that Lash provided. He no longer felt physically attracted to Lash and believed this was reciprocated. Theirs was strictly a business relationship, but he needed him now. More precisely, he needed three Lashes. He didn't have enough muscle. He must find some before the uranium arrived.

Buenos Aries
May 10, 2010
The Offer

The man entering the trendy outdoor café on Avenida Belgrano near the Plaza Domego carried a paperback copy of one of Rousseau's autobiographies so that the Pole could identify him.

He looked nothing like the typical conservatively dressed banker, the Pole thought. None of the Caesar Enterprises people did.

The Pole intuited criminal backgrounds in many Caesar Enterprises people, but you never knew. The bank employed presumably upstanding citizens as well.

This Caesars Bank representative, A tall, lanky, loose-joined man in his forties, spoke with a French accent, had crew-cut brown hair and blue eyes.

He introduced himself as René but did not give a last name. Most people the Pole met went by first names, and most of these were bogus.

Later, the Pole learned that René's last name was Oppenheim. "But I'm not Jewish," René had replied. "I'm nothing."

He dressed casually but neatly in a green Ralph Lauren polo shirt, Levis and tennis shoes.

The Pole glanced at René's paperback. "I'm not much of a Rousseau fan," the Pole said.

"Oh?" René said. "Why not?"

"Don't like his assumption that Man's an innocent, that Society corrupts him. Philosophically, I think one must start with Man," the Pole said. "Culture is Man's byproduct."

"Ah, but the byproduct, once it's created, becomes its own mimetic force."

"Interesting, and yes, I suppose that's so," the Pole replied. "I think it was the French theorist Girard who said that mimesis feeds desire. I'm not sure that desire and evil aren't intrinsic to man and hardly culture's fault. Culture is merely the facilitator."

"Don't usually have philosophical discussions with bank customers or contractors," a clearly pleased René said, "but delighted to make your acquaintance. You are Mr. Mannheim, are you not?."

"For now I am," the Pole said, grinning.

Now sufficiently comfortable with each other, the two men chatted as intellectually kindred spirits until the waitress came.

They both ordered salads and glasses of Chardonnay. After the wine and salads came, they each ate quietly.

****

"There's opportunity in selling arms," René said over coffee. "We've done rather well with this, but we should be doing better, because if anything, the market's expanding. For example, the U.S. just sold several billion dollars worth of missiles to UAR. Iranian, Armenian, African, Georgian and Chechen revolutionaries. We've identified more than 100 large crime groups in Italy, Romania, Mexico, Nicaragua, Somalia, Iraq, Nigeria, and Sudan in the market for arms. It can be a great business if run right."

"Where do you find weapons in large enough quantities?"

"Ah, that's interesting," René replied. "Generals in what used to he the old SSRs bootleg from their arsenals. Lots of shoddy Chinese arms remain in Albania from as far back as the 1960's. The Bosnian, Bulgarian and Hungarian governments are almost giving away free entire warehouses of weapons and munitions."

"Why?"

"The stuff just sits there rotting. Better to get something for it while you can; but not everything out there is old. Right now you can buy the latest Russian sniper rifle, known as the B-94, even though it's not yet been approved for the ordinary Russian soldier. Everything's for sale, to include missile launchers, grenades, machine guns, detonators, fuses, walkie-talkies, stun guns, mortars, anti-tank equipment, grenade throwers, Stinger missiles and Semtex, a pliable plastic explosive. That's a big seller. You name it and it's available."

"So where do I fit?" the Pole said

"We want you to help our bank, which is also your bank, get more of that business," René said.

The Pole smiled. "I don't have those kinds of contacts."

"We can help with that," René said. "We run five brothels in Hamburg."

"I thought this was about selling arms?"

"It is, but be patient a moment. The brothels are related. We buy girls from Russia, the Ukraine and Eastern Europe. The contractors supplying these girls also courier arms through the same conduits, meaning we already have a network in place. Both businesses come with similar problems. Shipments, human or inanimate, don't get through. Others get diverted. Couriers burn out or are arrested."

"Okay, René. But why me?"

"Because we know you," René said. "Trust is important. Also, you're not just muscle. You're bright and you've just redone yourself physically. That means that it'll take awhile for Interpol and others catch wind of you. Last year, we hired a Russian named Serge to grow the arms business. He hasn't worked out. We think he's skimming from the brothels. We've concluded that he's not ruthless or resourceful enough to grow the arms business to the size we want."

René leaned forward, his manicured fingers touching the edge of the table, his eyes fixed on the Pole. "First," he said, "We'd like you to take a look at our prostitution business. Should we keep it or get out of it?

We want your opinion."

"Okay," the Pole said, flattered but trying unsuccessfully not to show it. "What else?"

"The armaments business works for us. Not too much exposure from the bank's end. We want you to take our current guy's place and get the organization moving."

"Any competition to worry about?" the Pole asked.

"I was just getting to that," René said. "One of Europe's biggest arms dealers, nicknamed the Baron, works out of Hamburg. He's got CIA ties and their financial backing. We want you to muscle in on his business, convert his supply lanes to us, take over his business and take him out."

"What about the CIA?"

"They'll find somebody else, hopefully, or maybe even become a customer."

The Pole placed his coffee cup back on the table and thought about that. Did any of that make sense?

"At the end of three months," René said, "we can re-evaluate. We're bringing in some skilled and trusted Germans from Frankfurt and Munich who can help, once you have a plan. For every new $10 million dollars you generate in a year's time, we'll pay you $1,000,000. Then, if you choose, you're on your way to your next adventure. For starters, we'll place $250,000 in your account to demonstrate our good faith."

"What if I want to stay?" the Pole said.

"Everything's negotiable, "René answered, but the Pole detected conflict in René's face. Oh, oh, he thought.

"I'll think about it," the Pole said.

****

On May 12th, the Pole left Buenos Aires, flying

Lufthansa business class to Hamburg, Germany.

The night before leaving, to celebrate the beginning of his new career as a business developer, he got drunk in a bar and smashed a beer bottle into the bartender's face, broke the man's nose, knocked out four teeth and temporarily shut one of his eyes.

He also broke the arm of a bouncer who tried to throw him out and the wrist of the second bouncer who'd tried to help.

The Pole left the bar as he always did, with the awed and frightened crowd parting like the Red Sea to let him pass. The violence felt good. He'd held it in long enough.

Buenos Aries
May 13, 2010
Pursuit

Sammy would propose new searches as others grew cold. He'd outline the cost. Without argument, the mysterious intermediary would approve each new plan.

The intermediary's client clearly was relentless in his or her desire to find the Pole. Sammy had stopped wondering who or why, grateful for the work and the money.

In almost six months, he and his four companions had billed over $385,000 U.S.. This included salaries, bribes, travel, hotels, meals and interpreters.

"This gift keeps giving and hopefully will never end," one of Sammy's detectives said.

Sammy suggested they quit. "We know what he

looks like now," he told their intermediary. "He's a bad man. He'll turn up and they'll get him." '

"No," the intermediary ordered. "Continue. Find him."

****

Each day Sammy and the other detectives scanned the flight and ship manifests for the previous day. Finally, they got a hit.

On May 12th, a Maximillian Shroeder left Buenos Aries' Ezeiza International Airport at 7:10 p.m. on Lufthansa. His flight touched down at 1:45 p.m the next day in Frankfurt, Germany, before continuing on to Hamburg, its final destination.

Mr. Schroeder had deplaned in Hamburg. Sammy and his men would pick up his trail there.

Shanghai, China
May 14, 2010
Closing

Sitting behind her desk in her headquarters on Pudong's dreary outskirts, Dragon Motors CEO Tama Wu worried.

Months after her unfortunate trip to Montevideo, she'd turned down the chance to buy an old Fiat factory in Warsaw, Poland and build Dragon Motors vehicles there. Instead, she decided to export cars to Europe from Shanghai.

Her first Dragon Motors European dealership would open soon in Frankfurt, Germany. She planned to be there. She'd agreed to invest $100 million in Europe, with other dealerships planned for Paris, Amsterdam, London, Berlin, Moscow and Madrid. Now she was having second thoughts.

Her detectives believed the Pole might be in Hamburg. She did not want to be within 100 miles of him without protection. Then she got an idea.

She met at the American consulate with a local CIA operative, her request ending up on Chester Field's Langley, Virginia desk.

He promised to get back with her shortly. She hoped so. Without his help, she was under no circumstances heading to Germany.

The previous November, in Montevideo, Uruguay, the Pole's brutal beating of her required surgeries to replace both her knees. Seven months passed before she could walk normally. Her gait continued to feel unnatural and probably appeared that way to others.

In addition, the Pole had smashed her face with an iron pipe. The facial surgery had been agonizing. Skin and bone healed slowly and not to her satisfaction. It took three operations to achieve a physical semblance of her former self.

In the process, her face lost its once flawless color; the ridges over her eyes had been sufficiently altered to ruin what had been a lovely and balanced composition.

She believed the Pole's assault had taken part of her soul, a somewhat dramatic conclusion, perhaps, but in her mind true.

Early on, when the Pole's body failed to be found, it became clear that Deputy Director Alfredo Conrado and other Uruguayan Intelligence operatives lacked the resources or the will to continue their search.

So, while recovering from her knee operation and

facial reconstruction at Johns Hopkins Hospital in Baltimore, Maryland, Tama ordered Sammy Kan and four other Hong Kong private detectives to Montevideo to validate or invalidate the Pole's supposed demise..

She kept her obsession secret, letting a trusted vice president of her accounting firm act in her behalf. He paid Sammy Kan and the other detectives and provided her updates of their progress. He also checked receipts and other documentation to assure that Tama was not getting cheated.

Today, for the third time, she listened to a taped conversation between her intermediary and Sammy Kan explaining how pictures of the Pole's new self had been obtained and how they'd tracked him to Hamburg.

"And have you located the Pole in Hamburg?" the intermediary asked.

"We have not," Sammy answered. "We just learned about this. We're headed there now."

"He might not have stopped in Hamburg."

"True," Sammy Kan said. "We'll interview the airline's ground personnel. Even with all the physical changes he's undergone…and, as I said, we have photos…he's still a big, imposing, heavily muscled guy, easy to spot and easy to remember."

"When do you leave for Hamburg?" the surrogate said.

"Within the next hour."

"Good. This is getting expensive. Hopefully, you'll find him soon."

"We'll get him," Sammy Kan said.

Tama Wu shut off the recorder. The Pole and I have both suffered through painful plastic surgery, he to change his identity, I to restore mine, she thought.

Ironic.

Also ironic, surgery had failed both of them. Her beauty had not been restored. He'd not gained the anonymity he desired.

Hamburg, Germany
May 22, 2010
Paymaster

On a sunlit Saturday morning, a young, blond, middle class woman dressed conservatively and driving a late-model Volkswagen passed the brothel.

She'd driven by several times before when she had an odd moment, never stopping but on alert. This turned out to be her lucky day.

From the corner of her eye, she observed a flashily dressed man leave the brothel and get into a recent-vintage C Class Mercedes.

She recognized him! He'd arrive the same time each Saturday! He was the paymaster!

Not physically imposing, he preened as if he were God's perfectly designed male. In reality he was short, thin and resembled a drowning rat.

He'd strut through the brothel's back rooms casually looking about, writing notes, speaking with no one, preferring to spend most of his brief time talking with the manager in the office facing the street.

Whoever he was, he seemed to distain her and her fellow sex slaves. This distain evidently included the front office manager, who several times told backroom supervisors in her presence that the paymaster was, in his words, a flaming, gaping asshole.

Clearly, this paymaster reported to people who ran the syndicate, so she decided to follow him, always staying a few cars back.

In a western part of Hamburg she'd never visited, the paymaster stopped at another nondescript building and went inside. She noted the address and waited at the corner, car engine running.

He exited 20 minutes later carrying his satchel. He repeated this same routine three more times. She wrote down each address.

She returned the next weekend, this time waiting at the last house. The paymaster appeared on schedule, went inside, did his business and drove to a combination lunchroom/bar 15 minutes away, where he read a morning newspaper and enjoyed a Weiner schnitzel and a beer.

Two men joined him. She'd seen one of them before, and somehow remembered his name, Fritz. She'd seen him before in the brothel.

The third man was new to her. Tall and muscular, with a neatly trimmed beard, he wore dark glasses and dressed expensively.

She could tell by the paymaster and Fritz's body language that this third person, whoever he was, had higher rank.

The paymaster spent no more than a half hour eating with Fritz and the new man, and then got back into his car. She noted the time. Almost Noon.

She and Jürgen would visit the Art Museum later that afternoon. She had time to follow Karl the paymaster to one more destination.

He headed west, slowed, and drove around until he found a parking spot. He walked a block and into an apartment building.

Five minutes later, he appeared in the second floor window of what likely was his apartment. Good, she thought. Now I know where he lives. He's next.

Aitutaki, Cook Islands
May 22, 2010
Waiting

Captain Alfredo Gomez, 53, stood on the stone veranda looking down on rolling lush forest that extended maybe half a mile down to a rim of sand and the relatively calm blue Pacific Ocean.

A small, neat man with little fat on him, he had a weathered face, lots of dark hair immaculately barbered, large brown eyes and an expression of perpetual amusement, as if everything that happened was personally designed to entertain just him.

Overhead, a gaggle of small parrots perched on a telephone line that ran from the small general store behind him to the other side of the island. Occasionally, a parrot would squawk, mimicked quickly by others.

Alfredo wore a clean white undershirt, khaki slacks and sandals, his uniform when off duty in hot climates. He could see his freighter moored 100 yards off the island.

He wondered who owned the ship he commanded. Built in the Philippines in 1974 and almost 50 yards long, its Customs paperwork listed the owner as Robert Ordonez.

Googling this name uncovered a cruise ship catering company president and others of no particular relevance. Robert Ordonez, Alfredo concluded, likely was an alias.

Bored and restless, Alfredo debated whether to grow a beard. In such situations, frequent in his line of work, a beard felt right. Once he returned to the sea, he'd shave it off.

Such delays when carrying controversial cargo were typical. Customers agreed to deals and backed off. Intelligence services often were involved, and being bureaucracies, they frequently dithered. Sources were co-opted or murdered.

He'd often spent months at sea carrying concealed contraband, and had yet to be caught. He'd mention this when bidding for jobs.

Handling weapons grade Uranium was especially difficult. It could be detected without anybody having to uncrate anything. If caught, you might never again see the light of day.

Offloading and transporting weapons-grade cargo tripled and quadrupled the risks. Despite high profits, few chose to take the danger.

Thinking this, Alfredo watched the ship. Somebody had spent a lot of money refurbishing her. She could do 20-25 knots and carry up to 2,000 standard 20-foot-long steel, fiberglass or aluminum containers.

He'd checked. Boxten Maritime, Maersk and other trans well known oceanic carriers did not carry her on their books. He concluded that she was secretly owned by a governmental entity, private corporation or individual. He doubted he'd ever know.

His crew and he had been parked off Aitutaki going on 15 days, waiting for orders to continue. He had no idea why he was being delayed. No matter.

The island was a perfect place to drop anchor when carrying 'unusual' cargo. Tourists from surrounding Cook Islands and mainland Australia visited during days. Few stayed the night.

Islanders feigned no curiosity about the big freighter parked off shore. They were used to smugglers. They preferred to keep to themselves, ask and know as little as possible..

Evenings were spent in the island's only bar or with local women, none that appealing. Many nights, he and his crew were the bar's only patrons.

His wife of 24 years waited tables at a small pizza place in Palermo near their house. His two grown sons had each married and worked as merchant seamen. He saw them maybe two or three times a year.

The night he and his crew arrived on Aitutaki, a woman in her mid 40"s, overweight, balding and smelling of hair and sweat, serviced the crew, including himself. Now 15 days in, she no longer had takers.

In many ways, Alfredo mused, his situation was ideal. He got paid whether his freighter sat or sailed.

At his last port, Singapore, he'd dropped off 600 tons of Japanese machinery and taken on diesel, provisions and 300 20-foot containers filled with electronic goods.

His next official stop would be Punta Arenas, at the tip of South America, on the Chilean side, where he'd offload the electronics and lade new cargo.

His crew consisted of a cook, two engineers, four roustabouts and four security people, who also doubled as cleaners, kitchen assistants and loaders. Alfredo always sailed with five at rest while the others worked.

Some of the crew must have suspected he carried

contraband. While moored in the Sea of Japan, a long, black, needle-nosed boat had pulled along side and crew had winched a heavy create on to the freighter's deck.

Alfredo presumed the crew talked among themselves, but nobody said anything. Had they, his standard answer would have been, "I don't know what we've taken on or how risky it might be. We do our job, you get paid a double wage to keep your mouth shut, and that's how it will stay."

The ship had a double hull, not that unusual, especially in ships built after the early 1970's, plus a false floor not known to the crew, which *was* unusual.

A half hour before arriving in Singapore, an expensive 36-foot Sealine cruiser powered by two Volvo 260 horsepower diesels pulled along side.

Four men dressed in shiny black Latex boarded in open sea, disappeared below deck, cut through the false floor, and placed the crate holding the uranium in a new location.

While watching the men and keeping the crew away, Alfredo noted that already sitting beneath the false floor sat a large 'something' covered by a large shiny plastic, silver colored tarp.

Alfredo asked what that was. One of the men in black turned to him and said, "You'll find out in due time."

The men in black then sealed up the floor and covered it with heavy containers. Now you could not reach the secret place holding the enriched uranium unless you moved the containers with a winch.

Someone had taken a lot of time, thought and money, Alfredo mused, to fit this freighter for its current duty.

What was covered by the tarp? Something not supposed to be seen by him or the crew. What could that be? Hopefully, he'd learn more once the ship reached Punta Arenas.

Savannah, Georgia
June 14, 2010
Update

Chester Field called Rebecca on her cell phone.
"You, Barry and I need to talk," he said. "I may have a job for you."
"Don't be so abrupt, Chester. Don't you first want to know how we are?"
"Fine. How are you both?"
"Well, Barry recently had arthroscopic surgery on his left knee, the interior meniscus, thanks for asking, and he's had a tooth pulled. The children are due home from school tomorrow and I've been having terrible menstrual cramps, but otherwise we're well."
Pause.
"Incisive update, Rebecca, especially the news about your cramps. Hope they clear up, and give my best to Barry. But enough of this bull shit. I'm busy as hell and would really like to get to the business at hand, if that's okay."
"Okay, okay, Sir Grumpiness.."
Rebecca smiled, enjoying Chester's contrariness.
"Are you available?" Chester asked.
"Not right now. The kids are back and forth during the summer, but by late August, after Beth and Jason return to school, we'd be interested."

"Okay. Good," Chester said. "Remember that Chinese woman, Tama Wu?"

"Neither of us ever met her face to face," Rebecca said, "Although I saw her several times at a distance. I remember that she was very beautiful until the Pole got her."

"Well, she survived, and lots of surgeries later, she's active again. As for her beauty, can't comment on that." "Because you're being a gentleman?"

"No, because I haven't seen her."

"Okay. What's any of this have to do with us?"

"Maybe nothing. We'll see."

"Don't be so damn obtuse, Chester."

"Since when did you start using big words like 'obtuse'?" Chester said.

"Since living with Barry. It's his Harvard education. Every day I learn new words by osmosis. Go along to get along."

"I see. Well, say Hello to Barry and your kids for me."

"Our children don't know you, Chester, and I have no immediate plans to change that."

"Say Hello to them anyway."

Laughing, Rebecca hung up.

Aitutaki, Cook Islands
June 15, 2010
Deserter

Alfredo was lying in a hammock when his Iphone rang. While trying to extract the phone from the pocket of his Bermuda shorts, it fell to the ground.

Cursing, trying to reach the phone without tipping over, he tipped over, grabbing the phone on the sixth ring.

"Rested?" the Baron said. He stood in his Hamburg condo study, cradled his phone with chin and shoulder, stood, and dusted himself off.

"Yes, almost too much. My crew's going stir crazy. Hope we can get moving soon," Alfredo said.

"You can, the Baron said. "Let me know when you reach your next destination. Everything okay?"

"Some people boarded as we were about to enter Singapore. They secured everything, to include a big mystery something hidden by a tarp deep in the boat."

The Baron laughed. "That mystery object will be revealed in due course. When it is, you and your crew will be asked to evacuate."

"What?"

"You'll be paid and taken to shore by another boat."

"What about Customs?"

"You'll have fake documents by the time you arrive."

"I've run into a problem here," Alfredo said. "Crew member, name Tomas Polski, spelled T,o.m,a,s. He's fallen in love and wants to stay. He's a drunk, a roustabout and I'm not sorry to see him go."

Silence.

"What's he know?"

"Nothing. He's dumb as shit."

"Hope so, for your sake and mine."

"Don't worry. He won't be leaving this island for awhile, if ever."

After the Baron hung up, Alfredo felt uneasy. He

didn't like relinquishing the ship before reaching port.

What if this Baron, whoever the hell he was, didn't honor his promises?

The crew carried weapons. So did he. He'd wait to learn more, and prepare for the worst.

Hamburg, Germany
June 15, 2010
Betrayal

She'd been an 18-year-old virgin when seized outside her family's barn. Now 19, she'd yet to willingly participate in sex but knew this would be necessary if she were to build a lasting relationship with Jürgen.

Upon reflection, she needn't have worried. Jürgen was anything but sexually aggressive.

It took weeks for him to get the nerve to invite her to his apartment. She stayed the night and found him gentle, loving, traditional, and offering no surprises.

Initially, she found the sex uncomfortable. She tensed at certain moments and had to force herself to relax; but in succeeding weeks she began to enjoy and look forward to the intimacy.

Four months into their relationship, he invited her to live with him. He was 44, more than twice her age, but she liked and felt safe with him.

Her lack of passion bothered her. She did not want to hurt his feelings or emotionally short-change him and believed she had.

Jürgen told her later that he took her lack of passion for shyness. He believed her passivity was her true self and not what it was, an antidote to painful and recent memories of abuse.

She knew he loved her. This, too, upset her. She didn't love him but didn't want to hurt him, although she believed she eventually could.

He suggested she audit courses at the University of Hamburg. He had friends who taught there and would allow her to sit in for free. She enthusiastically agreed.

She chose art history courses. Looking at slides and reproductions of beautiful paintings filled her with wonder and calm.

Jürgen also helped her learn to write German. He patiently corrected essays on topics he assigned, amazed at how bright she was and how effortlessly she absorbed new material.

By now, she'd quit the Polish milk bar and immersed herself in auditing courses, learning more German, keeping house and cooking for Jürgen.

She paid 1000 euros for new fake working papers, using her original first name, and adopting the last name, Urbanska, of a girl in her high school class, also named Ania, who'd been killed in an automobile accident.

With Jürgen's help, she got a job in a travel agency that paid the equivalent of 27,000 euros annually, half of which she began saving.

Again with his help, she passed her driver's test, got a German driver's license and bought on time a black, four-year-old VW Jetta. The best news: she now had a bank account and had saved almost 3,000 euros.

She didn't find Jürgen's friends much fun. Like him, they were serious, left-leaning, idealistic, not ambitious, and did not swear or make personal judgments. Their wives and girl friends were much the same. None went out of their way to befriend her.

Three weeks into living with him, she wrote her parents to tell them she was safe, but did not provide them a return address.

Jürgen mailed her letter from Munich while there on business because she still feared retaliation from her former captors and wished to remain undiscovered.

Two months later, she got the courage to call them. Minutes into her awkward conversation, first with her mother and then with her father, she believed she knew: They'd sold her to her kidnappers. It was nothing they said but what they did not say. Her suspicions devastated her.

At Jürgen's insistence, and to be sure, she called the police station closest to her parents' farm to learn if she'd been reported missing.

No, a detective said. Her parents had never filed a missing persons report. When Ania's school reported her missing, her parents said there'd been a disagreement and she'd gone to live with an aunt in Wloclaw. The school and the police had not inquired further.

Ania's temporary enslavement taught her that she could withstand hard physical and emotional punishment and bounce back. Now she'd learned something additional about herself: She had no family. It had deserted her.

She told herself to persevere. She had a high IQ, exceptional physical attractiveness, a gift for language learning and a comfortable and relatively undemanding live-in relationship with a man she appreciated but did not love. In addition, she was resourceful, and cool under pressure. Not to be ignored, she also was a secret serial murderess.

So much evil happens without a response, she thought. Her parents sell her into slavery, she kills two men and the world moves on as if nothing happened.

She decided she'd never give birth, and wouldn't marry Jürgen. Killing those who'd ruined her would be her focus.

She'd take her time and follow the clues to the top of the evil pyramid. She'd act alone to revenge not only the permanent harm done her but the harm done to all the women currently stolen and those yet to become lost.

There were moments when her plans gave her pause. Was her decision not to bear children and become a loving husband to Jürgen tied up in this? Was she losing her humanity?

She promised herself that once her killing reached the top of the syndicate food chain, she'd stop, leave Germany, return to Poland, get a job, and happily live out the rest of her life. That was her hope.

Langley, Virginia
June 16, 2010
Inquiry

Chester Field hadn't heard much from Montrose Five, the lush who did contract work for him in Warsaw, Poland, so when he saw the man's callback number he quickly dialed it.

The connection took forever and sounded like it was coming through a tunnel with depth charges exploding around it. Finally, Montrose Five picked up.

"Thanks for the return call," he said. "Sorry I

haven't been in contact. I've been working on other stuff, but you should know that eavesdropping on that attorney's email finally paid off."

"Good. What have you got?"

"The Pole's estate has been settled, the furniture sold. Photos, paintings and stuff went for $145,000, the house for the equivalent of eight hundred thousand U.S., all of it deposited with Caesar Enterprises, an offshore bank in the Caymans. The net after real estate commission and..."

"Never mind all that. You have my attention. What else have you got?"

"The money went to a numbered account. Don't know whose, but there's seven million dollars sitting in it."

"Holy shit! How do you know that?"

"Because that's what the lawyer's correspondence stipulated."

"Whose name is on the account?"

"We're good but not that good. Couldn't get that. We do have an email address in Hamburg, Germany."

"Any idea who it is?"

"No, but one more thing..."

"Okay."

"Before the Pole left for Montevideo, he visited a Beata Zawardska in a local hospital here. She had AIDS. It almost killed her, but she survived."

"I hope this is leading somewhere, Montrose Five."

"It may or it may not, my friend. The same lawyer whose in-box I'm snooping in paid for this Beata's six-week recuperation at a clinic in Sopot, the money coming from the Caesar Enterprises account just mentioned."

"Okay."

"Well, she left Sopot yesterday, clean apparently. The lawyer sent her a first class ticket from Gdansk to Hamburg, Germany."

"Aha!" Chester Field said.

"So we have the Pole's estate run out of an attorney's office in Hamburg and the Pole's old girl friend heading there."

"Right," Chester said.

"Want me to continue snooping?"

"Yes!" Chester said. "Let me know if you get more."

****

An analyst stuck his head in the door. "Busy, Mr. Field?" he said. In his mid twenties, tall and brown haired, he wore a white shirt and paisley tie.

Another Ivy leaguer, Chester thought, unlined face revealing how much he still had to learn about man's inhumanity. Well, Chester thought, the CIA was a good place to get that education.

"What is it?" Chester said.

"It's about the Baron," the analyst said. Chester remembered.

"Okay," Chester said. He grimaced. For the past five years, the Baron had been the CIA's principal European contact for used and cheap Russian and Chinese armaments, and for the unloading of old American weapons.

As with all CIA suppliers, each year the Baron sat for a lie detector test. Each year he passed, until March of this year, when he failed. He was not told this.

Instead, he was left in place, only now the CIA began monitoring his land and cell phone usage surrepticously from U2 planes flying at the edge of space across the European continent.

"Intercepts suggest he's just brokered a deal to bring in weapons grade uranium," the analyst said. Chester looked up.

"Oh oh. Confirmed?"

"Not exactly, Sir. He never says this, of course, but the amount of money involved…and the innuendo used, it would have to be fissionable material."

"Who's buying?"

"The Iranians."

"Who's selling?"

"We don't know."

"Where's the uranium now?"

"We also don't know. No money's changed hands. Presumably the stuff's sitting somewhere or at sea. If it's at sea, they won't try to bring it through the Straits of Hormuz. It would never make it past Kuwait. Our base there can detect within a one-mile range now. Soon we'll be able to do a satellite scan, but not yet."

Chester thought a moment. "Russia, North Korea, Pakistan or India are likely sellers. I'll make some calls."

"Very good, Sir."

"How long before you get me translated transcripts of the Baron's conversation?"

"Early tomorrow morning at the latest, Sir. "

"Good. The Baron is generally careful, but he never did get enough training. I may recommend…"

Chester's voice drifted off. He did not complete the thought. Davidson left. Chester phoned a friend at the Indian desk to inquire. Nothing. Then he called Tokyo.

Hamburg, Germany
June 17, 2010
Replacement

The Pole, using the name Hans Deutsch, entered Serge's Hafen City offices. Serge had personally decorated his office with good-quality French regency furniture, the centerpiece an ancient, six-foot-high, dark wood cabinet with glass doors. Beautiful Persian rugs and polished dark plank floors completed the elegant interior.

The walls were red brick, the ceilings high and timbered. Three tall windows gave a nice view of the canal and cityscape beyond.

The Pole and Serge conducted business in two matching armchairs that faced a comfortable couch with beautifully carved wooden armrests.

Unknown to many of Serge's visitors, Serge's bodyguards sat in an adjoining office. Pressing a buzzer under the desk would summon them.

This afternoon, thanks to René Oppenheim, the bodyguards would not respond if Serge called. Each had been paid 1,000 euros to stay away.

The Pole, alias arms dealer Hans Deutsch, had been vouched for by René, who told Serge that Hans had contacts with Kurdish Iraqis and the Kuwait royal family.

That was enough for Serge, who immediately granted an exploratory meeting.

The conversation proceeded amiably enough until Serge sensed that something was not right. He started to get up from the couch.

Before he reached his desk, the Pole began strangling him.

Serge struggled, but he was considerably smaller, older and weaker.

"You can make this go more quickly if you just relax," the Pole said.

Serge's face reddened. Somehow he removed a knife from his pocket and slashed the Pole's hand.

Enraged, the pole pushed Serge away, evaded another stabbing attempt and flat-handed struck Serge at the base of his neck, which snapped. A second even more violent chop and Serge's eyes seemed to pop from his head. He fell lifeless to the floor.

The Pole bent down and checked Serge's body for vital signs. He found none.

He wiped prints from everywhere and everything he'd touched before leaving the building. Down the street and two blocks distant, he felt sick to his stomach. He leaned against a wall until his breathing steadied. Feeling marginally better, he took a bus back to St. Pauli, By the time he arrived, he felt ravenous. He dined well at a Hungarian restaurant he'd been curious to try.

Later, he phoned René to let him know that he was ready to assume control of Caesar Enterprises' Hamburg businesses.

At last, the strong-arm stuff is behind me, the Pole thought. I can build a business and begin a new, less violent life.

Tokyo, Japan
June 19, 2010
Confirmation

Frank Bishop was paying for carryout at a noodle shop near his apartment when he recognized a CIA contact known as 'Boots' entering. Boots asked him to come with him and Frank followed.

Boots drove him in a government-issue Chevy Malibu, parked and escorted him up metal stairs to the third floor of a nondescript contemporary building in Tokyo's Asakusa district.

The trading company offices easily suggested its likely occupants. Frank had seen hundreds of such places while in the army and later as a government civilian employee.

The room where they sat him had walls painted a flat white, cheap tile floor, standard issue metal desk and chair, and a photograph of President Obama on the wall.

On a side table sat a voice recorder, which one agent immediately turned on, plus a mystery device the size of a cigarette pack, its function unclear.

Frank doubted he was in any individual's office because he saw no photos of a wife or children. The room probably was used to interview people like himself, meaning it was not a holding cell, but if the conversation did not go right, a holding cell would be next.

He cooperated fully. He was an independent contractor who did a lot of CIA work and eater to please.

He'd tell the two agents what he knew as long as he needn't reveal his customers' names. That would quickly mean the end of his livelihood and possibly his life.

The mood was uncomfortable but not threatening. Nobody offered him coffee or tried to make small talk.

The agent assisting Boots didn't feel like a field agent. He seemed 'corporate,' detached and not all that likeable. He was easily over six feet tall and fat.

"Normally, we don't snoop into your private business," Boots said. "We agreed when we first hired you that you were free to take work from others. But if it's fissionable material, that's a national security matter. We can't just ignore that."

"Fissionable material? You mean like uranium, cobalt and the like?"

"Yes."

"I may have transported something like that recently. I never know for sure," Frank said. "Everything's always packaged to look like machinery, electronics or whatever. Back in mid May, May 15th, I'm almost sure, although I can check. I was suspicious. We loaded a smallish crate that was heavy as hell and dropped it off an hour later at sea."

"So it didn't end up on one of those islands or back in Japan," Boots said.

Frank Bishop smiled. "Didn't realize I was so predictable."

"It's one of your strengths," Boots said. "You stay within areas you know and use proven routines and checks. All of that's kept you alive."

Frank now realized what he'd suspected: the CIA monitored and back-checked every job they gave him.

"On that particular job, the hand-off was at sea," Frank said. "A Handimax. It had all been arranged by phone."

"Who was your initial contact?"

"A man from the North Korean Embassy. I've done several jobs for him."

"So he arranged for the pick-up, but what about the delivery?"

"The North Korean arranged that as well. I communicated with the ship's captain briefly. He gave me the coordinates where he'd be, and he was."

"What can you tell me about the freighter?"

"As I said, Handymax. Flag said Malta registration. Don't remember much else."

"Do you know where the ship was headed?"

"No idea. Didn't care. Just wanted to off-load and get the hell out of there."

Boots' briefcase sat on his lap. He put it on the table and picked up the mysterious black device the size of a cigarette pack, some cord and a variety of plugs.

"Let me have your cell phone," Boots said.

"What for?"

"So I can upload all your messages. Your communication with the ship's captain will be on there, yes?"

"Sure, but I'm not sure that's any of your business."

Boots sat back as if relaxing, sighed and then leaned so close to Frank Bishop that Fran felt the heat of Boots' breath on his cheek, the effect menacing.

"Of course you can refuse my request," Boots said. "I'm not going to try to wrestle your phone away from you. But I don't think refusing my request would be wise. You'd be dead within 20 minutes after leaving this building, and we'd take your cell phone anyways. We don't care whom you do business with, but we need to know when you're dealing fissionable materials."

"I told you, I'm not sure that's what I was dealing."

"So what do you think you were shipping?"

"Okay," Frank took his cell phone out of his pocket and handed it over.

Boots searched until he found the right connect plug, turned on the cell phone, pressed three buttons on the small black device, there was a blip, and silence.

"Now let me have your second cell phone," Boots said.

"How did you know...?"

"We have photos of you, lots of them. You carry two phones."

Frank handed over the second phone.

"Did the freighter have any markings?" asked the second agent. He had a southern accent.

"I couldn't see at night," Frank said. "It was a Handymax bulk carrier, had four winches, was maybe 200 meters long and carrying both 20 and 40-foot containers. That's about all I saw. I never boarded, so I could not see what they were carrying. Oh, before I forget, the ship had a Maltese flag."

"You already mentioned that. Did she look new or old?" the second agent said. He was thin, and balding. Although older, he did not act senior to the other agent.

"The hull had a fresh coat of paint, but as I said, I never even got on the deck. From the sounds of the engines, they were diesels."

"Who contracted for this delivery?"

"I told you. A Middle-aged Asian, code-named Rolph. He didn't give his nationality, but I suspect he was North Korean."

"Why did you think that?" the agent with the southern voice said.

"Because his suit looked badly made and he had an unhealthy, pasty face. His English was decent but sounded as if he'd learned it in a lab."

Both agents looked at each other as if they might know such a man.

"I met him here in Tokyo. Just a second and I can tell you when, but I need the first phone I gave you." Boots handed Frank Bishop the cell phone.

Frank fiddled with it. "Yes, here it is," he said. "I met this Rolph on December 15th of last year. He gave me the pick-up time and the coordinates."

"Do you have his number?" the older agent asked.

"We're getting into sticky territory here, gentlemen. If I give you that, I might as well quit what I'm doing. No one will ever trust me again, to include all of you."

"I guess it's come to that," the younger agent said.

Frank searched 'Contacts' on his phone, found Rolph's phone number and provided it.

"Thanks, Frank," the agent said. "We appreciate your cooperation."

"Before you start questioning or rolling up people, I need three days to clear out," Frank said. "You've shut me down."

"What if we buy your boat?" Boots said.

"I'd appreciate that," Frank said with anger.

"We'll cut you a check for $20,000 before you leave," the older agent said, "to show our appreciation for your cooperation."

"I've got over $200,000 tied up in it," Frank said. "Sorry. We're only authorized to pay you $20,000," Boots lied.

Frank left ten minutes later. He'd entered the building a successful smuggler and left without a trade.

It wouldn't take long for the arms smuggling community to learn that Frank Bishop had compromised them.

Two hours later, he left his apartment by the back way and took the bullet train to Osaka, hopefully without anyone observing his departure. From Osaka he'd fly somewhere. When he got to the airport, he'd decide. He didn't care where. His only goal: get as far from Tokyo as he could and quickly.

He had $75,000 in a numbered Swiss account and a check for $20,000 in his pocket. He knew a guy in Panama who'd put him up for awhile.

Hamburg, Germany
June 18, 2010
Identification

Sammy Kan patiently searched through 734 males who'd registered for driver licenses in the Hamburg area over the past two months. He paid 500 euros for the list from a Department of Motor Vehicles employee. None of names listed matched any of the Pole's known aliases.

Concurrently, Sammy and his four fellow detectives queried underworld sources. Slowly, over a six-week period, they assembled a list of 14 forgers and through intermediaries approached each with the photos of the Pole taken after his Buenos Aries' surgeries. Each forger was offered 15,000 euros for photocopies of fake documentation created for the Pole. None accepted the offer. No one even admitted they'd had the Pole as a client.

They sold secrecy, they said. Revealing their customers was tantamount to professional suicide and could, in certain circumstances, get them killed.

Their responses were pro forma and expected. That was how you played the game, especially if by chance your conversation were recorded.

Sammy Kan knew from previous experience with forgers that the right amount of money could be persuasive. The trick was to be patient.

Sure enough, a week later, coming out of a coffee shop, Sammy was stopped by one of the forgers, who said he was 72, had been careful with his money, and one hundred thousand Euros would allow him to retire.

He'd want the money deposited in a bank in Bad Tolz, where years ago he'd purchased a small, walk-up studio apartment.

Sammy, through his intermediary in Hong Kong, checked with Tama Wu. Sammy and the other four detectives had already spent close to $400,000 chasing after the Pole. Tama suggested further negotiation and set a cap at 75,000 euros, which sufficed.

The document exchange took place in Bielefeld, a five-hour drive south of Hamburg. Sammy and the forger met at a small neighborhood café of the forger's choice.

The forger produced copies of passports and driver's licenses for three men, Hans Deutsch, Heinz Czsylinski and Bernard Mannheim. The photo on each document was of the surgically enhanced Pole!

****

The search began. The addresses on the three driver's licenses differed. A week later, the detectives found the Pole.

He worked in a small suite of offices overlooking one of the canals in the Speicherstadt, an ancient warehouse district infiltrated by canals leading north to open sea.

One afternoon, three men unknown to Sammy Kan joined the Pole for lunch al fresco at a table outside an Italian restaurant several blocks from the Pole's office.

From a distance, Sammy took photographs of the assemblage, which included a rat-like younger man, a fat, well-dressed man in his thirties, and the Pole.

Immediately after they left, Sammy Kan walked to the Pole's vacated table and placed the knife and napkin used by the Pole in a plastic sandwich bag.

Questioned by the waiter, Sammy handed him a 20 Euro bill and walked out.

Sammy was known for being careful. This time he'd been careless. He didn't notice a gray S Class Mercedes with tinted windows move slowly by.

The Pole had retrieved his car from the parking lot next door and planned to head back to his office.

As his car cruised past the restaurant, he saw Sammy pocket the spoon and napkin and pay off the waiter.

The Pole turned the corner, stopped the car, dropped off his two bodyguards, and drove off.

The bodyguards tailed Sammy to his car and got his license plate number. Two more days and they were able to follow him to his hotel. One of them followed Sammy up to his room but continued down the hall while Sammy let himself in.

When Sammy left the hotel the next day, the bodyguards broke into his hotel room, searched and bugged it. The next day, they identified his four companions.

Another week and they'd assembled enough information to understand what Sammy was doing in Frankfurt.

He and his four companions had been paid to find the Pole and keep him under surveillance. It was not clear why, or when the surveillance would end.

Told this, the Pole kept his feelings and conclusions to himself, but deeper inside he felt emptiness and despair. Despite his surgically remade self and venue change, despite his effort to become a new and more respectable man, enemies had found him.

Hamburg
June 19, 2010
Pay Day

Ania's days passed pleasantly without major disruptions. She found work at the travel agency easy enough. The business didn't get much traffic. She used down time to practice speaking and writing German.

Nights, she audited Hamburg University art history courses and considered enrolling full-time in the Fall to study English.

Today, Jürgen was in Frankfurt on business and not scheduled home until later.

After work, she phoned to tell him she was going to study with friends at the university and might be home late.

Back in their apartment, she tied her natural straight blond hair behind her, put on Levis, glasses with tortoise shell rims, a white tee shirt, tennis shoes, and no lipstick.

In her backpack, she carried make-up, a change of clothes and shoes, plus the pistol taken from the backroom supervisor she'd killed on the brothel front steps.

As the sun set, she drove within two blocks of paymaster Karl Kleinholtz's apartment, parked on a side street, donned a red beret and waited patiently for darkness.

She'd given thought to how she'd proceed. Shooting Turku in the groin made the killing seem personal.

The killing of the second backroom supervisor on the steps looked more like a professional hit. From now on, every time she killed a syndicate person, if she could, she'd make his slaying appear similarly impersonal.

From the street, she watched Karl through his second-floor window, Ipod in his ear, gyrating slightly, apparently to music playing in his head.

She rang his doorbell.

"Who is it?" he said gruffly through the intercom.

"Can I come up?" she said. "A friend at LuLu's said you were definitely a hot guy who liked pretty girls."

She heard him laugh.

"Are you hot?" he said coquettishly.

"Definitely," she said, "But why not see for yourself. If you don't like me, you can ask me to leave and I will; but I'm warning you, I've yet to get a refusal."

The ground floor entry door buzzed, clicked, she opened it and stepped into the foyer of a well-maintained, pre-war building. She smelled fresh paint and shellac. As she climbed the stairs, she saw Karl on the second-floor landing, Ipod still in his ear, studying her.

"Did we meet a Lulu's?" he said.

"No," she said as she reached the landing. "But you definitely are hot!"

"You're not so bad yourself," Karl said. "Come on in!"

He stepped aside as she moved into his apartment. She heard the door shut behind her.

"You sound foreign," he said.

"I am. I'm an exchange student from Slovakia," Ania said. "Got anything to drink? I've been studying all day and could use something."

"Beer's all I've got," Karl said. He was grinning, unable to believe his good luck. She noticed a bulge in his pants.

"Then beer it is," Ania said. She set her backpack down and started to open it.

"Great!" he said. "Just a sec. I'll get one for you."

Still grinning, hardly able to conceal his anticipation, he turned away from her as he opened the refrigerator and bent down to get two beers.

She shot him in the back of the head. His forehead banged on an open refrigerator shelf as he did.

She removed a towel from the bathroom and wiped down the doorknob and gun. Holding the gun in the towel, she placed it next to him and stuffed the towel in her backpack. Next she looked for his gun, finding it in a kitchen drawer along with some stray bullets and cartridges and put them in her purse.

She activated his computer, which was on sleep mode, and eyeballed emails. She noted two from Fritz Engel, whom she'd seen Karl visit on two occasions, and one message from a Bernard Mannheim that Fritz had forwarded just two hours ago.

The name was new to her but she sensed from the message's tone that Manheim was higher up the syndicate chain of command.

The apartment was a mess, clothes everywhere, bed unmade. Methodically, she wiped down the computer and every available surface she might have touched, then left.

She passed a young couple heading up as she headed down the stairs. She and they nodded.

Outside, she stepped into an alley, removed her glasses, took off her red beret, let her long, straight blond hair fall to her shoulders, put on lipstick and donned an expensive light wool red jacket and pumps.

In less than a minute, she'd transformed herself from college student to sophisticated looking young middle class professional woman.

She left from the other end of the alley, walked two blocks, got into her car and drove home.

Jürgen greeted her as she walked in. "My, my, you're all dressed up! What happened to the study group?" he asked.

"At the last minute it was changed to a combination study group and birthday party. We girls decided to dress up," she said.

He nodded. "You look great!" he said. She could read his mind. He was wondering why she'd dressed up for a study group. His worried look suggested he feared she might be seeing somebody.

"We were going to a restaurant later. Waste of time and effort. Everybody said they needed to go home and study."

She kissed him on the cheek and he patted her rear, the worry gone from his face.

They watched the ten o'clock news on TV and read another hour, neither talking much, both in bed by eleven-fifteen p.m.

Jürgen woke her at two a.m. to have sex and she accommodated him, surprised at the ferocity of her response.

"My, what's gotten in to you!" he said.

"You," she said. She gave him another peck on the cheek and went back to sleep.

Savannah, Georgia
June 19, 2010
Cover

Barry heard the phone ring at ten-thirty p.m. Jason and Beth, who'd arrived from boarding school that morning, were visiting friends. Had something happened to one or either of them?

Barry, who'd just slipped beneath the covers, glanced at the phone, saw the caller's phone number and perked up.

"Calling rather late, aren't you?" Barry said. He shouted to Rebecca in the bathroom, "It's Chester."

"Yes, and I apologize," Chester said, "but I needed to get to both of you tonight"

"Why? What's up?"

"Is Rebecca on the line?"

"Yes, I've picked up," Rebecca said.

"Got a rather unusual call about two hours ago and had to check with my superiors before calling you," Chester said.

"Why?"

"Don't be so damned impatient. I'm getting to it."

"You're taking your own sweet time doing so."

"The call came from China."

"So?"

"Now you're being snippy and childish."

"It's bedtime. I'm sleepy. I need you to get to the point," Barry said.

"Okay, I will. The call came from Dragon Motors."

"Anyone we know?"

"Very funny. Tama Wu wants you to do some work for her."

"Really? How does she even know about us?"

"You sell yourself short, my friend."

"Always, but please clarify."

"Let's just say your work in Montevideo was admired and word spreads."

"Oh?"

"Oh, indeed. You got in and out of there and almost killed the Pole without anybody identifying or nailing you."

"The Pole can now identify me," Barry said, "assuming he's still alive. He was about to kill me if you recall. I have a scar on my heel as a memento."

"He's alive. It's confirmed. He has no idea who Rebecca is," Chester said, "although this is all beside the point."

"So what kind of work does Madame Wu want done?" Rebecca said.

"Her company, Dragon Motors, is opening car dealerships in various European capitols. The first will be in Frankfurt. As a result of her Montevideo experience, she's fearful when traveling internationally. She liked the way you operated in Montevideo, especially likes the fact she has no idea who you were or are."

"What's she want done?" Rebecca said.

"She wants you to give her cover while she's in Frankfurt."

"You serious? That's it?"

"That's it. She wishes to enter Germany incognito, meet her new people there, appear as herself publicly for the dealership's unveiling, and leave."

"Okay," Barry said. "Rebecca and I will talk things over. Anything else we should know?"

"I need a decision relatively quickly."

"Give us two days, Chester."

"Fine. Let me know sooner, okay?"

"Yes. Goodnight, Chester," Rebecca said.

"Goodnight, to both of you," Chester said. "Pleasant dreams."

****

Chester worked at his desk at home for another hour. No hints of fissionable material movement out of India, Pakistan or Russia, but the lead out of Japan got Chester's attention. Something valuable had been transferred to a Maltese freighter in the Sea of Japan on May 15th.

Where might such a freighter head? Using the

Suez Canal did not make sense. Too many inspectors and detection devices.

The ship, unless it off-loaded its cargo on any of a thousand islands in the Pacific, would likely head down and though the Magellan Straits at the tip of South America.

Analysts were now tracing the ship captain's cell phone. Soon they'd have a GPS read on the freighter.

Should he alert German Intelligence? Was the transfer even taking place in Germany? So many questions. He had Barry and Rebecca headed for Europe. He'd utilize them if killing was needed.

Hamburg
June 23, 2010
Cleanup

Brothers Hugo and Hector Spicers' bulk overwhelmed the two normal sized metal chairs facing the Pole, who sat imperiously behind his desk eying them.

Hugo and Hector had received terse emails from an anonymous source saying that Serge was returning to Russia to 'look after business interests and a new boss, Bernard Mannheim had arrived, had already met with Karl and Fritz, and now wanted to meet them.

That was all they were told, which did not surprise them. Not much ever got committed to writing by anybody they knew.

Unlike Serge, their new boss was huge and muscled, dressed expensively like Serge, but his face, which was partially covered by a trim brown beard and thick brown hair was unreadable.

"Okay. Start with Kleinholtz," the Pole said. "Then I want to hear about this Sammy Kan."

The name on the Pole's office door said Kapinski Associates," and beneath it 'Bernard Mannheim, President.'

The firm was registered as an importer and exporter of Polish furniture. Elsewhere in the same building, three legitimate firms brokered India rugs and exotic spices.

Kapinski Associates' dowdy looking office consisted of unpainted cement floors, brick walls painted white and dropped particleboard ceilings. It contained one room filled with desks plus a conference room. The firm shared an adjoining washroom on the same floor with two other trading companies.

The Pole noted with private amusement that neither Hugo nor Hector appeared impressed with his office. He was not surprised. Compared with his predecessor Serge's office and its Regency furniture, Kapinski Associates definitely was low rent.

It contained an old wooden desk, a table lamp with green plastic shade, a side table complete with Bosch Tassimo single-cup coffee maker, some boxes of Gevalia coffee pads, ratty looking cane-backed chairs, a Dell computer, HP printer, steel, floor-to-ceiling filing cabinets and absolutely no photographs or other decoration.

"Planning on hiring a decorator?" Hugo said. He smiled to suggest he was kidding.

"Nope," the Pole said. He'd recently owned an expensive condo in downtown Warsaw but always rented offices in low-rent industrial areas, not caring whom he impressed or did not impress.

He once asked himself why he did this, then decided such introspection would lead nowhere productive and never again asked himself the question.

Hugo shifted uneasily, not liking his new boss's lack of responsiveness. He'd been a Munich policeman for several years, but hadn't taken orders willingly. After he smashed a police captain in the mouth with the butt of his revolver, he was told to resign.

That said, he'd received good training, could pick locks, conduct surveillances, evaluate and clean up crime scenes, eliminate clues when necessary and use a variety of firearms.

Hugo's younger brother, Hector, a high school dropout, lacked such skills, but lifting weights had given him prodigious strength that made him useful as an enforcer.

Unlike his brother, Hector willingly followed orders as long as the orders came from big brother. With others he remained perpetually wary and reticent.

The Pole, studying Hector, was reminded of himself as a young man: He, too, had been brutishly strong back then. Hopefully, Hector did not share a similar youthful penchant for risky behavior.

A Caesar Enterprises source told the Pole that Hugo and Hector would gladly kill if asked, and always followed orders. Their only downside: they were prone to bar fights and soccer hooliganism. Each had a rap sheet stretching back to their preteen years.

The Pole continued staring silently at the two brothers. Hugo continued nervously shifting in his seat. He and Hector were a few inches shorter than the Pole, who stood 6'3," but both were heavier and blunter in appearance and speech.

The Pole had a PhD in Polish History and Literature. This extended learning had not quelled his viciousness but had exposed him to proper table manners and educated speech. His acculturation softened his face's blunt edges, giving him, especially in repose, a certain soulfulness.

The brothers stared back, trying unsuccessfully to form a connection. The Pole decided that he needn't play dominance games with them. They were too dumb to be intimidated, plus they were valuable.

Everyone in the brothel and sex trade world was exposed to drugs, kickbacks, bribes, and disease. Brothel managers and backroom supervisors changed frequently. Employees sometimes had to be killed. Same with the whores, many going crazy after spending a year or more cooped up, pawed and treated like trash.

Hugo and Hector made such problems go away. Time he loosened up with them.

He smiled to break the impasse and they smiled tentatively back.

Hugo and Hector were homely, unkempt men. He wondered how often they bathed. Neither had shaved that morning or bothered to comb their thick, greasy hair.

Hugo wore a wrinkled flannel shirt, and Hector a tee shirt and leather jacket. Each wore identical nondescript jeans held up by thick leather belts with big buckles, and wore heavy work boots. Both were easily 30 pounds overweight and in their mid thirties.

"Fritz asked us to check on Karl," Hugo began. "He didn't show for work or call in. We went to his place. He'd been shot in the back of the head."

"Forced entry?" the Pole said.

"No," Hector said. "Everything wiped down. No prints. Clearly a professional job."

The Pole noted the brothers' scarred faces, wondering how they'd gotten the scars.

They were closer to animals than men, he thought, psychopaths, as was he, but without his overall awareness of the world and how it worked.

"Had anyone called the police?" the Pole said.

"No," Hugo said. "We didn't either. We cleaned up the place. It didn't need much. I looked for clues to who did him, didn't find any and got rid of the body."

"How?" the Pole said.

"We have a moving van with all the necessary papers. We came back later as movers. Took some stuff, to include Karl wrapped in a rug."

"There's nothing else you need to tell me about this?" the Pole said. He assumed the body had been dumped somewhere and burned, but decided he didn't need to know.

"Yes, there is something you need to know," Hugo countered. "The gun found next to Karl belonged to the supervisor killed outside House One."

"How do you know that?"

"Because Hector and I provide guns to the backroom supervisors and the paymaster. It was one of ours."

"The Polish girl!" the Pole said.

"Looks like it," Hector said. "Or somebody else we don't know who doesn't like us. Turku was definitely done by the Polish girl. There were witnesses. The others? No way to know."

"Guns deliberately left at the scenes certainly implicate the Polish girl," Hugo said. "She first kills a backroom supervisor, then another supervisor, and now the paymaster."

"That's right," Hector said.

"Somebody could be setting her up so we focus on her," the Pole said.

"That's true," Hugo said.

"We need to find her," the Pole said. "Have you been looking?"

"When we have time," Hugo said. "But not really. There's just the two of us. We interviewed the owner of a Polish milk bar awhile back. A girl who looked a lot like her picture worked for him for about three months, but it's hard to be sure."

"How did you get her picture?"

"We take their drivers licenses when they come in, or take a photo. In her case, we took a photo. She didn't have a license when she got to us."

"Coffee?" the Pole said.

Yes," Hugo said. "You want some, Hector?" Hector nodded.

"I'll take some as well," the Pole said. "The French roast." He made no effort to get up and help.

****

Once everyone made coffee and took their previous seats, the Pole resumed his questioning.

"Okay," He said, "Now tell me about the Chinaman, the guy who picked up the silverware and napkin I used."

"There are five," Hugo said. "The guy was easy to follow. We're been hiring different people to watch him and them. We keep switching people. We've bugged their phones. Their contact calls from a Hong Kong number. Then, just recently, they began receiving calls from a

Shanghai number."

The Pole straightened. "Are the calls coming from, a private residence or a company?" he asked.

"A company," Hector said. "We traced it. Dragon Motors in Shanghai, China."

The Pole's face flushed. Hugo noticed.

"You know what this is about?" Hugo said.

"I may," the Pole said, "Continue." He seemed to momentarily lock up, chin down, then his chin rose and he looked directly at both men. "Other than looking for me, what are these detectives doing here?"

"We don't have a translator, so when they don't speak English, we don't know what's being said, but most of their correspondence has been in English; which is how we know what they're up to. For instance, one of them is staking out this building."

"What?" the Pole was furious. "How long has this been going on?"

"For about the last three weeks," Hugo said.

"Why haven't you told me?"

"Because we didn't even know you were in here, Boss. Serge had his office in Hafen City, about a mile from here. We just assumed you were using his office."

Somewhat mollified, the Pole nodded. "So they saw you come in..."

"Yes," Hugo said, but they don't know where we went. As far as they're concerned, we could be buying spices or rugs from one of the other businesses on this floor."

"Possibly," the Pole said, not mollified. "What else are they doing ?"

"They're also staking out the Kempinski Atlantic."

My hotel! The Pole thought. He and Beata

Zawardska had been living there for the past month, but Hugo and Hector didn't know that.

"Anything else?"

"No," Hugo said. "They were busy for awhile, but now they just seem to be sitting around waiting. They go to lunch, take walks, sit in coffee shops but aren't busy like they were."

The Pole suspected the Chinese detectives were idle because they'd found him and were awaiting further orders. What might those orders be? Terminating him?

"Have you had their Chinese conversations translated?"

"No, Boss," Hector said. "We had no boss for about ten days. Serge had left and you'd not contacted us. We tried to get a sit-down with you earlier but you were busy." The Pole nodded, irritated with himself. They were right. He'd been spending time introducing himself to people in the supply channels, visiting the brothels, learning from Fritz how the finances worked.

"Okay," he said. "We need a translator ASAP. I don't care what you have to pay. I want to know everything they're up to and what they're waiting for. Be careful whom you hire. No, wait. Get me the tapes. I'll get them to a source who's trustworthy."

"Okay," Hugo said. "Anything else?"

"Yes. I'm bringing in some people from Poland to take care of the Polish girl. She's a worrisome distraction. I'll ask these men to talk with you first to get oriented. After that, they'll know what to do."

He motioned for Hugo and Hector to leave. "I'll be in touch, and thanks for coming in. This was a good meeting."

"Glad we could help, Boss," Hugo said.

"One more thing, Hugo," the Pole said. "Have you ever torched or bombed a building?"

Hugo looked amused. "Who, me?" he said with mock seriousness.

"If you have, I've got a job for you. It means 20,000 euros for you if done right. You'd need to make it look like some radical group planned it."

"Been there, done that. No problem," Hugo said. He looked pleased. He and his brother, shoulders touching, psychopathic partners by predilection, knew it was time to leave, and did.

****

The Pole sat in silence. Okay, the bad news: Tama Wu had not only discovered he was not dead, she'd found him!

The good news: he'd discovered this before her arrival and she didn't know this. But Tama Wu was not his only problem. A mysterious rogue Polish girl was killing up the chain of command, meaning Fritz Engel was next. Should Fritz be warned?

No, he'd be the lure. Hugo or Hector could watch Fritz until the Polish guys arrived, which would be within the week, hopefully. They'd catch the Polish girl when she made her move.

Just yesterday, he'd read in the *Frankfurter Zeitung* about the Dragon Motors dealership opening in a Frankfurt suburb. She'd be in Germany for that. Ha! She was already as good as dead and didn't know it.

His mind drifted. He thought about Beata. Life with her was not going well. He liked to rise early. She liked to sleep late. She didn't like his friends but was not making her own.

He had no idea what she did with her days, if anything. She'd always been an indifferent lover, more interested in the act that in the preliminaries, and this frustrated him.

Last night, he'd been unable to get an erection. This uncomfortable fact challenged his self-imposed sense of masculine power.

Worse, Beata didn't seem to care. She just rolled over, said nothing, and went to sleep.

He wondered how much longer she'd stick around. He hated to admit the obvious: he needed her.

He dealt with scum all day. It was nice coming home at night to someone warm who smelled good and accepted him as he was, or so he thought.

Did she love him? He thought not. Neither he nor she handled intimacy well. Loving someone was no easier for her than him.

Did he love her? Yes. Unfortunately for him, his feelings for her were stronger than hers for him.

Hamburg, Germany
June 23 , 2010
Double

Ania found Fritz Engel's office in a relatively new but nondescript, four-story, glass-walled office building off Ludwig-Erhard Strasse, a block from the Stadhaus canal bridge.

In the lobby, she studied the building roster. It contained a dozen accountants, dentists and other professionals, to include Fritz, whose title was

Finanzielle Manager und Planer (Financial manager and planner).

She headed across the marble-floored lobby. It held a coffee table and three leather club chairs. She noticed a man sitting in one reading the *Hamburger Morgenpost*. She'd seen him before, but when and where?

Hector glanced at her over the top of his newspaper as she headed past him to the elevator, then went back to his reading.

The young woman he saw had dark brown hair, wore heels, glasses, wore a conservative blue business suit and carried a legal briefcase.

She looked like somebody's wife visiting one of the building's dentists or financial people and nothing like the small and very young, blond and likely emotionally damaged Polish whore he was told to apprehend.

Ania had taken two months to track Fritz to this location. By now, she also knew he lived in Altona and had a stay-at-home wife, suggesting that taking care of him in his office would be easier.

She got off the elevator on the third floor and headed down the corridor, glancing into offices.

Three doors from the corridor's end, she saw Fritz through his office's glass door. He sat behind his desk bent over his computer keyboard. He had no secretary!

She continued walking, then took the stairway to the ground floor, suddenly remembering where she'd seen Hector.

Two weeks after her arrival at the first Hamburg brothel, a supervisor argued with a client and beat him severely.

At the time, six clients were in the brothel. All but

the beaten man were asked to leave. Two huge, unkempt men Ania had not seen before arrived.

"Cleanup," one of the girls said in hushed tones. Terrified, Ania asked what that meant.

"These same awful men always come when there's trouble," she said. "They're enforcers. They clean up blood and they get rid of us when we're no longer wanted."

Ania asked no more questions. She went to her room and cowered, waiting until the two huge, unkempt men left.

She heard later that the aggrieved client accepted 1,500 Euros to keep quiet. He was escorted out a back door, taken to a clinic, and patched up. He presumably left Hamburg soon after.

Two days later, Ania and three other girls were moved to another brothel owned by the same syndicate. This apparently was standard procedure when a brothel experienced problems.

So, Ania thought, one of the cleanup crew she saw back then was the man sitting in the lobby now.

Should she reappear and give him a second look at her? Ania decided against this, walked slowly back up the stairs to the first floor and looked for another exit. None. If she exited it would have to be through the lobby.

She made a decision. She returned to the third floor and headed down the corridor to Fritz Engel's office, pulling on a pair of white gloves as she walked.

Fritz looked up as she entered, smiled, rose and moved around from behind his desk.

She'd concealed her gun by carrying it in the same hand as her briefcase. He saw the weapon too late. She shot him in the chest.

He collapsed, moaning, hitting his head on his chair as he fell.

Frantically, she looked around, rushed to the glass wall facing the corridor, found the controls and electronically lowered a plastic shade.

She returned and shoved the barrel of her gun against the back of Fritz Engel head and fired a second shot.

Still hurrying, she placed her gun, the barrel still hot, in her briefcase, searched through drawers, put an appointment calendar and Fritz's cell phone in her purse, checked Fritz's computer, printed out emails to him from a Bernard Mannheim, and headed back to the elevator, her high heels click-clacking on the hard tile floor, carrying her gun against her side, her briefcase concealing it.

In the lobby, Hector continued to read his newspaper. He glanced up.

Quickly, seeing nobody in the lobby and no pedestrians passing by outside, Ania made a decision.

As she moved past Hector toward the revolving front door, she turned and shot him. The bullet hit him high in the chest and threw him backward.

He slid slowly off his seat and on to the floor. He struggled to get up but could not.

Coolly, she approached as close as she dared and fired again, hitting him just above the mouth. Blood shot from his face.

She wiped her gun of fingerprints and left it beside him, found his weapon, a Glock holstered under his left arm, and with difficulty extracted it, checked to see if it were loaded, saw that it was, and walked out of the building into the late morning, turned the corner and moved with deliberate speed towards the corner, her heart beating, terrified someone had seen her.

She entered the Metro stop and waited for the next train. She didn't care where it went. While she waited, she moved into a corner away from the magazine stand and removed her brown wig, heels and glasses, took off her two-inch heels and put on tennis shoes. She heard the warning bell that announced another train arriving. She got on.

As she grabbed a strap to steady her as the train left the station, she looked out the window and saw two policemen rush on to the waiting platform looking wildly around.

Whew! She thought later. That was too close. She must plan better. She'd stop killing for awhile.

She returned to the travel agency where she worked. There, she read the Bernard Mannheim emails.

Each dealt with financial matters, a lot of the material coded. She did not understand most of it.

No matter. She'd confirmed what she'd suspected: Bernard Mannheim was the syndicate's boss. He would be her final kill.

Hamburg, Germany
June 27, 2010
Hugo

Anxious and unsettled, the Pole crossed streets, took cabs, ducked into and out of department stores and doubled back on himself to make sure he was not followed. He hoped that Hugo had taken similar precautions.

He'd driven by the old Regency-style building in Hamburg's old town near the corner of Medenheimer Strasse and Neustadt, noting and admiring it. Although he preferred interiors with a contemporary feel, he loved classic, well maintained exteriors, the older the better.

He and Hugo met inside the building in a small, disappointing second-floor, walk-up apartment containing two small bedrooms and a single bath.

The narrow, dark living room had dirty carpeting and a single window that looked across the street at a similar building. The place belonged to Hugo's uncle, who was at work. It smelled of stubbed cigarettes, poverty and loneliness.

Hugo and the Pole sat together on a black Naugahyde living room couch across from a credenza displaying an unappealing collection of tacky flower girl and dog figurines.

A copy of Dali's melting-pocket-watch painting hung on a far wall. Dirty dishes sat stacked on the galley kitchen counter.

Once seated, and already anxious to leave, the Pole asked Hugo if the police had contacted him.

"Yes," Hugo said nervously. "They did. I had to go to the morgue and identify my brother's body. It was the hardest thing I ever had to do."

He paused, looked away, wiped a tear from his eye, and continued, his voice almost a cry for help.

"Hector was shot point-blank in the chest," he said. "She shot him with Fritz's weapon and took his. She'll be coming for me next."

No, probably me, the Pole thought.

"I'm sorry about your brother," the Pole said. He sounded as if he meant it. Hugo glanced up briefly, face filled with gratitude.

"We've got to catch her quickly," the Pole continued. "As promised, I've brought four Poles in from Warsaw. They'll find her, and when they do, we'll hold off killing her so you can have a few private minutes with her."

"You'd do that for me?"

"I take care of my people," the Pole said. "Do the police have any idea who did your brother?"

"They seemed to think it's a mob hit."

"And you didn't dissuade them."

"I did not."

"They'll keep an eye on you, which means you and I cannot meet again for awhile. I can't be connected with you. You'll take over the paymaster's job along with clean-up duties. You may want to hire somebody to help with that."

"I have someone in mind."

"He's reliable and trustworthy?"

"Yes. If there's a problem, I'll remove him myself. Will the paymaster job mean more money?"

"It will. As of this moment, I'm giving you a 30% raise. I'm appointing one of my men to replace Fritz. His name is Macek. He'll be contacting you tomorrow. He doesn't speak very good German, but his English is good."

"My English is not so good," Hugo said, suddenly worried.

"You and he will be okay," the Pole said. "Each of you knows the other's responsibilities. Macek will take care of the money. You take care of collecting it and cleanup duties. How much do you want to pay this man?"

"I was thinking 400 euros per week to start."

"Done," the Pole said. "I'll tell Macek. No need for me to meet your guy, not yet. Once the Police either catch Hector's killer, or lose interest, then we'll resume normal business. Understood?"

"Yes, Sir," Hugo said, "And thanks for the promotion."

****

As the Pole left the apartment building, he looked up and down the street but saw nothing suspicious. Unknown to him, he'd missed Ania, who'd called in sick from her job and watched him enter the building from inside a drycleaner's across the street.

She assumed he was Bernard Mannheim, whose name, address and company, Kapinski Associates, was listed in the materials she'd taken from Fritz's office.

She'd forget Hugo, she decided. His brother, Hector, had been an opportunity target and too great a risk. She'd not make another mistake like that.

She'd wait for Mannheim to leave his office, tail him and learn his routines. She'd figure out how and where to kill him. She'd been lucky so far. She could only hope her luck would hold.

Punta Arenas, Chile
June 28, 2010
Threat

Alfredo hired a pilot to navigate the Magellan Straits. He believed he could do the journey on his own, but for insurance purposes, he played it safe. In fog and rain, islands appeared as if out of nowhere, tides could be dangerous and winds treacherous.

His ship now rested in a repair facility off Avenida Costanera, two miles north of town center in Punta Arenas, reputedly earth's southern most city.

He knew settlements existed further south on the island of Terra Del Fuego. He'd been to one, Ushuaia, where he'd spent one night two years ago in late June.

He was about as far down as he wished to go. Another day's travel south and he'd be in Antarctica.

Alfredo and his crew had been sleeping on the ship but spending days on land while their freighter's diesel tanks were flushed and new fuel added.

Earlier, Alfredo walked around town, surprised at how normal such a place down near the bottom of the world seemed.

As he thought this, his phone rang. He'd just had his hair cut and stepped into perpetually overcast sky and windy, 35-degree light rain. He opened his phone and glanced at the phone number, which he did not recognize.

With his collar jacket zipped tight and parka hood covering his head, he moved quickly down the street into a small restaurant not far from his docked freighter and answered the call.

"Alfredo here. Who's this?"

"Remember me?" the voice said. Whoever it was sounded young, drunk and truculent.

"You'll have to speak up. I can hardly hear you," Alfredo said. "Who is this and where are you calling from?"

"I'm calling from Singapore, Captain. I'm the

sailor you left in Aitutaki."

"Oh, yes. We left you there at your request, did we not?" Alfredo said.

What was the sailor's name? He remembered: Polski, Tomas Polski, a strange name for a French Canadian from Trois-Rivières. He visualized a small person with a face like a whippet.

Tomas had fallen in love with an islander. How anyone could find anyone in such a low life place attractive was curious, the Captain thought.

"You forgot to pay me my entire wage," Tomas said.

"You didn't stay with us all the way to Hamburg, Son. I paid you for the days you worked and stayed on the island."

"Not good enough, Captain. I want the full wages promised me or you'll regret it."

"Oh? Why will I regret it?"

"Because I know what you're carrying." The captain felt fear but stayed composed.

"Good for you, but I have no idea what you're talking about. Any sovereign nation can board me any time it likes, so if this is attempted black mail, take a hike!"

"I saw the secret compartment, Captain. I saw them put that crate down there and cover it up. I saw that you had to use the winch, that four men couldn't lift it. I stayed below in the shadows down there all the time. You never saw me."

"Okay. How much?"

"Five thousand dollars."

"That's ridiculous."

"Suit yourself."

Alfredo thought quickly.

"Perhaps something can be arranged," he said. "Call me back in four hours."

"Will do, Captain. Glad we can come to an agreement."

****

Alfredo immediately phoned the Baron, explained the situation, gave him Tomas Polski's cell phone number and probable Singapore location.

An hour later, the Baron explained the problem to Lash, who easily made a Gulf Emirates' 2:35 p.m. flight from Hamburg, with a three-hour layover in Dubai, arriving at Singapore's Changi International Airport the next day at 1:45p.m.

The Baron then called Tomas Polski.

"Where can I wire the money to you?" Alfredo said.

"I'm way ahead of you, Captain. Wire it to Tomas Polski, Citibank, Great World City, One Kim Seng Promenade 237994, Singapore. Make it 5,000 dollars and addressed to the attention of Rodger Lim, who's a bank officer."

Alfredo repeated the address, and being told it was correct, said, "Will do, Tomas. I've been promised that the wire will arrive around three p.m. your time tomorrow."

"It better," Claude said.

Alfredo smiled, thinking 'What a dumb sonnavabitch!

****

At seven p.m. the daily download of the Baron's monitored telephone conversations was reviewed in

Langley by an analyst on the night shift.

She noted the call from Alfredo to the Baron. Who was this Tomas Polski? Why was he calling Punta Arenas? Who was Captain Alfredo?

Per instructions, she phoned Chester Field. He'd already left the office, so she called Chester's cell phone number. Chester answered and listened carefully to a summary of the Baron's conversation.

"So we know the call came from Singapore, right?"

"Yes, Sir. I ran the trace before I called."

"Where to again?"

"Punta Arenas."

"Aha! And the sailor was a former crew member, yes?"

"Yes, he'd apparently been left behind. I could play the tape. He's trying to blackmail the captain. He mentions a small but heavy cargo."

"Yes, yes, I got that. Send the tape to record on this phone after I leave."

"Do you want the whole day's conversation?"

"Is there a lot?"

"No. Once I compress it and remove the dead air, it'll be a five minutes' worth. The guy's not a heavy talker."

"Is it in English?"

"Yes."

"Sure. Send it all. The blackmailer's going to show up at Citibank in Singapore at three p.m. tomorrow, right?"

"Yes."

"Okay, got it," Chester said. "Good work, young lady. I'll handle it from here.

Hong Kong
June 28, 2010
Cover

Five days ago, Barry and Rebecca welcomed their children home. That evening, to honor them, Rebecca prepared Spaghettios, hamburgers, raw onions and root beer, a favorite going back almost ten years.

Three days later, the reunion ended. Jason left for soccer camp in Tennessee and Beth for six weeks to live with a family in Brest, France.

Once both children were gone, Barry and Rebecca drove to Atlanta, ordered new disguises built, and booked flights.

They stayed the night at the Ritz Hotel in Buckhead and the following day, using aliases, flew on different airlines to San Francisco.

They treated themselves to a suite at the Fairmont Hotel on Nob Hill on a high floor overlooking the city, bay and Golden Gate Bridge.

The next day, after massages and a late breakfast, they talked long-distance to Beth and Jason, who both sounded petulant and irritated by the parental interruption. That evening, Barry flew to Hong Kong and Rebecca to Hamburg, Germany.

They each knew from experience that wherever an assignment took them, an unanticipated unpleasantness might be waiting, so to avoid surprises, they meticulously planned their entries into new places, took different modes of transportation, arrived on different days, dressed plainly so as not to bring attention, used multiple disguises and stayed at separate hotels.

If possible, they never appeared together or

allowed themselves to seem linked in any way.

They wore disguises, changed hotels and hotel rooms frequently and used multiple fake identities.

Tama Wu was paying them to provide her cover during her stay in Germany. In Intelligence circles, 'cover' meant an outer layer in addition to the close-in protection of bodyguards.

To provide this cover, the first task was to pinpoint who might be watching. Sometimes, your client knew. Sometimes additional work was needed to identify interested parties.

You'd announce that your client was staying at such-and-such hotel. You might pay the hotel manager to assign your client to a specific room or suite on a specific floor, then bug the manager's phone to discover what he did with such information; or you might conceal a camera in the room to see who visited before the client's arrival. It was now Tama Wu's turn to learn what 'cover' involved.

****

Barry moved briskly along Hong Kong's busy harbor front and up to the Kowloon's Peninsula Hotel entrance past one of the hotel's fleet of Rolls Royces, its trunk lid raised.

Hotel staff dressed in immaculate white, beautifully creased uniforms and white gloves unloaded an Asian family's luggage.

Barry smiled as he saw the expensively dressed, middle-aged father and mother's two pre-teen children fidget and complain.

Despite rooms costing $550 to $1,300 per night, and formidable local competition from the Ritz, Four Seasons and others, the Peninsula, since its 1928 opening almost always stayed full.

Unknown to Barry, Tama Wu and her bodyguards had landed at seven p.m. the previous night on the helipad atop the Peninsula Hotel's newer rear building.

There, the General Manager and four white-suited attendants welcomed and brought her, her entourage and its luggage to adjoining suites in the older building.

At four p.m., Barry and Tama met for afternoon tea in the Peninsula Hotel's high-ceilinged lobby. Tama wore simple black with pearls, her hair tied with a festive red bow behind her neck.

Two young Asian males flanked her, each easily a foot taller than her. Both kept an assiduous eye on the crowd. They dressed identically in blue suits, white shirts and blue ties.

Their straight posture and shaved heads suggested they were military or ex-military. Barry could tell by the slight bulge under their left arms that each was armed.

He introduced himself as Todd Seymour. He wore a body suit that added 20 pounds, most of it around his middle, make-up that gave his skin a dark, almost Negroid cast, an artfully fitted gray wig, coke-bottle glasses and special shoes that made him walk slightly pigeon-toed.

A waitress escorted them to a corner table where they could have privacy.

Tama's two bodyguards sat at an adjacent table, watching everything that moved. Tea was brought, no bags, just tealeaves swimming in a pot. Barry selected two fruit pastries and a small ham and cheese sandwich. Tama Wu chose a chocolate chip cookie.

"I'm glad you're here," she said. "I'm going to share something with you. The Pole survived and is now in Hamburg. To put it mildly, he doesn't like me."

"The Pole?"

"Oh, please. Mr. Seymour. You know very well who the Pole is. Your confederate supposedly killed him."

"Miss Wu. I don't like the Pole any more than you do, but I didn't hire on to deal with him."

"Nobody's asking you to. All I want is to get into Germany without him knowing. I'll attend the opening of our first European dealership in Frankfurt as myself. Then I must again disappear. I need somebody to manage all of this for me and have my back. Is that the right American idiom, having one's back?"

"Yes. And okay, as long as you and I are clear on this. I'll sneak you into Germany without attracting anyone's attention, and I'll get you out, but this will require a lot of work from you."

"Fine. What kind of work, Mr. Seymour?"

Tama nibbled at her cookie, took a sip of her tea, grimaced and waited.

"Harsh taste?" Barry said.

"Very. As you were saying, Mr. Seymour…"

"We want you to dress down, wear Levis, tennis shoes and try to look like a typical Asian office girl on vacation."

Tama Wu smiled. "That might be fun," she said. "Go on."

"You won't fly directly to Hamburg. Too obvious. You'll fly back to China, wait a few days, then, with your new identity, fly a roundabout route to Munich. We'll prepare a fake passport, visas and whatever else you need. In Munich, I'll rent a car and drive you to your hotel, which will be a Best Western, Holiday Inn or a similar mid-market place."

He watched with amusement as Tama Wu wrinkled her nose, not relishing a stay at such a down-market hotel, but she did not verbally protest.

"Once you're settled," Barry continued, "we'll disguise you again and move you to a private apartment further away. By then, we'll be properly set up to provide you external cover while your bodyguards provide…"

"Internal cover," Tama Wu said, looking amused.

"Yes, that's right."

"That's well thought out, Mr. Seymour," she said, "but why the subterfuge? Nobody in Hamburg is expecting me."

"That's not true. You're opening a dealership in Frankfurt. That will generate press coverage. The detectives you hired know you're coming. The intermediate you used to shield them from you knows you're coming. They just don't know when. We need to know more about your detective, Mr. Kan. As we speak, a friend of mine is checking to see if anyone's following him."

Tama Wu laughed. "So devious, and so distrustful," she said. She paused, then smiled. "I also like the idea of playacting as somebody else."

"You'll do fine, Miss Wu, but you must always let me or my partner know in advance where and when you're going somewhere. Otherwise we can't guarantee your protection."

"That won't be a problem," Tama Wu said, but she knew it would be.

****

"While you're helping out the Chinese broad, find out all you can about the Pole," Chester Field told Barry by phone. "Tama Wu's detectives probably have a lot of useful information on the bastard. Once we have him in our sights, we can assist you better."

"Assist me in what?" Barry said.

"Help you stay out of his way if that's your wish," Chester said.

"You're being disingenuous," Barry said.

"I take offense at that," Chester said.

"Then take offense. You want us to kill him. The Tama Wu cover stuff is just to get us over there."

"Believe what you will. You're not being paid to take out the Pole, so relax. I suspect that Miss Wu will do that for us. On the other hand, something else is going down in Hamburg that we might want to involve you in."

"Not interested."

"Could be a big paycheck."

"How much?"

"Couple of hundred thousand."

"Okay. Let me know when you're ready to provide more details."

"If we involve you, it will be done with a cut-out in Hamburg. I know these phone conversations are safe, and I fervently admire our technical people, but this job's too sensitive to mention even on these secure lines."

"Now you've aroused my curiosity."

"My intention, Sir. Talk to you soon. Good luck getting Tama Wu to her dealership opening."

Chester hung up.

****

"I think it outrageous that Chester was not up front with

us," Rebecca said when Barry called. "He's got us involved with the Pole again."

"We can back out of the assignment with Tama Wu," Barry suggested.

"No, that wouldn't be honorable, although we could argue that we took the job under false pretenses."

"I've already argued that. But while providing cover for Tama Wu…"

"Yes, I was thinking the same. She's going to try to get him."

"Chester said exactly that."

"If she screws up, we may have to finish the job."

Singapore
June 29, 2010
Bamboozled

Tomas Polski returned to the Citibank offices in Great World City, one of those typical, multi-block, look-alike complexes that filled the densely populated island.

Completed in 1997, the group of buildings contained a 400,000 square foot, three-story shopping mall, 18 stores of offices and 35 stories of apartments in two beautiful, brown-skinned skyscrapers sheathed partially in blue glass.

Just that morning, Tomas bought a Grateful Dead tee shirt at a store across the mall from the Citibank's retail center, where Tomas now waited a few minutes inside the bank for the next available bank officer.

"Mr. Polski," a voice finally said. Tomas looked up, flattered. Few people called him Mr. It was the bank officer, Rodger Kim.

"Your money has arrived," Mr. Kim said. Tall, pale-skinned, in his late-20s, the bank supervisor stood smiling to Tomas' left. "Come with me. We have some formalities before handing you the money."

"What sort of formalities?"

"We fingerprint and photograph you, that's all. It's just for our records. Protects against fraud."

Tomas paused, wondering if this were so. He'd never received a money order before.

"Okay," he said.

He followed Rodger Kim through glass doors and down a thickly carpeted corridor.

As he passed the third office on his left, he failed to notice a crew-cut Caucasian man in tie and suit get up, leave this office and follow them.

At the third office on the left from the corridor's end, Rodger Kim motioned for Tomas to enter. As he did, he turned to see two crew cut men standing behind him and two others waiting inside the office.

The taller of the two men behind him said. "Hello, Tomas. You're coming with us."

****

Lash's 17-hour flight from Hamburg arrived on time. Twenty minutes later, he left Changi International Airport in a taxi, and by 2:30 p.m. was lounging outside the entrance to the Citi-bank retail center.

At five minutes to three p.m., a thin, smallish young Caucasian male with blond hair and a narrow face headed purposely towards the Citibank offices. He wore Levis and a Grateful Dead tee shirt.

The young man entered the retail center. Lash followed him in. He heard Rodger Kim greet the young man and address him as Mr. Polski. Lash congratulated himself.

He left the Citibank retail center and parked himself outside the door. When Tomas Polski exited with his money, he'd engage him.

What happened next depended on Polski. Care must be taken. Singapore was a police state run by a dictator.

He'd smuggled a deadly poison into Singapore inside his anus. He'd use that, or find a quiet place to strangle Mr. Polski.

By four p.m., Lash began to worry. At five p.m., employees began to leave. At 5:45 p.m., someone put a 'Closed' sign on the door and locked it from the inside.

Lash continued to wait. At six-thirty p.m., as evening settled, lights automatically turned on inside the store.

Rodger Kim and three other managers walked out, Kim locking the door from outside. He and the others then headed presumably for home.

Meanwhile, Tomas Polski had disappeared.

Lash phoned the Baron with the bad news.

"Okay. You'd better come home," the Baron said.

So someone else knew about Tomas's presence in Singapore! Who?

Was somebody tapping into his phone calls?

Worried, he called a specialist who said he'd be by in the morning to check.

Milan, Italy
June 29, 2010
Protection

The Pole entered an upscale clothing store in the Golden Quad, an ultra luxe shopping area framed by Montenapoleone, Sant'Andrea, Monzani and Della Spiga streets.

He found himself flanked on both sides by wooden, floor-to-ceiling racks holding folded suits, vests, leather jackets and three-buttoned blue blazers.

Further inside, in what appeared to be an added-on room, additional shelves had been stocked with rolls of beautiful wool, cotton, silk and a variety of high-end synthetic fabrics.

An attractive, smartly dressed women in her early forties greeted the Pole there dressed in frilled white blouse, a beautiful knobby linen red jacket and skirt. She had teased blond hair. Her big smile revealed beautiful white teeth.

"What can I do for you?" she said in good English.

"I've heard that you know something about heavy duty couture," the Pole said.

"Yes, I do, and this shop does. Come with me," she said. She introduced herself as Alessandra.

The Pole followed her into a large rear workroom at the rear of the shop.

He stopped to admire its domed ceiling painted a light yellow. Thick plush red carpeting covered the floor. The walls had been painted robin's-egg blue.

In one corner, he saw an espresso machine and table holding cups, sugar and milk next to a contemporary white leather couch, Plexiglas coffee table and matching armchairs.

A long wooden bench dominated. It displayed sewing machines, needles and spools of colored thread.

Alessandra introduced the Pole to Aldo, a thin, middle-aged bald man whose delicately patterned white shirt sleeves were rolled to the elbows.

His beautifully draped brown pants held a nice crease and his Gucci loafers looked freshly shined. The Pole noted liver spots on the backs of his hands.

"I'm Aldo Carbone," Aldo said, also in excellent English. "I'm both the owner and master tailor. I have three assistants, who are on lunch break, but it is I who will take your measurements and make sure you're satisfied."

"You're aware that our clothing does not come cheap?" Alessandra chipped in.

"I am," the Pole said.

"I apologize for my wife's directness," Aldo said, "But many people don't realize that what we sell is unique, proprietary and we can't just give it away."

"Of course," the Pole said.

"We can make you anything, use any material you prefer," she said. "Or we can fit you from something off the rack." She studied him a moment, admiring his muscular build, walked to a shelf and returned with a grayish metal panel a foot square.

"This, essentially, is what we place in any garment you might buy from us," she said. "It's a mix of nylon and polyester."

She handed the panel to the Pole. He picked it up, surprised at its lightness.

"I don't know if you've ever worn a Kevlar vest," she said. "Almost everyone in law enforcement has worn one at one time or another. The material doesn't breathe and it's quite heavy. The panel you're holding is stronger and one-third as heavy as Kevlar, and it breathes. Let me give you a demonstration."

Alessandra picked up a leather jacket that the Pole assumed sat there for demonstration purposes. She held it up inside out to demonstrate how the panels fit inside, put it on, zipped it up, reached inside a drawer, took out a long-barreled Mauser C96 semi-automatic, and handed it to the Pole.

"It's loaded," she said. "Shoot me in the stomach."

The Pole checked to see if the gun were loaded. It was.

"Are you sure you want me to do this?" he said.

"Yes," she said. "It's how we make every sale."

"Okay," the Pole said. He placed the tip of the barrel no more than two inches from Alessandra's midsection.

He pulled the trigger, and the gun fired, the noise momentarily deafening.

Alessandra took a step back, stopped, smiled, unzipped the jacket, took it off, and with a pair of long-nosed tweezers removed the flattened bullet from the leather.

"Don't touch the bullet, it's still hot!" she said.

"That was amazing! Sold!" the Pole said.

He decided against having suits and jackets custom made. Aldo and Alessandra fit him easily enough with off-the-rack clothes, but extensive alterations were needed to account for his chest size, and the thickness of his upper arms.

While waiting for the completion of alterations, he left the shop and down the street bought Beata a

$15,000, 18-carat gold, jeweled seahorse pendant at Cusi, a fourth-generation jeweler on Via Monte Napoleone.

He ate lunch at La Verando inside the Four Seasons Hotel on Via Gesù, dining on breaded small squids with artichoke flan, veal ossobuco in parsley sauce with risotto, followed by a pear-flaked chocolate tartlet washed down by thick, dark, African-bean coffee.

Sated, he walked aimlessly for two hours, stopping once for an expresso. At four p.m., he picked up his altered leather jacket, dark blue sports jacket with gold buttons, and a vest, spending almost $35,000.

"The protective panels should be removed before dry cleaning," Aldo said. "You may find the garments difficult to get used to, but in time you'll adjust. In the meanwhile, you'll feel considerably safer."

The Pole wrote a check on one of his Cayman accounts, waited almost 20 minutes while Aldo confirmed its validity, shook hands with Aldo and Alessandra, left the store, and two hours later was on a flight back to Hamburg.

****

That evening, the Pole sat with Beata in the living room of his Kempinski suite watching a Slum dog Millionaire DVD. She put the movie on pause to go to the bathroom. When she returned, the Pole turned to her.

"I got something for you in Milan," he said.

Beata looked over at him, tilted her head coquettishly and smiled. He handed her the small tiny and elegant purple-domed box.

Opening it, she exclaimed. "Oh, my, oh my!" She jumped on his lap and gave him a big hug.

"It's beautiful, the most beautiful thing I've ever

seen!" she said.

She gave him a big kiss and disappeared into the bedroom. He could hear her fumbling around, opening drawers, then silence.

Minutes later she reappeared naked with the pendant dangling between her large breasts. He touched the pendant, then his hand moved elsewhere.

****

They'd made love vigorously for almost and hour. The Pole's chest was heaving.

Staring at the ceiling, he asked, "Ever wonder what might have happened if you hadn't been a political protestor?"

Beata turned to him, resting her head on her hand, smiled and appeared to give the question some thought.

"What made you ask that question at this particular moment" she said.

"No particular reason," the Pole said." Just curious."

"I have thought about that," she said. "For one thing, had I kept quiet, I'd have avoided jail. Maybe I'd have finished my university education. On the other hand, I was pretty fucked up back then. My father molested me. My mother. Well, you know the story. I'd have acted out regardless."

"I didn't have your excuses," the Pole said. "My father was ineffectual, but he loved me. So did my mom."

"Com'on, your father beat you!" Beata said.

"Only when he was drunk, and he always apologized later."

"And your mother cheated on him multiple

times."

"It's not that uncommon," the Pole responded. Beata looked away, annoyed.

"My point," the Pole said, is that here I am, almost 40, running a business and good at it. I could have been a success in the legitimate world if I hadn't been so violent early on."

Rather than verbally comfort him, Beata merely nodded.

"Best we accept ourselves as we are, faults included," she said.

The Pole got up, upset, turned the movie back on and sat up in bed to watch, no longer touching her. He'd bought her jewelry to show his love. In return, he wanted her to say she loved him. She had not.

Hamburg
June 29, 2010
Bugs

While Barry prepared Tama Wu for her trip to Germany, Rebecca got busy in Hamburg. First she met the Baron for an early 11 a.m. lunch at the Fairmont Vier Jahrezeiten Hotel restaurant overlooking inner Alstar Lake, the meeting arranged by Chester Field. She and the Baron had communicated in code using a fictitious Face book page.

The Baron chose a corner table by a window where they could not be overheard. She found him attractive, especially his graying hair, which she liked in men in their 50's.

The gold buttons on his loose-fitting dark blue blazer gleamed. He wore a light blue, open-neck shirt with buttoned, monogrammed cuffs and cream colored, pleated slacks.

His handshake was soft, almost feminine. All he needed to be the baron of her child's imagination was an ascot.

The restaurant fit the image he clearly wished to portray. Flooded with light, Flemish Gobelin tapestries hung on rich looking wood-paneled walls accompanied by handsome baroque and Renaissance furniture, all of it old, of good quality and meticulously maintained.

"Glad you could make it," the Baron said. He rose from his seat and extended his hand, Rebecca shook it and sat.

She'd prepared for their meeting by dramatically altering her looks. Contact lenses changed her eye color from blue to brown.

Tiny, skin-colored hooks disguised by make-up and partially hidden by her hair pulled the edges of her eyes wider, giving them a slight Asian cast.

She'd applied bright red lipstick and wore a gray wig with a pageboy cut. The upper torso suit worn beneath her light blue silk blouse gave large, sagging breasts that hid her natural B cup. The torso suit also thickened her waist.

After exchanging introductory pleasantries, Rebecca whispered a request.

"Chester said you could get me two Glocks, two sniper rifles with scopes, ammo, electronic hotel room lock readers, mace, Semtex, wireless detonators and bugs."

"Not sure I can remember all that," the Baron

said. She smiled. Was he were serious or merely trying to be amusing?

"Then get what you can remember and I'll keep reminding you," she said, sounding cross, which she'd not intended. The Baron did not seem to take offense.

"I can code you the list," she added, her voice gentler. The Pole nodded.

"Are you doing business with the Pole?" she asked.

"Funny you should mention that," the Baron said. "The Pole and I have a business meeting tomorrow, although he doesn't know I know who he is."

"How do you know who he is?"

"A mutual friend told me," the Baron said.

Aha! Rebecca thought.

"Be careful," she said.

"Oh, I will. And you?"

"I'm going to avoid the guy if possible."

"You're not here to help me with him?"

"No, I'm here on another matter."

"Which you can't discuss…"

"Yes."

"I see." This news demonstrably upset the Baron, but he recovered quickly." Let's order," he said.

He held up his hand. A blond, crew cut, stiffed-backed waiter in his 40's wearing black shoes and pants, white shirt and red vest, approached, showing not an ounce of deference.

"Have you both decided what you want?" the waiter said in crisp German-accented English.

"We have," the Baron said. The waiter took their salad and bottled water orders and hurried away.

The Baron leaned toward Rebecca. "I have some concerns," he said. "The Pole's trying to muscle me. He's not done so directly, but he's offered a ten percent premium if my clients switch their business to him."

"Why would he do that? Rebecca said. "He likely knows you have CIA backing. Won't he assume you'll meet any price?"

"Yes and No. What he's really doing is showing my clients that he's got money and is a worthy competitor."

"Meaning you've been the only game in town?"

"No, I'm not the only game in town, but for large shipments of newer weaponry, I have been. I'm told he's rather menacing in person. I'll find out tomorrow."

"Do you have protection?"

"Yes, of course, but I'll be missing it tomorrow. I was counting on you."

"Did Chester suggest this?:

"No, he did not. I assumed it."

"I'd help, but for the moment, as I told you, I have my own assignment that comes first. I'm leaving tomorrow and will be gone a few days."

"The Pole's brought in some rough trade from Warsaw, four of them," the Baron said. "He's set them up in his offices as salesmen, although they're anything but. He's assigned them territories. So far, that's what I know. Nothing's happened yet, but it's about to."

"Are you preparing contingencies?"

"I talked with Chester. He won't help. I don't know why. I'm currently Chester's biggest and main source for armaments in Europe, at least I think I am. I've told him that if he can't help, I may soon be out of business."

"Surely, you're not giving up that quickly?"

"We'll see," the Baron said.

Rebecca read resignation in his voice. He's over his head, she thought. Not good.

****

That afternoon, a long blond-haired, big-gutted German electronics expert in his 60's gave the Baron his report.

"There are no physical bugs in your cell phones or land lines in your apartment or in your offices," he said.

"That's a relief."

"But I still think you have a problem. When I turn on any of your phones my devices detect interference. I don't know what's causing it. I suspect some sort of receptor picks up your calls. They could be buried in your walls, although I checked in your office and found none. Both your apartment and office share common walls with other rooms. That could be where you're being intercepted."

"Any way to know for sure?"

"Not without physically entering every room that in any way abuts any of yours."

The Baron thought about that. "What if I conduct conversations away from home and my office?"

"That would likely work; but cell phones operate on open frequencies. If someone is intent enough, they can find a way to listen in."

"So what do I do?"

"There's sophisticated new stuff out there that might help. I can investigate."

"Please do," the Baron said.

****

That evening, the Baron sat in his apartment, a glass of sherry in hand, thinking.

He had a new and physically threatening competitor with heavy financial backing from unknown sources.

He likely was being overheard every time he picked up a phone.

Lash would not be back until late the next evening, meaning he, the Baron, was defenseless until then.

The Pole had soldiers. Lash, tough and ruthless as he was, worked alone. There wasn't enough money to hire more people. He already spent every dime he made.

Maybe he could do a deal. The Pole couldn't sell to the CIA. He could. The Pole could be a secret partner supplying needed muscle for a piece of the uranium deal. He'd suggest that when they met.

Hamburg, Germany
June 30, 2010
Search

The Baron turned out to have a good memory. Late that evening, Rebecca received the armaments and other materials she'd requested. When Barry reached Frankfurt, she'd let him have his choice.

Also, Chester provided her with an address and phone numbers for Sammy Kan. She chose not to contact him. Instead, she shadowed him.

He proved predictable. He left the hotel around 8:30 a.m. with the international edition of the *New York Herald*, took breakfast alone at a more expensive hotel down the street, read the newspaper and did its crossword puzzle, then returned to his room.

He ate lunch at one-thirty p.m. each day with the other four detectives at an outdoor Italian place two blocks from his hotel, sometimes spending several hours drinking wine and later coffee with what were now clearly not just work mates but friends.

His carefree actions and those of the other detectives suggested that his work was done, that there was no point in any longer checking for tails, that he was planning to enjoy the city as long as his per diem continued.

Such carelessness worried her. Twice, in two days, she saw the same ill-kempt man loitering near the hotel. The second time she spotted him, she kept going, doubled around and watched him from a safe distance.

Sure enough, when Sammy emerged from his hotel, the ill-kempt man moved, staying well enough back to be unobserved.

The next day, Rebecca searched Sammy's room while he was at lunch, a propitious time. Maids were busy on other floors.

She used an electronic room opener to get in. She found the room immaculate, bed made, papers stacked neatly on the desk.

She checked for bugs, standing on the bed to check the first light. A bug!

She checked the telephone. Another bug! Sammy was now certified careless in multiple ways.

Who was doing the bugging? What information had been divulged? She decided it made no difference. She'd turn her discovery to her advantage.

She added two bugs of her own, then, plugged an electronic transposer into the wall and its universal adapter into a slot at the back of Sammy's computer, which lay open on the desk.

She waited, continuing to check her watch.

Twenty-five minutes later, the transposer beeped, informing her that she'd now downloaded all of Sammy's files.

She left the room just as a maid came down the hall. The maid gave Rebecca a careful look, and continued walking.

Three blocks from the hotel, Rebecca used a restaurant bathroom stall to change out of her disguise.

She carefully folded and put her glasses, a brown wig, work shoes and Levis in her briefcase, donning a pretty blue and white print dress, leaving as a completely different person, long blond hair swaying behind her.

That night, she phoned Chester.

"Are you bugging Tama's detectives?" she asked.

"No," Chester said. "Should I be?"

"Don't know. Somebody is. Thought it might be you."

"Well, it isn't me. Don't bother me until you learn who."

"Try not to be so grumpy, Chester."

"I'm having a lousy day. Goodbye."

Next she phoned Barry.

"Tama's detectives are compromised big time, Bear," she said. "Bug in the phone, one in the light. I placed another in the bedside lamp. Also, the lead detective's being followed. Chester says his guys aren't doing it. I'm going to tail the tail tomorrow. Maybe I can find out who's doing the bugging."

"Good, Becs. Had some problems here."

"Oh, what?"

"Let's just say that Tama Wu's idea of how a middle class, low level female supervisor dresses was not convincing." Rebecca laughed.

"So how did you solve that?" she said.

"I took photos of women around Hong Kong, showed them to her, got her sizes and went out and bought her new outfits."

"How'd she like that?"

"She acted as if I'd bought her the clothes as personal gifts."

"Oh, oh. Do you think she has a romantic interest in you?"

"Naw. I'm fat around the middle and wear funny glasses, walk pigeon-toed and am too old for her."

"I certainly hope it stays that way."

"It will, Becs. She's not that appealing. She's emotionally fractured and defensive. Definitely messed up, lonely and loaded with anger, bright as hell but not very companionable."

"Has she come on to you?"

"No, damn it. I must be slipping."

"She'd better not."

"Don't worry. She's not my type."

"How'd she look after all that surgery?"

"Like she's had a lot of surgery."

"Not so good, huh?"

"No. You look at her and you can see that everything's not aligned right but you can't tell what it is."

"I miss you, Bear."

"I miss you, too, Becs."

"Wish you were here so I could nail you."

"I don't like it when you talk like that."

"Okay, I wish you were here so that I could experience your charms in person."

"That's better but sounds old-fashioned." '

"Okay, I wish you were here so that I could make passionate love to you."

"That's better."

"San Francisco was fun. You should do what you did more often."

"A few times a year for the surprise. It's enough," Rebecca said.

"I'm envisioning you right now walking into our hotel room naked below the waist, your...."

"Enough! Got to go. I'll call the minute I reach Hamburg. The gaps between when we talk and talk again always leave me anxious, and right now I'm feeling horny."

"Okay. How about this: I enter the hotel room and you're bending over. I lift up your skirt and you're not wearing any underpants."

"That can be arranged."

"Changing the subject, anything new on the kids?"

"No, I'm going to give it three more days. Maybe they'll have settled and won't be so crotchety."

"Did you pay the orthodontist?"

"Oh oh! I forgot."

"You want me to?"

"If you would. Thanks."

"Okay, and Good luck. Can't wait to see you in Germany. I'll be in Frankfurt for Tama's dealership opening, then, hopefully, I'll put her on the plane back to China."

"I have a feeling that she's not going right back to China."

"We'll deal with that, if it happens, although I haven't decided how. Can't wait for you to get here,

Bear."

"Love you, Becs."

"Love you, too." She hung up, feeling sad. She decided to go through Sammy Kan's downloaded hard drive and see what she could learn. Two hours later, she'd learned a lot.

Most of the hard drive contained notes and other material written in English.

She quickly deduced that Sammy and his crew had found the Pole, knew where he lived and worked, and had catalogued the arrival of the Pole's mercenaries, Marek, Lech, Kristoff and Andrzej.

Sammy had taken fuzzy photographs from long range of them and unidentified others seen talking with the Pole.

Tomorrow morning, she'd tail Sammy Kan's tail. Hopefully, this would lead her to the Pole. Did Sammy already knew about the bugs and the man tailing him? Could he be preparing his own trap?

Hong Kong
June 29, 2010
Flying

Tama Wu flew alone from Shanghai to Tokyo's Narita International Airport, deliberately avoiding Barry, who arrived from Hong Kong on a different flight.

Each took the same British Airways 12-hour flight from Tokyo to London.

Tama sullenly watched Barry board ahead of her in Business Class, 15 minutes later taking her seat in

Economy Class near the back of the plane.

After a five-hour layover at Heathrow, still ignoring each other, they boarded another British Airways plane for the two-hour flight to Munich, Germany.

Throughout the journey, Barry remained in the same disguise used during their initial meeting in Hong Kong's Peninsula Hotel.

He wondered how Tama was holding up, amused at the thought of such a powerful woman masquerading as an office girl.

Tama wore designer jeans, tennis shoes, crisply ironed white blouse, and a jaunty flower in her coal black hair, which she no longer tied in back. She carried a de rigeur Louis Vuitton purse favored by Asian shop girls on vacation.

From Munich's Franz Josef Strauss International Airport, she and Barry took separate taxis into town and checked into separate rooms on different floors at downtown Munich's King's Hotel on Marsstrasse across from the railroad station.

Once in his room, Barry phoned Rebecca to tell her that the trip had been uneventful, he and his guest had arrived in Munich and that they planned to head for Frankfurt tomorrow.

That evening, he ate dinner alone in the hotel's small restaurant. The odd and disappointing menu featured hamburgers, Wiener schnitzel, bratwurst, French fries, warm potato salad, several types of lettuce salads, and, unaccountably, a choice of ten different types of asparagus.

A tall, shy, blond-haired teenage girl wearing a red dirndl with white bodice and lace sleeves waited on him.

Just before his food came, his cell phone rang. He stepped away from the table, listened intently, spoke softly, nodded, hung up, and then phoned Tama.

"A friend just called," he told her, "with news that will interest you."

"What?"

"I'll tell you in a moment. How was your flight?"

"I'd rather have been in First Class, of course, the food was execrable, but everything was actually okay. The seat next to me was empty and the old Japanese lady on the aisle was uncommunicative, which was fine with me. Besides, I'm small. Leg room was not a problem. Okay. Now tell me about the phone call."

Barry told her about Sammy Kan's room being bugged. She seemed to take the news well enough.

"Maybe they know about the bugs but left them in so they could feed false information later," she said.

"Quite possible," Barry said.

"When will I get a chance to meet your partner?" Tama said.

"You won't. We work in concert but separately."

"For security purposes, I presume."

"That's right."

Tama considered that. "How can you be in love with someone and run a business with her. How do you make that work?"

"I don't understand."

"I can't conduct business with someone I'm interested in," Tama said. It doesn't mix with the softer, more vulnerable side of me."

"We manage okay," Barry said, wondering what Tama's softer side might be. "Guess we've been lucky."

"You have been," Tama said. "I envy the both of you."

After the meal, Barry went to his room and started a new Lee Child book he'd bought at Heathrow, but had difficulty concentrating. He knew what bothered him. He found Tama Wu attractive.

Feeling guilty, he phoned Rebecca again and they talked again briefly. "Miss you," he said. "I sure hope we have time to get together after the dealership reception."

"We'll see," Rebecca said. "A lot going on here. Love you a lot, Bear."

"Love you, too, Becs."

Around ten p.m., still restless, he walked downstairs. As he passed the bar on the way outside to take a walk, Tama Wu exited the bar, her arm around the waist of a heavy, blond German man in his 40's. Ignoring Barry, she and her new friend headed up the stairs, presumably to her or her new friend's room.

****

By earlier agreement, the next morning, Barry bought pastries and coffee for himself and Tama at the train station across the street, then, watching for suspicious persons, took the elevator to Tama's floor and entered her small room at seven a.m.

She greeted him wearing a bathrobe. As they sat, he in a chair and she across from him on a small settee, her legs opened, momentarily revealing a dark, inviting patch of glistening, curly black pubic hair.

She pretended to be unaware of her exposure, demurely sipping her coffee and pronouncing it to be 'mediocre.' "But your taste in pastries is good," she said.

She studied Barry, tilting her head, looking both

flirtatious and amused, watching him do his best to keep his gaze centered on her face.

Nonchalantly, she readjusted the robe to cover her legs, surrepticously glancing at his crotch to see if he had an erection. He did.

"Did you sleep well?" Barry said.

He took a bite of his blueberry muffin, embarrassed by his arousal and wondering if it were obvious.

"Yes, I slept okay. Why?"

"Just making conversation."

Tama re-crossed her legs, her face alive with pixyish amusement.

"You slept well?" he asked.

"I did. I'm not looking forward to getting back in character. It's fun being unnoticed. The dealership reception won't take long, but afterwards, I have to have some serious discussions with the European director and the dealership manager. You can attend if you wish."

"Thanks, but I'll hang around outside. I'll have a compatriot also watching."

They left 15 minutes late for Frankfurt but Barry figured the trip could be done in less than four hours. The reception began at one p.m. They'd arrive in plenty of time, do the reception, then head to the hotel.

During the drive, the mood quickly grew testy.

"How was he?" Barry said.

"How was who?" Tama Wu said.

"The guy you took to your room."

"Oh, him."

"Don't you think that's a little dangerous?"

"You jealous?"

"I repeat. Isn't such behavior risky?"

"I don't know, is it?"

"Look, Tama, I've gotten you to Germany without anyone, to include any possible enemies of yours, knowing."

"Yes, so far you've done that very well, Mr. Seymour. I've learned a lot."

"I'm going to get you to your dealership opening on time as well," Barry said, "keep you protected there, and then get you back to your hotel. That will be the most stressful period. Advertising and articles in local and national German newspapers have announced your presence. You'll be giving a press conference at the dealership. Anybody wants to get at you, that's when."

"My German security will be at the dealership when I arrive," Tama said. "It's all arranged."

Security and hit squad, Barry thought.

"Once I'm there and have made contact with them, your responsibilities end," Tama said petulantly. "No return trip to Munich necessary. I'll get back to China on my own. As for my picking up strange men in bars, you're right, it was risky; but I needed a little recreation, got it, and got away with it, so there!"

"My concern has nothing to do with morals," Barry said, privately thinking that it did. "When you do that, when you take risks, it's difficult for your protectors because you introduce new and unvetted people into the mix."

"So what if I do?" Tam said. "What business is it of yours?"

Her continuing petulance irritated him.

"Because that's a great way to get yourself compromised and killed," he said.

"I know that," Tama said. "I had to take care of

some urges. I took care of them and should be okay for the rest of the trip. You're very attractive, you know."

"What's that mean?"

"It means I see through your disguise. I can see that despite the bulge around your middle, which is likely some sort of body suit, you don't have an ounce of fat on you. I've watched how you move. You're athletic. About 50, I'd say."

"Don't see that any of this has anything to do with…"

"Oh, but it does," Tama said.

She unbuttoned her blouse. He tried to look away but could not. She wore no bra, which he already suspected. Her breasts were not large but hung nicely, the skin much softer than her redone face, the nipples a dark brown, puffed and hard.

"Cover yourself!" he said.

"You don't want me?"

"That's not the question. First off, I'm a married man who loves his wife."

"What's that have to do with anything?"

"It means she's enough. She loves me and I love her."

Tama Wu made a face. "A little fun, in secret, never hurt anyone," she said.

"It would hurt me. I'd think about it. I'd feel guilty. Eventually, I'd tell my wife, and that would mess us up."

"So you've done this before…"

"I've been tempted before. I've had women come on to me."

"And you've never strayed?"

"No."

"Aha! I don't believe you."

The car went silent. Tama sat, her arms across her chest, glaring straight ahead.

"You're not much fun," she said. "I really like you. You're bright, you're funny, and you're not afraid of me."

"My job's to protect you," Barry said. "I'm here to do my job."

For another hour, they rode in silence.

"Look, Tama," Barry said as they got their first glimpse from the Autobahn of Frankfurt's towers in the distance, "I do find you attractive. You're bright, accomplished and…"

"Never mind," Tama said. "Part of your attractiveness, Mr. Seymour, is your inaccessibility." She went silent for a moment. "Now, as for my future safety, you needn't worry. Unlike in Montevideo, I'm prepared. I've got four Germans watching the dealership. I talked with Lothar, their leader, twice before leaving China. He's in contact with Sammy and the other detectives. I now have a small army. Get me to the dealership, we'll say goodbye, a romantic opportunity missed, perhaps, but a job well done on your part. I thank you for that. I have no hard feelings, and no reluctance in using you and your partner again."

"Okay," Barry said. He turned their rental car off the Autobahn and headed into Frankfurt.

Hamburg, Germany
June 30, 2010
Tracking

A week had passed since Warsaw residents Marek, Lech, Kristoff and Andrzej arrived in Hamburg. The Pole gave each a key to their own room at the Kronprinz Hotel across from the railroad station. Each man also got a key to the Kapinskii Associates offices.

    The first day, he left them free to get familiar with the city. That was his first mistake.

    Lech, a 5'10", heavily muscled blond with thick lips wandered by mistake into a Turkish bar, was drugged, rolled, dumped in an alley and picked up by the police. An attorney hired by the Pole got Lech out.

    Their second night in town, the Pole and Beata hosted a dinner for the men at the Kempinski Atlantic's elegant, ground-flour Alstersalon. Another mistake.

    The four men looked thuggish and out of place. They had long greasy hair. Lech's face was covered by bandages. Each wore identical poor-quality leather jackets. Curious and clearly disapproving diners turned to watch their entry.

    Minutes later, the Pole had to tell Andrzej and Kristoff to talk more softly because they were disturbing other diners.

    The group's manners quickly became an embarrassment. They talked and ate with their mouths open. As a result, service seemed to slow, the wait staff behaving with increasingly haughty diffidence.

    The Pole hurried through dinner quickly, said goodbye to Beata, told her he'd be home in a few hours, and took his men back to his office, where they talked business until ten p.m..

The men were told that their first and most important assignment was to find the Polish girl who was murdering syndicate members.

They were shown the only photo of her in syndicate possession, taken upon her arrival.

"She's an amateur but with a creative imagination. She's a good gauge of risks, at least so far. Don't underestimate her. Put yourself in her shoes," the Pole advised them. "If you spoke only Polish, and you were trying to stay alive, where would you go and what would you do?"

Marek raised his hand.

"I'd try to find other Poles to help me, people who spoke my language," he said.

"Good," the Pole said, "Start there."

****

Late the next day, Kristoff, a prematurely gray-bearded, tall and sinewy Pole stumbled upon the Polish milk bar where Ania once worked

Shown Ania's picture, the old man with coke-bottle glasses who owned the place said that she'd worked several months for him. He asked why Kristoff wanted to know.

Kristoff said she was his younger sister who'd run away.

"Oh, my, too bad. She was a nice girl," the old man said, "And an excellent worker."

"Why did she stop working for you?" Kristoff said.

"I don't know," the old man said. "One day she came in and gave two-weeks notice. She'd been studying German at night. She rented a studio apartment in an apartment building not far from here. My cousin's the apartment manager there. She was getting by okay."

"Do you know where she is now?" Kristoff asked.

"No," the old man said.

"Do you know where she was studying German?"

"Some church, she said. "Probably one close to here, but which one I can't say. I'm not all that religious."

"Do you have her apartment address?"

"I do. Say, young man, why again are you so interested?"

"I already told you. She's my long lost sister," Kristoff lied, showing a touch of annoyance. "There were problems with our parents. She ran away. I have no idea why she came to Germany."

"To find work, most likely," the old man said. "Still not much of that back in Poland, I hear, unless you have an education."

"True," Kristoff said.

An hour later, he showed up at the address the old man gave him.

"Yes, I remember her," the apartment manager said. Also Polish, he was of medium height, approaching 60, and stooped, with white hair. He had coke-bottle glasses exactly like his cousin's and acted suspicious.

Kristoff repeated his story about Ania running away and the man nodded.

"Your story doesn't surprise me," he said. "Wish I could help you, but I don't know where she went. She was secretive and acted fearful much of the time. She didn't have a lot of people to talk Polish with, except at the milk bar. I never remember her having anybody visit her or go inside her apartment. She could have confided in me, but she didn't. I assumed she was in trouble with the law, if not here, then in Poland."

"Do you know where she went?"

"No. One morning she comes to me, says she's leaving, asks if she owes any money, and I say she's good to the end of the month and still has another week to go. She didn't have a lot of stuff. I watched her lug a big suitcase on wheels out of the building. Everything she owned was in it."

"Did she get a lot of mail?"

"No, just circulars and flyers. I'd find them in her trash. Never a personal letter in all the time she lived here."

This memory seemed to make the man sad. "I still think about her," he said. "She was a pretty little thing, sweet at her core but developing an emotionless and wary exterior. I hate to see that happen. You see it in stray dogs if they don't get adopted. But I'll tell you this. She was resilient. I could sense she had her mind set on something."

"Any idea what that was?"

"Not a clue," the apartment manager said.

The next day, Kristoff found a nearby Lutheran church offering German lessons at night, the course taught by a Jürgen Hodel.

Hamburg
June 30, 2010
Discovery

Kristoff, because he did not speak German well, brought the Pole with him to the Lutheran Church 15 minutes before Jürgen's class began. The Pole did the talking.

"This man's sister," the Pole began, referring to Kristoff, "whose real name is Ania, had problems with her parents, left home and somehow ended up here in Germany. She worked for a while at a milk bar not far from your church and started taking German lessons here, I'm told. I have a picture of her and wonder if you've seen her?"

He showed Jürgen the photo. Jürgen pretended to study it, then too quickly handed it back.

"Yes, there was a Polish girl who took lessons here," he said, looking nervous. "She was a good student, one of my best. But she stopped coming months ago and I haven't heard from her since."

"Did she have any friends in the class, anyone else who might know her whereabouts?" the Pole asked.

Jürgen pretended to consider this. "No," he said. "She was a loner. She just upped and disappeared."

The Pole and Christoff left.

Outside the church, the Pole turned to Kristof and said, "The man's lying. He's hiding something. Look into it."

"Do you want me to rough him up?"

"Let's wait on that. Tail him and see what you can learn."

Hamburg, Germany
June 30, 2010
Discovery

Rebecca devoted the day to following Sammy Kan's tail. She picked him that morning as he left for breakfast, After Sammy finished his meal and returned to the hotel, the tail walked away, got into a Mercedes and drove off.

She emailed the tail's license plate number to Chester and five hours later got a response.

The Mercedes was registered to Halberstadt und Sohnen, a car and truck rental agency located in the warehouse district.

When Sammy went to his usual restaurant for lunch, she ignored the tail and searched instead for the Mercedes. She found it parked illegally on a side street.

From her purse she removed her car keys and pretended to begin opening the Mercedes driver's door, then pretended to drop the keys, bent down, and while picking them up attached a GPS device to the car's underside.

She waited. The car stayed parked until past five p.m., when her linked GPS device blinked and vibrated to tell her the car was moving.

She drove her rental car past Sammy's hotel, noticing that another man similarly dressed had taken the first tail's place.

She caught up with the rental Mercedes as it neared Alster Lake, continued over a bridge, and a second bridge, finally stopping on Am Sandtorkai, a block from the Mattenweite Bridge.

The man got out and walked into a tall, ancient

looking nine-story old building faced entirely in brick with a domed top that reminded her of houses she'd seen in Amsterdam.

She liked the area. It was undergoing massive redevelopment. She noted new contemporary architecture sprouting next to buildings easily a century old. She saw newly built foot and paved walks along the water.

Tomorrow, she'd investigate the building the man entered, but that proved unnecessary.

****

By eleven p.m., her usual bedtime, she'd spent two hours reading Sammy's computer files. In them, she found the Pole's office address, the same address she'd followed the Mercedes to earlier that day. She also learned that he and his woman lived at the Kempinski Atlantic.

Sammy Kan even found the hotel where the Pole's rent-a-thugs thugs stayed, plus their names: Marek, Lech, Kristoff and Andrzej. They were billeted at the Kronprinz across from the railroad station.

She found a photograph and the license plate number of the Pole's S Class Mercedes, and noted that the four Warsaw thugs had rented cars.

Sammy even knew that Andrzej and Marek had been assigned to watch him and his fellow detectives. Photographs of all four Warsaw men were included, most taken at long range and photo-shopped.

Impressed, Rebecca put down the file. Sammy had not gotten sloppy. Clearly, they were suckering the Pole. They would feed false information to move the Pole to where Tama and her little army would kill him.

Frankfurt, Germany
June 30, 2010
Smoking

A few minutes after midnight, night watchman Henrik Richter, 45, a friendly, fleshy, blond-haired man of average height crouched guiltily between two SUVs in the small parking lot next to the new Dragon Motors dealership and smoked a cigarette. He did not wish to be seen because smoking was forbidden on the job.

To Henrik, each new cigarette registered his progress through the night. He always tried to wait an hour before lighting up again but cheated more than he wished to admit.

As a teenager, he'd begun air-conditioning technical training but had problems with authority, lost jobs, and found mindless guard duty a decent way to make a living without actually having to work hard or learn a skill. That money, a rent-controlled apartment and free health care, and a wife who worked provided enough to survive.

Best of all, as a night watchman, he didn't have to answer to a boss on premise. Each night, he could be alone with his thoughts.

At the end of each shift, he typed out a report on a laptop the company provided, noting the time he arrived and left, plus any abnormalities spotted, such as scratches on cars, hoses not put away, or trash accumulated.

Much of his night was spent slowly walking the fence line, part of it enjoying computer porn, and part smoking cigarettes.

Most fun was leaning against the dealership's

front window watching cars head into Bornheim's Stattmitte, where mostly young people nightly gathered in bars.

He'd started work May First. The building had once been an Opel dealership. Its position on Bergerstrasse near the edge of Frankfurt am Main's Bornheim district was not particularly good for foot traffic but within walking distance of the town's entertainment district.

Henrik had never heard of Dragon Motors, but was impressed by how much the company had improved the facility, to include new digital signage, shiny silver, cutting-edge diagnostic equipment and an expanded showroom.

The new sales manager told him that the Bornheim location came with problems, the most egregious a lack of interior or exterior storage space.

Dragon Motors had shipped 300 cars to Germany, but most continued to sit at the Hamburg port, he said.

Due to lack of dealership space, only three could be displayed in the small showroom and another 16 behind the dealership, leaving six parking spots in front of the dealership for visitors.

After a soft opening five weeks ago, only four cars had been sold, the rest stored in a vacant lot near the Frankfurt Airport. Regardless, management continued to appear optimistic.

Tomorrow, the dealership officially opened with a band, press conference in which the Dragon Motors President would speak, and an open house for the public with refreshments, balloons for the children and door prizes.

Henrik been invited and planned to come with his

wife and two children. If his wife couldn't get off work, he'd bring the kids himself.

"We've spent almost $2 million getting this place ready," the General Manager told Henrik at an employee meeting the week before.

Henrik finished his cigarette, squashed the butt with his heel, and stepped between the two cars to begin a tour of the building, stopped, returned, picked up his cigarette butt and flicked it in the trash can directly behind the back wall.

As he turned the back corner, he saw a shadowy figure dart around the far side of the building.

"Hey!" he shouted. He pulled his gun and started chasing.

As he rounded the building's far corner in the dark, he missed seeing small lumps of plastic explosive with tiny antennae stuck in them pressed tightly at set intervals against the base of the building's rear wall.

Even in bright light, unless you knew what you were looking for, you'd miss them, or, if you saw them, would think they were some form of repair patching.

Breathing heavily, Henrik reached the front of the building and looked around. Several young couples chatted animatedly on their way to town center.

Momentarily blinded by the soft glare of the neon street lights, Henrik did not see the shadowy figure across the street in the dark between two buildings, also winded.

Another group of young people passed. Seconds later, a shot was fired.

Henrik did not die immediately. Unconscious, he felt himself dragged by his armpits, and lifted into the back of a van. He lay there in the dark, heard the van start up and accelerate.

Time passed. The van stopped. He felt himself dragged across wet grass, then felt the liquid poured on him. He heard a match struck and quickly felt the heat.

He heard the van's tires leave the grassy area, felt the flames consuming his face, thinking how odd that he felt no pain.

Frankfurt, Germany
July 1, 2010
Surprise

At eleven a.m., Tama and Barry arrived at the Best Western Hotel on Karlstrasse in downtown Frankfurt. Tama signed in.

Barry followed her to her room, inspected it to make sure there were no bugs or other surprises, and left, telling her he'd pick her up at 11:45 a.m. and drive her to the new Dragon Motors Dealership. The reception there was to begin at noon with a brief press conference at one p.m.

Barry then met Rebecca in her room on the third floor, hugging and kissing her enthusiastically, wanting to do more but knowing there was not time.

"Take your pick," Rebecca said. On their bed, she'd laid out the arsenal the Baron had procured for them.

Barry chose a Glock, which, thanks to the padding he wore around his middle, produced no tell-tale bulge under his right arm pit.

He stood before the mirror in the bathroom, pleased that the weapon could not be seen. He also took a sheathed knife, which he concealed in his right sock.

"Your disguise sucks," Rebecca said as she watched with amusement. "How much longer you going to wear it?"

"Until after the reception. Any problems on your end?"

"No. I'm going to check the dealership before everyone arrives. What time are you bringing Ms. Wu?"

"I'll get her there about five minutes before her speech. How long a drive?"

"About fifteen minutes with traffic."

"She's going to have some sort of meeting with staff after her press conference. Also, before I forget, and this is important, she's got four German thugs protecting her. She says they'll be at the dealership when she arrives. She's emphasized that once I get her there, our responsibilities end."

"You don't want to stay and go after the Pole?"

"What's the point? She's got five detectives and four German paratrooper types to help her. Let her have the honors."

"Want to visit our place in Villefranche before heading home?"

"Great idea, Bear."

"Okay. A few more hours. This, for a change, has been one of our easier assignments. Thank God for that. After Montevideo, we deserve one."

"Amen," Rebecca said.

Frankfurt
July 1, 2010
Boom

By the time Rebecca parked, it was eleven-thirty a.m. Approaching the new Dragon Motors dealership, she heard a German oompah band warming up.

As she got closer, she saw six old men sitting on chairs outside the entrance dressed in Leiderhosen, white blouses with red suspenders, white socks almost to the knees, thick-heeled shoes and green hats sporting pheasant feathers. Below a huge neon-lit Dragon Motors sign, a banner announced:

> Grand-Openint Öffentliche willkommen'
> (Grand opening. Public welcome).

Across the entrance from the oompah band, a small banner above an unoccupied booth announced free raffle tickets, the winner to get a new Dragon Motors Scorpion.

Rebecca looked around, checking to see if anything seemed out of place. So far, nothing.

Maybe a dozen people milled around inside. She saw Sammy the detective talking with an expensively dressed Chinese man she assumed was a Dragon Motors senior executive.

Three mechanics dressed in white uniforms looking ill at ease chatted with a young German professional woman and two men in suits and ties who looked like newly hired sales people.

Tama and Barry had yet to arrive but her German army clearly had. Rebecca quickly picked out all four. Their physical fitness, wary state of alertness, inexpensive but neatly pressed civilian clothes and short haircuts screamed former military.

Her practiced eye also detected the slight telltale bulge under their left arms that suggested they carried weapons.

She entered the dealership display area and walked around. Two cars, polished to the nth degree, sat gleaming in the middle of the room, both green, one a coupe and the other a four-door sedan.

Neither car appealed to her. They looked to be what they likely were, cheap, sturdy, basic transportation.

On one side of the room, a makeshift bar had been set up. Two caterers, a blond woman and equally blond man, both wearing white shirts, red vests and dark trousers, busied themselves placing plastic glasses and bottles of liquor in rows on the table in front of them.

A squatting young girl in another corner used a machine to blow up balloons, which she released into the air. The balloons rose slowly and circuitously to the ceiling and stayed there, jockeying playfully with each other.

Rebecca walked back into the service bay and stopped to admire it. She counted 16 individual work stations, complete with hoists, diagnostic machines and shiny new tool racks. The glossy gray floor glistened with silver flecks.

She exited the back of the service area and stepped into a back lot containing several rows of new Dragon Motors cars in various colors.

Nearby, a group of giggling Chinese teenagers practiced fitting themselves into a long, multi-colored paper dragon, soon to be a part of the festivities.

She walked the perimeter slowly. Something caught her eye. She glanced down, continued a few steps, stopped, walked back, went to her knees and touched the soft plastic pressed along the bottom of the dealership's back wall.

Looking more closely, she spotted less than an eighth of an inch of protruding wire. Oh oh!

She got up, walked quickly through the service area and back into the showroom, seeking the most important looking official she could find.

She spotted the expensively dressed Chinese man and whispered to him, "You've got to evacuate the building immediately! The place has been mined, plastic explosive's been attached to be base of the back wall."

"What? Who are you?" the man said.

She had no answer for that. She rushed out of the dealership, past the loud and festive oompah band and lottery ticket booth, which was now manned.

Across the street, sheltered from the noise and crowd, she dialed Barry.

As she waited for him to answer, she watched the expensively dressed Chinese man say something to one of the mercenaries, who looked across the street to where she stood, then walked back into the service bay and outside, apparently to check her information.

"We'll be there in five minutes," Barry's voice said.

"Stay away!" Rebecca said. She watched as the mercenary returned to the selling floor and whispered something to the older Chinese man, who looked alarmed.

"I found plastic explosive. I tried to get people to leave but no one will listen," Rebecca said. "Have Tama call and evacuate the building, please, hurry!"

She heard a rustling as Barry relayed the message to Tama, who said something Rebecca could not hear. Too late.

The explosion, loud and close, blew out the dealership windows.

Something flammable she missed must have been sprayed, painted or dusted inside, for the entire building quickly became consumed by fire, the glare so intense she had to shield her eyes.

Terrified, she crouched, waited, turned and looked up through her fingers, horrified. The Dragon Motors dealership began to collapse upon itself.

****

A visibly shaken Tama Wu held her press conference outside the Frankfurt Police Headquarters. Before speaking, she'd tried to learn if anyone survived.

A police official in plain clothes told her that because the building had collapsed upon itself and still burned, no one had been able to search through the rubble. She was told that might take days.

Tama assumed that her European director was dead, along with Sammy and her four German mercenaries.

She asked the only supervisor at Dragon Motors European Headquarters who'd not attended the opening if cars stored at the Frankfurt Airport were okay. When told they'd not been touched, she looked relieved.

"To honor memories of all those who lost their lives today, we will rebuild on the same spot," she told reporters, although privately she was not sure.

Asked if she felt bitter about having her business singled out, she responded, "Of course. But we will not be so easily defeated. We came to Europe to establish a beachhead, and that is what we will do."

Hours later, police found flyers headlined 'Death to Capitalists' and 'Chinese go home.' The next day, two groups, one Marxist and the other Islamic claimed responsibility

Privately, Tama Wu announced to Barry, "That bastard will rue the day he fucked with me."

The words sounded hollow. She no longer had her mercenary Germans. The leader of her detectives also was dead.

She turned to Barry. "You and I know who did this," she said. "Help me kill the Pole and I'll give you a million dollars."

"Killing him is worth that much to you?" Barry said.

"Yes," Tama Wu responded.

"I'll talk with my partner," Barry said. "I'll give you my answer tomorrow."

"In the meanwhile, you'll still provide cover?"

"Yes," Barry said. "We will."

Hamburg
July 1, 2010
Caught

Jürgen arrived home to his second-floor apartment tired from teaching his German class to find Ania had dinner waiting.

As they ate cold cuts and fresh salad under soft light at the kitchen table, Jürgen mentioned the visit before class by a tall, powerfully built Pole named Bernard Mannheim, and a smaller man named Kristoff.

"The big man had good German but it was not his native language," Jürgen said. "He scared the hell out me. He was no more than 40, about 6'4," heavily muscled with a clipped brown beard. Once you meet a guy like that, you don't forget him. His eyes looked as if he didn't give a damn about anything."

Alarmed, Ania asked, "What did they want?"

"The smaller man, Kristoff somebody-or-other, said he was your brother," Jürgen said. "He said that you'd run away from home and he was looking for you! I knew you didn't have a brother, so I played dumb."

Ania had turned pale.

"What did you tell them?" she said.

"I told them that, yes, you'd been a student, but that several months ago you stopped coming and I had no idea where you you'd gone. The big man, Mannheim, gave me his card."

"May I see it?" Ania said.

Jürgen removed the card from his pocket and handed it to her. She glanced at it, saw a phone number but no address. She kept the card.

"They're getting close," Ania said. "I'm going to have to leave, Jürgen, and right now. It will be for just awhile, I promise you, Sweets."

She got up, her chair scraping against the linoleum floor, went to her room and frantically began packing.

****

Outside the second-floor apartment and down the street, standing in shadows, Marek had watched Ania and Jürgen sitting next to their apartment window having diner.

Bingo!

He turned and walked jauntily back to his hotel.
****
Ania, pulling a large suitcase behind her awkwardly down two flights of stairs, left the building by the back way.

Two blocks distant, she got into her Jetta and drove away. She'd hole up in a cheap hotel, Maybe, after Bernard Mannheim was dead, she'd return to Jürgen, and maybe not.

Hamburg, Germany
July 1, 2010
Decisions

The Pole and René Oppenheim sat on the terrace of the Jacob Hotel enjoying a breakfast of fruit compotes, coffee and toast. A pleasant, cooling breeze blew gently from the North.

The terrace sat across a highway and a treed swath of green fronting the Elbe River. Big ships moved majestically past. The temperature had already reached 70 degrees Fahrenheit, suggesting a hot day to come.

One of now-deceased Sammy's fellow detectives watched the meeting. From across the street, he photographed the two men together.

"Nice spot," the Pole said, "But kind of far from the center of town."

"It's relaxing out here," René said. "I love these old hotels. You've got to try the Engle, it's a five-star place on a houseboat about five minutes from here. Great food, service, atmosphere, and, of course, the river traffic."

René leaned back, placed his manicured fingers on the table, signaling to the Pole that he was done with small talk.

"Go ahead. Tell me your 'take' on the arms business," he said.

"I've gone over everything Serge did," the Pole said. "The guy was bypassing small and medium-sized sales, trying to assemble and package larger and larger groups of weapons to attract the biggest clients. Did you know he was doing this?"

René shook his head. "Hadn't given it a thought. We basically watch revenues and don't get involved in much else. But assuming that's what he was doing, do you have a problem with that?"

"Yes. Contacts complained that Serge turned down perfectly good deals to hook the biggest fishes. Worse, he was mixing in a lot of Chinese munitions from Albania dating back to the 1960's, much of them bad. He'd remove identification so he could unload less desirable stuff at a higher cost."

René frowned.

"Fix that immediately," he said.

"It's fixed. I gave the complainers a rebate on new orders and apologized. Good thing I did. We have competition."

"Who?"

"The Baron."

"Noted. He's CIA, you know."

"Didn't know that. You sure?"

"Almost positive. I doubt he's in their actual employ, but I do know that he sells a hell of a lot to them and for them."

"I'm going to talk with him shortly," the Pole said.

"You've put me here to build the business. That means getting rid of competitors fairly or by other means. I've brought in people. Serge was doing everything himself. He didn't appear to trust anybody."

"Not bad strategy in the arms business," René said.

"No, but there are ways. Who was it that said 'Trust but verify?'"

"Ronald Reagan," René said. "Had something to do with Russian arms negotiations."

"So there you go," the Pole said. "An apt quote. When I'm done here, you'll have a structure in place. That'll allow you to do your own trusting and verifying. I'm also developing new channels. I'll be attending the IDEX conference in Abu Dhabi next month. I'm told I'll find a lot of business there."

"You can. Every arms dealer on the planet will be there, most of them not who they say they are."

The Pole laughed. "I won't be who I say I am either. As for Hamburg, give me three months, that's all the extra time I need," the Pole said.

"You have a year," René said, "But a check-up in three months sounds good. Now, talk with me about our other business."

The Pole sipped of his coffee, put the cup down and said, "You had good people running thr brothels. Unfortunately, Hector and Fritz aren't with us any longer."

"What?"

"An escaped hooker murdered both of them. I've located her. The situation's being taken care of."

"Okay." René looked worried.

"I don't like the brothel business," the Pole said.

"Why?"

"Too messy. Human beings are a lot more unpredictable than guns and ammo."

"That's a given," René said.

"What I'm saying is that I don't want to run it," the Pole said. "I hate all the personnel shit, the drunks, drugs and suicidal hookers. I like clean transactions, and moving and housing hookers isn't clean. I have no moral concerns. My objections are strictly practical. I'll give you back half the $250,000 you've deposited in my account if you wish. I want to concentrate on the arms business. I'm developing channels that don't require an additional business to make them profitable. Keep it simple. That's what I'm recommending. I know a man in Poland who can run the girls in and out for you if you wish."

"No, never mind," René said, thinking quickly. The German brothel business netted almost $3 million annually. He could find somebody to run it.

"Okay. Concentrate on the arms business. Keep the deposit, but you'll need to generate $3 million more to make up for the brothel revenues you'll be giving up."

"Understood," the Pole said.

"Who's running the brothels now?" René asked.

"I am, but while you're looking for a new overseer, I'd like to make some changes."

René said nothing.

"Most of the girls are Roman or Orthodox Catholic," the Pole said. "I want, within limits, to keep them borderline content. Let them keep religious symbols in their rooms. Introduce incentive programs. Over ten customers a day and the girl keeps 25% of the gross. That policy alone should jack up revenues."

"The brothel managers, most of them Muslim, won't like any of that," René said.

The Pole ignored this. "Get rid of the present managers," he said. "I can arrange to have them gone by the end of the year. They're all from the same small towns in Turkey. It's incestuous. I'm getting reports of physical abuse by backroom supervisors. Replace them with tough and experienced female managers."

René seemed amused. "You're more the enlightened feminist than your reputation would suggest."

"This is business," the Pole answered. "I've been in a lot of whorehouses. The ones run by women have a better atmosphere."

****

Later that afternoon, the Pole met with Mahmoud in a hotel room on the second floor of the Kempinski Atlantic.

"I occasionally need to dump older arms," Mahmoud said. "I can let you know and you can bid."

"I prefer not to bid," the Pole said. "I'll pay you more for an exclusive."

Mahmoud pretended to consider this. "No, I don't want to be locked in," he said. "But I do have a proposition for you."

"I'm listening."

"Have you ever trafficked yellow cake or any isotopic metals?"

"No," the Pole said. "but there must be a lot of money in that."

"There is, commensurate with the risk. I know of a shipment coming into Hamburg."

"When?"

"Hard to say, and if I knew wouldn't tell you. I know who it's going to and where, but not when. I won't know when until 12 hours or less before it arrives."

Stone-faced, the Pole absorbed the information, wondering how much money was involved.

"Most such shipments never make it," Mahmoud said. "Countries are getting exceptionally sophisticated in tracking, sometimes from miles away; but let's assume that this operator is able to get such materials into the country, avoid Customs and electronic searches."

"Okay."

"The seller wants $35 million for what's coming in. A fair price. Do you know a man called the Baron?"

"I do."

"The Baron has an enforcer he thinks no one knows about."

"I assumed more than one," the Pole said,

"He's created that impression, but he's only got one, a brutal homosexual who the Baron seldom meets in person."

"Are they lovers?"

"I don't know. Maybe once. It's not important. We've had the Baron followed off and on for over a year. To help, I'll remove his muscle for you."

"Won't he just get somebody else?"

"No, he's already panicking. I sense it. With his enforcer gone he won't be able to handle the shipment. I'll suggest you."

Hamburg
July 1, 2010
Shot

Around five-thirty p.m., Ania left work and drove past her old apartment. Its lights were on, meaning Jürgen was home.

She noticed a man standing on the corner, leaning against a building staring up at the light.

Not only did he look like a thug, something about him said he was Polish. His haircut, shoes, cheap leather jacket and the way he slouched convinced her.

A half hour later, she drove by again and saw him still in the shadows watching the apartment. Was he waiting for her return?

She looked for a parking place, finally giving up and paying to park in a garage.

Standing far down the street, she spotted the man staring up at Jürgen's apartment, a cell phone to his ear. She wondered what he had in the leather case resting by his feet.

She could see Jürgen through the second-story window. He was taking something out of the refrigerator.

She felt a moment of affection, sadness and then panic as a familiar feeling of coldness spread across her skin.

She took out her pistol, concealing it in the same hand that held her purse and headed quickly down the street towards the stranger, trying to look distracted and unaware of her surroundings. She doubted he could tell who she was in the dark.

She got to within ten feet of him before he

recognized her. He reached into his pocket.

She shot him in the heart, the nose of her weapon inches from his chest.

As he fell, she grabbed his leather case, started to leave, stopped, reached inside his jacket pocket, found his cell phone, revolver and wallet. She took them. The leather case was heavy. She'd just managed to lug it around the corner when she froze.

A police car drove leisurely past. Had it turned the corner, it would have seen the recently shot man. Fortunately for her, it continued in a straight line heading away from her.

Staying out of the streetlight as best she could, she lugged the heavy leather case to an all-night diner. Her forehead and underarms perspired and her heart still beat fiercely.

At the diner, she drank coffee, then walked with the leather case to the parking garage and got into her Jetta.

In her hotel room, she opened the wallet of the man she'd just killed. His driver's license identified him as Marek Ogrodski. He had a Warsaw address.

She opened the leather case. Inside she found a disassembled sniper rifle, telescopic sight and ammunition. Tucked inside Marek's wallet she found room key 243 for the Kronprinz Hotel. Aha!

She checked his cell phone address list. It contained 20 names and phone numbers, one of them a Bernard Mannheim.

The syndicate's identified me, she thought. They'll try to get to me through Jürgen, meaning I can't contact him again until the threat is gone.

What should she do? She couldn't kill them all.

This Marek was likely but one of many. Bernard Mannheim could keep bringing in new people until they finally found and killed her.

She must kill Mannheim quickly. She'd never be able to resume a normal life until he was dead.

As she started to put Marek's cell phone in her purse, it rang. She glanced to see the caller's name in the phone's address file. A Kristoff was calling.

Should she go back and kill more of them? She now had a sniper rifle. She could take care of matters at a safe distance.

She went across the street to another hotel and used the pay phone in the lobby to report the murder and its location, then hung up, walked away from the hotel, around the block and back into her hotel through a side entrance that opened on to the bar.

She stayed for a few minutes in the bar, then returned to her room.

She used the dead man's cell phone and called Bernard Mannheim's number. The Kempinski Hotel desk answered. She immediately hung up.

Tomorrow, she'd call in sick at the travel agency, check out the Kempinski. She'd also talk with doormen at similar luxury hotels. She'd find him.

Hamburg, Germany
July 1, 2010
Vulnerability

Half inebriated but alert, Lash left the Boyz und Fun gay bar stuck down an alley off the Reeperbahn. He'd had sex twice in the stalls with anonymous strangers while rap music thumped and boomed.

He wore a loud, short-sleeved Hawaiian shirt to show off his muscled, tattooed arms. His freshly washed and pressed Levis fit tightly, emphasizing what he considered an A-plus 'package' and comely rear end.

That morning he'd had his hair clipped close to his head. He'd used a light and almost imperceptible rouge on his face and lots of lotion to smooth his rough skin.

Almost 35, he continued to flirt and get flirts but was beginning to dread the approach of obvious middle age. He could see lines forming around his mouth and on his forehead. He'd ask the Baron pay for a facelift soon.

He walked jauntily towards the nearest metro stop, thinking about stopping at another place for a drink, no flirting, no hookups, just a chance to unwind before returning to his dismal studio apartment.

If the Baron didn't come up with something soon, he'd have to manufacture something on his own. He had a friend who could get him a job on a freighter.

He didn't have a union card, but that could be finessed if you knew the right people. His friend said he did, not to worry, the pay was good, you were at sea no more than six weeks before returning to Hamburg, wouldn't be spending much money while at sea, and had a chance to save up and get a little ahead.

As he thought this, he felt dizzy, assuming that

two earlier ingested Mojitos were speaking.

He stumbled, his legs gave way and he fell to the sidewalk. A crowd gathered. He was aware of going into convulsions and blacked out.

EMTs failed to revive him. He had no pulse and no heartbeat. They assumed he'd died of an embolism or heart attack.

At the hospital, an orderly began calling telephone numbers found in his cell phone. The third call was answered by the Baron.

****

The Baron stared at Lash's lifeless white face, and listened without comment to the morgue doctor's explanation of how Lash had died. He told the hospital he'd pay for an autopsy.

The Baron left the morgue distraught, not for the loss of love, but because he was now alone and defenseless in a dangerous world. Without his arms business, he had no way to continue the expensive charade needed to command attention and respect. He thought of suicide, remembered he had the chance to make $1 million on a $35-million deal. This thought made him even more tense. How could he do that without Lash as backup?

Two days later, after his attorney conferred with police and hospital authorities, the autopsy was done and the cause of death determined.

Lash had swallowed less than one microgram of radioactive polonium, or the substance had been introduced into him by other means. The polonium didn't kill him, but it likely triggered the heart attack that did.

Salvador, Brazil
July 1, 2010
Pause

Alfredo biked along Todos dos Santos Bay, the day sunny and warm. He spent an hour at Porto de Barra Beach looking at the trim bodies of young males and females.

He'd docked several times in Rio de Janiero and Recife, but this was his first time in Salvador.

Yesterday afternoon, he'd unloaded cargo taken on in Punta Arenas. Then he'd given his crew leave.

Salvador reminded him of older areas of Goa and Macau, which he'd expected. Salvador was once an ancient Portuguese colonial port. Along the docks, much of its 17th century architecture remained.

As he walked and enjoyed the feel of the sun on his face, he wondered what had happened to the sailor who'd tried to bribe him. The money had been returned from Singapore, meaning Polski never got it. Odd.

The latest news: He'd been ordered not to dock in Hamburg. He was to anchor in international waters and wait for instructions. What the hell was that about?!

To hell with it. He had the rest of the day in Salvador. He'd forget his worries and enjoy himself.

The freighter would be provisioned, diesel engines checked, enough fuel added and he'd be ready to sail by seven p.m. and darkness. He'd checked the progress of the work earlier in the morning. He was told everything was on schedule.

A tug had met and led him in and then vanished. That had been the extent of his official greeting.

Officialdom obviously had been bribed to stay

away. How else to explain the fact that no inspectors radioed instructions or boarded?

From Salvador, he'd try to average 20 knots the rest of the way, a nautical distance of almost 6,000 miles without stopping.

His estimate of seven to eight days, assuming they were not boarded and there was no engine trouble, seemed reasonable.

He ate lunch at a no-name restaurant. Instead of seafood, which he ate twice and sometimes thrice daily on board, he ordered a deep-fried bread called acarajé, rice with spicy jerked beef, plus desert of sliced bananas, and dark Brazilian coffee. It all tasted delicious.

Full, he left the beachside boardwalk and headed into the lower town.

On an escarpment several hundred feet above where he walked, he could see a newer part of the city complete with skyscrapers.

He had no interest in going up there. Almost 3.5 million people lived in metropolitan Salvador, many in shanties stuffed four to a room. No thanks.

He rented a bike and peddled happily across cobble-stoned streets past marinas filled with sail boats, boat repair facilities, stores selling uniforms, small 24-hour cafés, an open farmer's market and a choice of merchant banks.

The facades of old colonial houses painted a variety of cheerful pastels came to street's edge on both sides. Occasionally he had to stop for a car or person unexpectedly exiting a building.

Lonely, he rented a woman for an hour in narrow three-story combination small hotel and brothel near the open market. A racial mix of negro and Spanish named

Carla, she smelled heavily of perfume and was an indifferent lay. He finished with her in less than an hour.

The rest of the afternoon, he sat and let his mind wander. He'd receive a bonus $40,000 cashier's check plus his regular captain's pay at trip's conclusion. He'd use some of that to take his wife and children on vacation, but where?

He'd been almost everywhere on earth? Maybe they'd settle for a nice resort. He and his wife could discuss this.

He thought of phoning her, but the whore's sweat and perfume still hung guiltily to him. He felt a sense of emptiness he could not shake.

Usually, he had hassles. Inspectors wanted bribes. Work didn't get done right. Something always prevented him from leaving on time. So far, none of this had happened. Everywhere he'd docked, the way had been greased for him. That took some powerful entity's planning and connections. Even a sailor's attempted blackmail had been handled without him lifting a finger!

He looked up and saw his cook walking down the street with a plump young negro woman. He checked his watch. The man had another four hours before he had to return to the ship. He'd let him be.

Often, when you got ready to sail, crew failed to show. They got thrown in jail for being drunk, disorderly or both, overslept with a woman, or just decided they'd had enough.

His crew, with one exception, had stayed. They were being paid double for the run and that likely explained their reluctance to leave. Plus, all but two of them had families. Family men were more reliable, although arguably more set in their ways.

Eight more days would take him to July ninth or tenth. Then it would end and he could go back to making normal runs and not worry about carrying such dangerous cargo.

A straight shot up the coast of Africa, past the Azores, and then skirt the coast of northern England and Scotland, then a turn into the North sea.

Frankfurt, Germany
July 1, 2010
Aftermath

A grim but seemingly resilient Tama Wu soldiered her way through a press conference held in the downtown police station auditorium, expressing the right sentiments, answering questions directly.

As many as 50 people, to include children, had been burned or crushed to death when the Dragon Motors dealership's walls imploded and the roof collapsed.

After the press conference, Tama stoically and bravely sat for another hour of police questioning, to which she responded glumly.

As she and Barry left the station, more reporters accosted her with questions. It was all she could do to remain civil, but she managed.

Her vulnerability and pluckiness made him feel sorry for her, an emotion he'd never guessed he'd associate with such a tough, infuriating and uncompromising woman.

All the while, he worried about snipers, his eyes

wildly scanning every window of every building in the vicinity while also watching every passing car.

Tama's four remaining detectives rushed to the dealership the moment they learned of the explosion. Told of Sammy's almost certain death, they became disorganized and emotionally lost, but stayed for the press conference, even though in Barry's professional opinion they did not act alert and focused.

Afterward, before entering the police station, Tama introduced her detectives to Barry, who gave them instructions.

They were to watch the area and keep their boss safe. When she exited the police station, they were to phalanx her and check for snipers.

Barry did not mention Rebecca. She'd conduct her own surveillance, plus check the vicinity of Tama's new hotel before Tama arrived.

Barry and Tama argued in the car after leaving the police station.

"I'm tired of staying in cheap places," she said. "I deserve better after all I've just been through."

"It's necessary you don't stay at well known places," Barry told her, "They attract attention. What are your plans?"

"What do you mean?"

"Are you returning to China?"

"No. I still have work here."

"Are you referring to the Pole?"

"Yes. Can you help me with him?" Tama's eyes searched Barry's face as if expecting to find the answer etched there.

"I've got to talk it over with my partner," Barry said

"The one you won't let me see," Tama said petulantly.

"The one I don't let anyone see," Barry replied. "I'll drop you at your new hotel...it's been checked out. You should change into your salary girl disguise before we get there."

"Right now. Here in the car?"

"Yes."

"So you can see me naked?"

"I'm not suggesting you take off your clothes, just ditch the suit and go back to being Salary Girl. It's a great disguise. I'll keep driving around while you change. I'll use the time to check for tails."

Tama unbuttoned her skirt, raised her rear off the seat and pulled down her skirt. She wore pantyhose but no underwear, her furry vaginal area again on display through the panty hose material. At the corner of his eye, he saw large, ugly scars running across both knees. The legs themselves, he noted, were flawless.

"You like this?" she said. She thrust her hips several inches off the seat, wiggled and held them there.

He surreptitiously admired the lovely curve of her thighs. He forced himself to focus on the road.

Tama quickly abandoned her body's awkward position, which attracted the attention of a passing trucker, who blew his air horn in an appreciative salute as he passed.

She bent over, unzipped her Vuitton bag on the floor between her legs and removed the skirt she'd worn on the plane

Again she raised her hips off the seat, this time to remove her panty hose. Her sexual scent filled the car. She pulled on underpants, stopped, and with her legs wide reached her hand inside.

"Sorry. got an itch down here," she said, "and I'm very wet." She stared at him. "Come on, Mr. Seymour. Say something!"

Laughing again, she slipped on the skirt, tucked in her blouse, then buttoned and zipped the skirt, put on tennis shoes, tied them, and loosened her hair, which fell softly, covering her ears.

She took out a compact, opened it, studied her face, took a tissue, removed her lipstick, checked her face again, fluffed her hair and took a final look.

Satisfied, she shut the compact and put it and everything she'd just taken off into the bag, zipped it shut and leaned back.

"Satisfied?" she said.

"You look great," he said. "And no tails. Now we can head for the hotel."

Hamburg, Germany
July 1, 2010
Bedfellows

In the Kapinski Associates office, the Pole listened intently as the Baron explained the situation.

"I've had a good run," he began "made a lot of money and now I'm ready to quit. This is good news for you, Mr. Mannheim, since most of the business I usually get will, if we can work this out amiably, go to you."

The Pole wondered: Was the Baron's muscle already neutralized?

"You want to sell your business, is that right?" the Pole said.

"I do. I'll provide you contact names, sellers and buyers, but only after making sure they're okay with this. I'"ll even make the introductions and vouch for you. I have 16 channels that last year generated almost $3 million in sales. Plus, I have a job coming up that will net a $1 million commission. "

"I hear that upwards of 60% of your business is done with the CIA, is that so?" the Pole said.

The Baron looked uncomfortable. "Yes, I do business with them," he said. "Is there any reason they wouldn't be happy doing business with you?"

"I don't have good relations with them," the Pole said.

This, the Pole knew, was an understatement. He'd killed at least three known CIA agents and perhaps others contracted to the CIA but unknown to him. He'd also turned one CIA agent into a quadriplegic.

"Then perhaps we can't do business," the Baron said.

"No," the Pole said, "It doesn't necessarily mean that. Your eastern European and Russian suppliers would be useful, assuming they're proprietary."

The Baron considered this. "I think that for $2 million I can let you have everything. You can sort it out yourself."

"How many buyers do you have that aren't CIA-sponsored?" the Pole said.

"Sixteen," the Baron said.

"How much did they alone generate last year?"

"$1.5 million," the Baron lied, plus the upcoming $1 million commission is not CIA-connected."

"One million dollars," the Pole said.

"One million five and the deal is done," the Baron

said.

"I'll think about it," the Pole said, "And give you an answer within three days."

Frankfurt, Germany
July 1, 2010
Chatter

"My. Oh my," Rebecca said. "That was wonderful!"

Her naked body flush and covered with sweat, she rose with effort from the bed.

Entering the bathroom, she glanced back coquettishly and saw that Barry was ready to go again.

"You were fantastic, Bear, so eager and attentive!"

"There was that time in Genoa, after I almost got shot," he said.

"Yes, but this time you lingered in a few places where you usually don't!" she said. "It was glorious. I loved all of it. Thanks, Bear."

He'd literally started with her toes and worked his way inch by inch up her body. He'd penetrated and worked her awhile, pulled out, licked her, re-entered her, finished, rested, and started again. He agreed that he'd been fantastic.

He listened to her pee, worried that his animal intensity might upon reflection unsettle her.

Most of their sex happened before sleep. One or the other signaled by touch they wanted intimacy and within ten minutes they were done, hugs and a kiss given, and each turned to sleep.

"We have to talk about what we do next," Rebecca said.

She stood in front of the basin washing her hands and staring at her face, which was still flushed.

She fluffed her hair on both sides just as both her and Barry's cell phones rang, announcing immediately who it was.

"You do the honors," Rebecca said. "I'll listen in on my phone."

"It's Chester," the voice said.

"We guessed," Barry said.

"So you're together, are you?"

"Yes, we are. Technically, we've finished the assignment here, but something's happened and we need to talk."

Barry told Chester about the explosion, the killing of Tama's lead detective and her four mercenaries, the press conference and questioning by police.

"You should have let me know," he said. He sounded angry.

"We had more urgent priorities, Chester," Rebecca chimed in. "Her security was killed. We got her out of there and she's back in disguise and safe for the moment at a new hotel."

"Good, because something's come up," Chester said.

"Before you get to what you want, we have some questions for you, too, Chester. Tama Wu has offered us one million dollars to kill the Pole."

"You going to take it?"

"We haven't discussed it."

"Well, I may have some added incentive for you."

"Okay."

"We've got computers that listen in on cell phone and land line international conversations."

"Must take a lot of operators to do that," Barry said.

"Very funny. The computer listens for certain words, like 'bomb,' 'attack,' etc., in a variety of languages…"

"I assume one of those is Arabic."

"Yes, Smarty. Farsi and Urdu would be others. We picked up chatter about a shipment of Uranium 235."

"The kind used in bombs?"

"Precisely. We've talked with a sailor who was on the ship that's carrying the stuff."

"Jeez, how did you do that?"

"Not necessary you know. The boat's scheduled to drop off the material in Hamburg."

"Why there?"

"How the hell do I know?! It's as good a place as any. It's in the Azores about now and should be arriving near where you are in five or six days."

"Why don't you just have Navy Seals board it?"

"For one, we haven't located it precisely, but we're about to. We're doing U2 flyovers that can detect the minutest radiation. A few more hours, I'm told, and we'll have her located."

Didn't know U2's were still flying. Thought Gary Powers crashing one in Russia ended that."

"You'd be wrong. We want to bust the entire network. We want to see how they get the stuff into the country and what they do with it."

"Sounds like a potential screw-up and career ender for you, Chester."

"What's that supposed mean?"

"Aren't you risking that the stuff will get by you?

That happens and you'll be running Aleut agents out of Nome."

"Not funny. I have no intention of letting that happen," Chester said. "Plus I have my orders; but I didn't call to get scolded about risks. Here's what's happening."

"Okay."

"The Baron is point man on this. We've been monitoring his conversations, which he clearly doesn't realize."

"Not the brightest bulb in the room, I presume," Barry said.

"That may well be, but he's been an on-time supplier and his business ethics, such as they are, more closely resemble the norm than others in his trade. We talked with him and let him know our concerns."

Barry laughed.

"We told him to contact a Bernard Mannheim," Chester said. "He runs his own arms outfit along with some brothels in Hamburg."

"Sounds like a nice fellow."

"He's not. His real named is…"

"Mannheim is the Pole," Rebecca chimed in. "I've read Sammy Kan's hard drive. I even know where the sonnavabitch lives and works."

"Then we're on the same page," Chester said.

"What the hell does that mean, Chester?" Barry said. "I hate clichés like that."

"Okay, fine," Chester said. "Now you've annoyed me. Keep an eye on the Pole. I'll get back with you once the ship docks, okay?"

Obviously angry, he hung up.

"What do you make of that?" Rebecca said.

"He's clearly in a bad mood, which is not that unusual," Barry said. "I'll stay with Tama here. The Pole's never laid eyes on you. You should watch him."

"Okay," Rebecca said. "But first let's fool around some more."

Hamburg
July 1 2010
Problems

The Pole rose from behind his office desk and angrily threw a magazine across the room, just missing Kristoff's head.

"What do you mean he's dead!"

"He was shot and left on the sidewalk to die," Andrzej said. "I'll bet anything the Polish bitch did it."

"Fine!" the Pole said, for the moment dismissing any threat from the Polish girl. "But why did you let the police beat you to his body? Now his ass is in the goddamn morgue and we can't go anywhere near him! How could you not know something was wrong? Didn't you check in?"

"We did, Boss," Lech said. "When he didn't call in when he was supposed to, when his cell didn't answer, that's when we went to check."

"And?"

"We got there and saw police cars and the area cordoned off. They'd already found him."

"Oh, Shit! What did he have on him?"

"Don't know, Andrzej said. "Cell phone, wallet with license. Gun. Suspect that's all."

"His gun? Did he smuggle it in with him?"

"No, he picked up it and a sniper rifle in town from the guy you gave us."

"Good, then it's unmarked and we're okay," the Pole said, then, as if he'd merely rested a moment, he again angrily erupted.

"His fucking cell phone!" the Pole screamed. "The police will track down the phone numbers. We're all in there either coded or otherwise!"

"We don't know that for sure," Lech said.

"Well, I know this. We're all going to have to change addresses, and quick. That includes me. We disappear, understood?"

"You mean leave Hamburg?" Andrzej said.

"No. We've still got work here. Clear your hotel immediately."

"Right now?" Lech said..

"Yes, right now. Find an alternative place or places to stay. I don't want to know where."

"How will we contact you?" Andrzej said.

The Pole thought about that.

"Okay," he said. "We'll all get new cell phones with new phone numbers. We'll use a simple code. Everybody have pen and paper?"

Everyone but Andrzej nodded.

The Pole opened a desk drawer, found a note pad and tossed it to Andrzej, who fumbled and dropped it. The others laughed.

Red-faced, Andrzej picked up the note pad, took a pen from his jacket and nodded that he was ready.

"Okay, here goes," the Pole said, "And I'm doing this on the fly. When we need to meet, use the alphabet. Midnight will be the numeral 175, 250 will be one a.m., 325, two a.m. Oh, Screw it. Here's a better idea. We all get new cell phones. Tomorrow morning we meet in my hotel room at the Kempinski Atlantic. We exchange the new telephone numbers, hold a short meeting and split. The minute you leave, you break the phone you have and leave it somewhere out of the way. Otherwise, they can track where you are with them."

"Okay," Kristoff and Lech said simultaneously.

"Any of us can call a meeting," the Pole said, "But if anyone but me calls one, it better be important. If you only need to meet one of us, say that name. I'll be Mickey Mouse, Andrzej, you'll be dopey, Lech, you'll be Sandman, and Kristoff will be Snoop Dog."

"Any significance to any of these names?" Andrzej said.

"None," the Pole said. "I just pulled them out of my ass, which is better. There's no obvious system to be decoded, and anyone listening will spend a lot of useless time attempting to find one. Okay, everyone copy the hour and its number."

"So," the Pole said, "If I say 430 Sandman Mickey Mouse," what does that mean?"

"That you want to meet with Lech at four-thirty p.m.," Andrzej said, frowning. "That has to be the worst..."

"Very good," the Pole said, cutting off Andrzej. "One more piece of information. One-on-ones, strictly for message exchanges, will be in the ground-floor men's room of the Holiday Inn Express. It's a big, businesslike place with lots of traffic, and easy to find."

"Which one, Boss?" Kristoff said. "There are two!"

"Good, good, that's what I like to see!" the Pole said to cover his error. "The one in St. Pauli near the Reeperbahn, the one near city center. Everyone got that?"

There were nods.

"I'm going to be gone three days to meet with clients and prospects," the Pole said.

This elicited worried looks from all but Andrzej, who seemed preoccupied with tying his shoelace, which brought an irritated look from the Pole.

"But when I get back," the Pole said, "we'll meet. In the meanwhile, find the Polish girl and take her out. I expect that to be done by the time I get back."

"What if we get contacted by the police?" Lech said.

"You tell them that you're salesmen for Kapinski Associates, are in training and that our dead friend Marek was as well."

More nods.

"Any other questions?" the Pole said.

There were none. The men filed out.

"Make sure you memorize the name and time codes," the Pole said as they left.

****

As the Pole and Beata packed suitcases, Hugo called and using euphemisms told the Pole about the successful detonation of the Frankfurt Dragon Motors dealership.

"Did you get the bitch?"

"Missed her by two or three minutes. I was watching the place with binoculars. Some woman discovered the explosive. I read her lips as she told some older, official looking dude, who alerted what looked like a retired storm trooper. The charges were set to go off with a phone call. I made the call."

" I've got a new cell. Get my number from one of the Poles. I'm heading out of town and won't be reachable for awhile. Everything okay with the houses?"

"Far as I know."

"Good. Talk with you later, and congratulations. Well done."

"Thanks boss."

Hamburg
July 4, 2010
Travel

The Baron waited on the sidewalk outside an abandoned building in a construction zone. He wore a blue windbreaker and waved as the Pole and Beata in the Pole's gray S Class Mercedes slowed to a stop. The Baron got in.

"Good that you reached me when you did," the Pole said as they drove away. "We're checked out of the Kempinski. I'll be away talking to clients and potential clients for the next few days."

The Baron nodded, noting that Beata looked upset.

"Can I talk in front of your friend?" the Baron said.

"Yes. Of course," the Pole said. "Beata is my confidant, aren't you, Kochanie!"

He gave her hand, which was on her lap, a friendly tap. She ignored the gesture.

"The package arrives July 12th," the Baron said. 'Do you still want to buy my business?"

"So, you're definitely getting out?" the Pole said.

"Yes, but if you're not interested, I have another buyer," the Baron lied. "Regardless, in the short term, I'd like to contract for back-up to protect the package while it's in transit."

"You want me to protect you?"

"Yes."

"No. Not interested," the Pole said. "Where can I drop you?"

"The Park Hyatt would be fine," the Baron said. He looked momentarily stricken. "Sorry we can't do business. Call me when you get back." At the Park Hyatt, the Baron disappeared inside the hotel's revolving glass doors.

"That was odd," Beata said as they drove down Elbchaussee Strasse and up to the Louis C Jakob Hotel. Beata had booked a suite there overlooking the Elbe River.

"Odd?"

"Yes. Why would he want to cut you in on anything that lucrative? Doesn't he have his own muscle?"

"Not any longer," the Pole said smugly.

"Are you going to help him?"

"Haven't decided," the Pole said. "I might actually do a legitimate business deal like the big boys do, buy his list from him and use him temporarily as a consultant. I've got to think about it. In the meanwhile, I'll let him stew."

"You can be cruel," Beata said. "What am I supposed to do while you're gone? We have no social life. Are we going to have any time for each other, just us?"

"Yes, later, after all of this is settled," the Pole said.

"After what's settled?"

"I've got somebody tracking me and trying to kill me," the Pole said. "I've also got a business to build, and that's suddenly become a lot more difficult."

"If you don't think you're succeeding at it, maybe you should get out before anybody finds out, especially whoever's tracking you. You can go back to doing what you were doing."

"Oh, were it that simple," the Pole said. "I've spent almost $60,000 changing my physical looks, added new identities, moved to a new country, and still people have found me."

"Let me go with you now. Let's just leave, the two of us. We can go back to Poland, settle around Krakow somewhere. You have enough money. You don't have to work another day. Why keep doing what you're doing?"

"Because I have to," the Pole said. She studied his face and saw genuine anguish there. "Because if I don't keep moving, if I stop, I'm dead. I've made too many enemies."

Beata sighed, thinking that her needs always would be secondary. She'd enjoyed Hamburg, loved the Kempinski, and had fun buying clothes. Her suitcases in the Mercedes' trunk were filled with them.

She knew her faults. She was not domestic. She didn't cook. She wasn't romantic; but he also was no bargain, an often rough and not always considerate lover who demanded obedience.

She owed him a lot and was grateful, but she resented his money and power over her. She felt like a captive bird. Time to leave.

"As much as I love you, I can't continue with you, Kohanie," she said.

The Pole said nothing. He wouldn't look at her. He sat with his hands on the wheel, staring through the windshield, turned the car around and headed back into

Hamburg.

In front of the hotel, he released the trunk. The doorman removed Beata's suitcases. The Pole heard and saw the trunk shut. He drove off, knowing that by the time he returned, Beata would be gone.

Hamburg
July 4, 2010
Hook

Chester was about to go to bed. He and Mary, their son and daughter-in-law had taken the grandkids to July Fourth fireworks in the town park, then the kids and their parents left.

Exhausted, finding it stressful being pleasant for a full day, Chester had just brushed his teeth and put on fresh pajamas. He and his wife had changed the bed and added fresh sheets that morning. She was waiting for him there.

His cell phone rang just as he was coming out of the bathroom. He went back inside the bathroom and shut the door so that his wife would not be disturbed.

He was tempted to let it ring. Early on in their marriage, his wife complained, but they'd been married almost 35 years and she now understood that lonely and often desperate lives in foreign places depended on connecting with her husband and him with them.

Chester immediately recognized the Baron, who didn't bother with small talk.

"The hook is in," he said.

"Good," Chester said. "You have the photographs of his new people?"

"I do, and thanks. One of them was murdered. There are only three left."

"Who was killed?"

"Marek."

"Who did it?"

"Don't have a clue."

"Okay. Be careful. I have two excellent people now in the city. The last one just arrived. Keep your fingers crossed, and keep in touch."

****

"Was it important?" his wife said as he moved next to her beneath the covers.

"Yes, it was," Chester said.

"Are you okay? You look worried."

"I'm okay," he said.

He shut his eyes, trying to envision Hamburg. He'd not been there for three or four years. They'd begun building Hafen City about the time he'd left. He imagined quite a lot had changed.

"Come to bed," his wife said. "I don't like seeing you so tired and worried. Grandchildren and children can be a lot of work. I'm not always comfortable with the way they parent."

Chester slid under the sheets, turned and hugged his wife.

"Something far away is about to happen," he told her, "If it doesn't turn out right, they'll retire me."

"Would that be such a bad thing, Chester?"

He thought about that. "No, I guess not," he said. "Thanks."

"For what?"

"For sticking with me all these years." "You're welcome," she said. "Time to get some sleep."

She pecked him on the cheek, turned and shut her eyes. He did the same.

Hamburg
July 5, 2010
Torture

For the past half hour, Jürgen existed in a state beyond personal humiliation. Chin on his chest, two upper front teeth gone, he'd peed in his pants.

Barely conscious, he sat, gagged, his left arm tied behind a kitchen chair, his ankles and knees also tied, his right arm secured to the chair arm by ties at the elbow and wrist.

His right palm, nailed to the chair's wood armrest, was not bleeding but turning blue.

Kristoff and Lech stood in front of him, Lech holding a pair of giant pliers.

"Your woman killed one of us," he said. "We protect and avenge our own, got that?"

Jürgen showed no reaction.

Lech put his hand under Jürgen's chin, raised it and looked into the terrified man's eyes. "Understand that?"

Jürgen gave no response. Lech took his hand away and Jürgen's chin resumed its previous position.

"Since your girl friend's not around, you're going to pay!"

While Kristoff held Jürgen's upper arm, Lech attached the ends of the pliers firmly on Jürgen's fingernail and yanked.

Because Jürgen bit his fingernails, the pliers didn't have a good enough grip. Lech tried again, nodded to Kristoff, who gripped Jürgen more tightly, and this time had success.

He held up the bloody fingernail and smiled.

"You had enough?" he said.

Jürgen nodded. Blood poured from his finger down the chair and began pooling on the floor. The room smelled of blood, piss and sweat.

Kristoff opened Jürgen's cell phone and scrolled down a list of numbers.

"Which one is hers?" he said. "That one?"

Jürgen nodded.

Kristoff dialed the number. It rang five times but was not picked up, so Kristoff left a message in bad German.

"Wir haben Jürgen," he said. "Kommen-sie jetzt zu seine Platz oder Jürgen ist tod. Sie haben eine Stunde oder Jürgen ist tod." (We have Jürgen. Come to his place or he's dead. You have one hour.)

Kristoff hung up.

"Now we wait," Kristoff said. "Andrzej will cover the back. I'll post myself in an alley down the street."

"You think she'll come?" Lech said.

"Trust me, she'll be here shortly."

"We going to kill her?"

"After we all fuck her, maybe," Lech said. "First, stop Jürgen's bleeding. It's beginning to piss me off!"

"What about the Boss?" Andrzej said.

"What about him?"

"Won't he be upset we took matters into our own hands?"

"Not once we cap the Polish girl," Kristoff said.

"That'll be one less thing to worry about."

"So you think he'll be happy?" Lech said.

"Once he sees what we've done, he'll be glad," Andrzej said.

"What about Jürgen?" Lech said.

"We'll wait until she shows." Kristoff said.

"He can ID us," Lech said.

"I know," Khristoff said. "We'll have to ice him. Andrzej, go on downstairs and cover the back for us, okay?"

"Consider it done," Andrzej said.

Hamburg
July 5, 2010

In Frankfurt, Tama Wu's four remaining detectives provided her with a knife, a Glock, and ammunition.

She told them to leave her and head for downtown Hamburg, and to call if anything important happened.

She explained that their constant presence would only draw attention to her. The detectives nodded and said they'd call her once they arrived in Hamburg.

Tama then accompanied Barry to a gun club, where she practiced firing the Glock.

"It's too heavy for me," she said.

Barry showed her how use both hands, one steadying the arm that held the gun.

After less than an hour, she pleaded fatigue.

"You only need to use the weapon in self defense," he told her. "So don't worry about it being too heavy."

Tama thanked him. He watched as she fired off her final six shots and noticed that four hit the target.

They got take-out salads on cardboard plates from a nearby Turkish hole-in-the-wall restaurant and ate at small tables next to a glass case containing baklava and German pastries.

Then they drove to Hamburg, checking into the Holiday Inn Express, a gray building built of stacked prefab modules resembling a prison, although inside, the hotel's interior appeared contemporary, business utilitarian and adequate.

Tama's small room contained two single beds, not the queen she asked for, but she decided not to complain, a rare concession for her.

Her detectives had given her directions to the Atlantic Kempinski, where the Pole and his girl friend presumably still lived, and to the Pole's Kapinski Associates address in Hafen City.

She left the hotel without telling Barry, who was sleeping.

She spent the afternoon driving around Hamburg, passing the Kempinski Hotel and Kapinski Associates, becoming familiar with which streets were one-way, and following certain roads to see where they went.

While orienting herself, she considered what she'd do next. The Pole's hotel attracted too much lobby and outside traffic, so killing him and getting away without being caught would be difficult.

She could walk right into the Pole's office down by the canals and shoot him. Her altered appearance and the 'surprise element' would facilitate that, unless, of course, others were there and armed.

She returned by car to the canal area, got out and while walking around with the lunch-time crowds, entered the Pole's building and saw the sign on a glass door that announced Kapinski & Associates.

She peered inside but the lights were out and nobody in.

That evening, she walked two minutes to the Reeperbahn, where she ate at cheep meal of Weinerschnitzel and beer, enjoying her solitude and anonymity.

She returned to her hotel around eight p.m. thinking she liked her alternative self better than her traditional business self.

In her present disguise, if she met someone like her business self, what would she think? She'd not like that self, she decided. It was to harsh, judgmental and self-focused.

But as a salary girl I am nothing, she thought. Isn't it better to be somebody than nobody? She left the question unanswered.

She phoned the detectives and checked in with Barry, whom she assumed was spending time with his female companion.

She watched CNN on her room's TV, fell asleep and woke up at 3 a.m., realized the TV was still on, got up, turned it off, peed, washed her hands and returned to bed. She slept well into the morning, forgetting for a few blissful hours that she was about to attempt murder.

Hamburg
July 5, 2010
BuAnia

Ania listened to the second message left on her cell phone. Panicked, she drove by her apartment, saw a man she'd seen before lingering in the shadows, glanced up, and noted the shades drawn over the window where she and Jürgen sat during dinner. She and he never pulled that shade at this time of night.

She ruled out climbing the fire escape. It did not reach the street and could only be activated by someone coming down. Besides, using it would be noisy and she could easily be seen.

She could enter by the back entrance, but it likely was covered by Bernard Mannheim's people, and assuming that she got in the back way, she could climb the stairs to her floor, but then would have to walk down a long corridor and get through the front door.

Then the solution hit her.

At a public phone inside a Turk's small general store, she dialed 911 and reported in a panicked voice that a Mr. Jürgen Hodel was being held captive by at least two men who threatened to kill him if she didn't come.

She gave Jürgen's address. When she sensed the operator was trying to keep her on the line too long, hung up.

She thought about killing the look-out down the block but decided that might distract the police.

Five minutes later, she heard the sirens. When they got close, she left.

Five minutes later, she drove slowly down the

cross street adjacent to her apartment and saw a police car parked there. The lookout was gone.

A half hour later, she parked three blocks from her apartment and warily moved down the street, stopping in a small store to buy a candy bar and a newspaper.

The Turkish storeowner recognized her as a customer. "You just missed some excitement," he said.

"Oh, what happened?" she said.

"They took somebody out of the second-floor apartment down the street. Drove one guy away in an ambulance and another hand-cuffed in a police car. A customer said a third man was shot by police around back."

"Wow!" Ania said. "I've seen the middle-aged man who lives up there. Seemed like a nice guy. Is he okay?"

"Don't think so," the storeowner said, "Maybe it will even make TV tonight on the 11 o'clock news."

"Too late for me," Ania said, pretending indifference. "I'll be asleep by then."

The storeowner laughed. "And me as well," he said.

Upset, Ania left. She'd wait until morning, start calling, and try to find out where Jürgen was.

Lodz, Poland
July 6, 2010
Oh oh

The Pole took the train from Warsaw, got off and walked to a dingy two-room bar two blocks from the Lodz train station, where he met a Slovak arms dealer.

It had been two years since he'd ridden in a Polish train. Nothing seemed changed. Same old cars, same elderly ticket takers, the cars clean and well-maintained but not up to the newer, glitzier standards of French and German trains, with their bars and meal cars.

Going from Warsaw to Lodz was more a long commute than a journey. He enjoyed the trip. It felt good to be back in his native country.

Even Poland's overgrown, weed-filled highway meridians and public spaces, meticulously landscaped and watered in more prosperous northern countries, made him feel at home. He believed such disregard affirmed Poland's renegade mentality.

His meeting didn't go well. The weasel who met him spoke no Polish and bad German and English. Hard to tell what he was peddling. The meeting ended inconclusively, but overall, the trip had been successful.

In Warsaw, he'd made two good contacts, one a Ukrainian who offered newer Russian arms, and a Russian offering the same. Now he needed buyers, which made him think about the Baron again.

The Baron had buyers. He should buy the Baron's list. Then his phone rang.

"It's Kristoff.," the voice said. His voice trembled. The Pole braced for bad news.

"What?"

"We've run into a problem."

"What is it?"

The Pole fought to remain calm. Why was it that when people brought bad news they took so long to deliver it?

"It's Andrzej and Lech," Christoff said.

"Okay, okay. What about them?"

"Andrzej's dead and Lech's in police custody."

"What?"

"We sweated out the Polish girl's boyfriend. We got him to call her. We had the trap set but she didn't show! The cops shot Andrzej on the back stairs. Lech was with the boyfriend. The police broke down the door and took him!"

The Pole said nothing.

"So now two of you are dead and one of you is in police custody."

"Yes, Boss, that's right. What do you want me to do?"

"Find Hugo. Get with him. Stay low. Will Lech sing?"

"Who knows, Boss? They caught him with a guy strapped to a chair and his hand nailed to it. I don't like his chances."

"Maybe you better get the hell out of wherever you're staying," the Pole said.

"Already done, Boss."

"Shit."

"I know. We didn't think the girl would call the cops. We didn't think she'd risk it."

"Go away! You're fucking useless to me by yourself."

"Sorry, Boss."

The Pole angrily shut his phone.

On impulse, before entering the Lodz train station, he called the Baron and told him they had a deal, that he'd pay $1.25 million U.S. for the Baron's business plus office furniture. After a minor hesitation, the Baron agreed.

"Glad you're coming aboard. When do you return?"

the Baron said.

"Tomorrow."

"Good. I'll give you a partial list then and we can discuss the commission job. I've just learned that it'll arrive within the week."

Finally some good news, the Pole thought; but like the Baron, now I, too, lack needed muscle, although the Baron doesn't need to know that.

I might even make the CIA a client. I can work through cut-outs. They don't ever have to know they're dealing with me.

The Pole waited 15 minutes and got back on the Warsaw train, his mind still filled with delusional possibilities, wondering if Beata would be around when he returned.

Hamburg
July 8, 2010
Set-up

In early morning, Ania staked out the Kempinski Atlantic, but the Pole never showed. She spent the rest of the day chatting with doormen from Hamburg's most exclusive hotels, giving them each 50 euros and a phone number to call, then returned to keep watch at the Kempinski.

As dusk fell, she learned why she'd not seen her quarry at the Kempinski.

The Louis C Jacob Hotel doorman phoned. "The man you inquired about, a Mr. Mannheim, big man with beard, gray Mercedes S Class?" he said.

"Yes?"

"He just checked in."

"Thanks. I appreciate your help."

"And I appreciate yours, Fraulein."

She checked her watch, thinking she'd not eaten for nine hours. She found a small restaurant two blocks from the Kempinski, where she had coffee and ate a bratwurst on rye. Tomorrow she'd kill the Pole.

July 10, 2010

Hamburg
9:15 a.m.
Return

Tama Wu's sexual frustration continued. She was beside herself. She'd temporarily alleviated the problem twice that morning and felt the urge again but did not have time.

She'd talked with Barry, who said the Pole had disappeared, and, yes, he, Barry, and his partner would accept her general offer and take care of the Pole for her.

"I'd like to be present when you kill him," Tama said.

Barry told her that might not be possible.

Where had the Pole gone? Tama fretted about that. Then one of her detectives watching for Beata at the Louis C Jakob Hotel phoned to say that Beata and left but the Pole had checked in.

Hamburg
2 p.m.
Double

Barry changed disguises. He added a hump in his upper back, wore a white longhaired wig, and big horn-rimmed glasses with thick lenses. He painted his eyebrows white, and used a lift in his left shoe to help him walk with a convincing limp.

He and Rebecca alternated watching the Pole's office building. This morning it was her turn.

For the first time since that Montevideo night back in November when she believed she'd killed him, she saw him in reconstituted form.

Just as she arrived to begin her shift, he exited his office building. Even with his beard and other work done to change his appearance, she sensed the essence of him in the shape of his upper body and how he carried his head.

She felt an adrenalin rush. She wanted to kill him immediately but caution restrained her.

As the Pole reached the sidewalk, Rebecca saw a young blond woman in tennis shoes come around the building.

The Pole didn't see her in time. Fifteen feet from him, she shot him in the chest.

To Rebecca's amazement, the alarmed but unprepared Pole stopped but did not go down.

The young woman shot him a second time, again in the chest. Rebecca thought she saw the flattened slug bounce off him.

Surprised and clearly frightened, the young girl fled.

The Pole tried to chase her but she was too quick. He removed his revolver from under his left arm, but before he could stop, aim at the girl and pull the trigger, Rebecca squeezed off three bullets from long range, hitting him in rapid succession three times in the back.

Again, he didn't go down.

Realizing that the young girl was now too far away to hit, the Pole wheeled around.

The frantic look on his face would have been comical were the situation not so dangerous.

He raised the pistol and fired. From 50 yards there was little chance he could hit her. To narrow the distance, he charged towards her bobbing and weaving as he fired.

Rebecca responded by quickly squeezing off three more rounds, every one missing.

The Pole got within 20 yards of her. She raised her rifle to shoot him again. He fired before she could squeeze the trigger.

She fell, blood oozing from her stomach.

The Pole reached her, studied her face, seemed puzzled, shot her one more time in the chest, and then, hearing a car approach, ran, disappearing into a labyrinth of side streets.

Tama Wu **had** parked her car a block away. As the Pole disappeared, Tama rushed to Rebecca's side, knelt, called 911, ripped open Rebecca's blouse and stuffed both ends of the expensive silk scarf from around her neck into the bullet holes in Rebecca's chest.

"Help's on the way," Tama Wu whispered. "Hold on."

North Sea
7:15 p.m.
Delivery

Alfredo moved his ship into position past the Netherlands coast and less than 45 minutes by sea from the port of Hamburg.

At seven a.m., he got instructions from his North Korean contact to hold tight, that he'd receive new instructions later that night.

Alfredo alerted the Baron.

At eight p.m., having waited all day bored and nervous, Alfredo heard a speedboat approaching.

Its Pilot provided the proper codes and requested permission to board.

Eight men of assorted sizes and nationalities quickly climbed the rope ladder extended for them and assembled on deck.

"I'm Hans," the oldest said. "We need all your crew on deck, so we can explain what we're about to do."

Alfredo nodded. He sensed a tense wariness in Hans, who spoke English with a Scandinavian accent.

More than 20 minutes passed before all the crew assembled.

"This is all of them?" Hans said.

Alfredo counted. "Yes, nine. We're all here."

Alfredo heard and saw weapons drawn. He watched Hans' men coolly shoot to death his entire crew. Then stood helplessly as Hans shot him.

A nearby 20-foot container was emptied of electronic goods, filled with the bodies of Hans and his crew, sealed, lifted by winch, and dropped into the sea.

Inside the container, Alfredo, still alive, tried to

breathe as his tomb grew cold. He felt movement. Others also were alive! Seconds later, he lost consciousness.

****

Below deck, Hans' men unsealed the uranium cargo and removed the large tarp to reveal a wingless drone aircraft, which they used a winch to move, along with the uranium, up onto the deck.

Next came the drone's wings, which had been packaged together. Each was the length of the fuselage. It took less than 20 minutes to attach both.

Two men poured diesel fuel into drone's tank, enough, to fly the unmanned plane a little more than 300 miles, more than adequate to reach its target.

Six men labored to lift and place the crate containing the uranium inside the drone's belly.

Two technicians examined every inch of the drone for flaws. Several times the moon passed through clouds, turning the night black then light again as the moon re-emerged.

At nine p.m., a technician handed Hans the control panel, which looked much like one used to operate an ordinary TV, but twice as long.

In the less than the two hours it took from boarding to this critical point, no moments had been wasted.

Hans started the drone's engines by remote control. Rotors at the drone's tail slowly began to turn.

A hatch on top of the drone's fuselage automatically slid open. A metal pole rose through the opening. At its top, like unfolding flower pedals, two sets of propellers emerged.

Hans slid a lever on the remote control and these

propellers began rotating faster. Everybody stood back and silently waited.

The drone rose vertically, shakily hovering no more than 50-60 yards above them for almost three minutes as if unable to decide what to do next, while Hans and his men craned their necks to watch.

The drone's rear propellers began to move it almost imperceptibly forward.

The mid-fuselage propeller shaft slowly bent in half backwards, enabling its propellers to provide additional thrust.

The drone seemed to drop a few feet, gather force and then noisily headed under radar toward the German shore.

North Sea
9:10 p.m.
Launch

The newly modified U.S. Trident nuclear submarine tower broke the surface quietly 100 yards from the anchored Handymax.

Two of the sub's missile tubes had been converted to lockout chambers, which now held a team of six Marine Special Forces personnel.

The Trident's hatch opened and four men in wet suits crawled out and stood on to the sub's flat surface, their feet wide apart to keep from falling.

Once oriented, each in turn reached down to take gear handed them through the hatch.

Finally, two of the men climbed down the sub's side, and once in the water inflated a small rubber dingy. Four more men followed, seated themselves and rowed slowly but steadily towards the freighter.

As they pulled along side, they heard what sounded like a winch grinding. It took six tries with a pneumatic rope launcher before the men succeeded in looping a rope around one of two protruding anchors at the freighter's rear.

A Marine quickly scaled this rope, secured it, then tied a second rope to the base of the freighter's rear railing. All six Marines then scaled the side of the ship and gathered silently on its rear deck.

They spread out and approached slowly and carefully, continuing to avoid detection, which was not made easier by the almost full moon, which unpredictably appeared and disappeared behind clouds.

They froze when they heard the unexpected clattering start of airplane propellers and looked up.

Stunned, they watched a white drone with its unmarked white belly and long, pointed wings rise vertically above them.

It seemed to hover magically and then head to the northwest and a likely destination somewhere in northern Germany.

One of the Marines crouched and radioed, "The freighter just launched a drone. It's just left."

He glanced at his watch, which told him the time was precisely 9:20 p.m.

Hamburg
9:22 p.m
Tip-off

The Baron heard a buzz, rushed into his den and picked up his cell phone, which he'd left next to his computer.

The North Korean source, his English terse and anxious, gave the Baron his identifying codes and the Baron responded with his.

"The package will arrive within one hour and 45 minutes, so you don't have much time," he said. "You'll offload the material in a farmer's field five miles out from Pinneberg, approximately 18 miles northwest of Hamburg." He gave the coordinates.

"We'll have two men there to help. From Bredenholtz Road you'll see an old manor house. Don't worry. It and the property will be empty. The delivery will take place in back. We've already deposited half your $1 million broker fee in your account. If something goes wrong, we know where to find you. As for the buyer, the electronic payment will be made by cell phone at time possession is successfully transferred."

The Baron immediately phoned the Pole with the information, then contacted Mahmoud. Less than two hours to go. Should he go to the site and watch?

No, he decided. Mahmound would have people there, to include a scientist to authenticate the shipment. The Pole would supply the muscle. Better he stay home and hope all goes well.

Fifth Corp Headquarters
Heidelberg, Germany
9:24 p.m.
Intercept

The CIA intercept of the Baron's call quickly sparked a series of linked actions.

An Army special forces team of ten heavily armed operatives at Ramstein Airforce Base near Kaiserslautern, Germany, in camouflage and night-vision goggles, scrambled into a four-bladed UH-60L Sikorsky Blackhawk helicopter and headed for the outskirts of Pinneberg.

The German Air Command at Ramstein prepared to scramble fighters to cover the Pinneberg's air space.

In Pullach, a small town outside Munich, officials of Germany's Bundesnachrichtendienst, or Federal Intelligence Service, popularly known as the BND, went on alert, its agents near Hamburg prepared to block all roads leading out of Pinneberg.

The chances of something going wrong, due to possible lack of coordination between German and American groups, became clear soon enough. The unexpected news: A drone, presumably carrying uranium 235 was heading under the radar across the North Sea toward Pinneberg.

Hamburg
9:16 p.m.
Dénouement

The Pole left the Louis C Jacob Hotel alone in his S Class gray Mercedes.

Per an earlier agreement, Mahmoud would pick up Hugo, Kristoff and the authenticator in a rented van.

They'd head to the Pinneberg Railroad Station, where they'd meet on site the Pole and two hired emissaries of the North Koreans, who'd referee the exchange of uranium for Mahmoud's $34 million payment.

The Pole worried about meeting men he did not know and the weapons they likely concealed. Anything, a misinterpreted word, a misunderstanding of payment terms, or a trigger-happy underling could start mayhem.

Once he arrived at the Pinneberg train station, he'd see who showed. The key moment would be when Mahmoud used his cell phone in front of the North Koreans' emissaries to transfer $34 million into the North Korean account.

Then, Mahmoud would have the uranium. But what then?

He'd observe how everything worked, tomorrow pay the Baron $1.25 million U.S. for his customer list and immediately double the number of his potential arms brokering channels.

The Baron would stick around to offer advice for no more than six months, just as was done in the legitimate business world.

At the end of the six months, he'd either kill the Baron or let him retire. He doubted he'd kill him. Time to wean himself from such old thinking.

In the meanwhile, he needed more muscle. Who'd run the brothels? Hugo? No, he wasn't bright enough. Nor was Kristoff. He'd discuss this with René soon.

As he turned a corner on to the highway that hugged Lake Alster's shore, he noticed a white Jetta behind him, but a few moments later he glanced in his rearview mirror and the car was gone. A Jetta was not a fast or agile enough vehicle for tailing an S Class Mercedes. Probably just my overactive imagination, the Pole thought.

He noticed that his gas gauge registered almost empty. He spotted an Esso station underneath the Stellenberg railroad overpass and pulled over.

Checking his watch, he determined that it would take less than 20 minutes to reach Pinneberg. He had time.

He paid for 25 liters inside the station, bought a candy bar and stepped outside, pocketing change before heading to gas up his car.

Again, this time because it was dark and an approaching car's lights temporarily blinded him, he did not see her in time.

She'd learned her lesson. She shot him in the legs, three bullets, one missing, the other two hitting high in his thighs.

He fell, but as he did, he reached out and grabbed her ankle, causing her to lose balance. As she fell backwards, she fired directly into his face. Blood clouded his eyes. He hit the ground, releasing his grip.

In the fog that ensued, he thought how this small young person had ended his life while powerful organizations could not. Was it meaningful that a lone woman killed him and not a man?

Where was Beata? Had she returned to Poland? How long would it take before she found somebody else?

He'd messed up. He was just about to complete his first legitimate business deal. He was easing himself out of a life of violence only to die violently. Ironic.

This thought, experienced as if in a receding in a colorless vacuum, was his last.

****

The gunshots brought a crowd. Two men started to close on Ania, who scrambled to her feet. She pointed the gun and both men, truck drivers by the looks of them. They backed off.

Glancing over her shoulder, she ran as the crowd coalesce around the fallen Pole. Someone used a cell phone, presumably to call 911.

Gun back in her bag, she ducked down an alley, turned the corner, got back into her Jetta and drove in the opposite direction from whence she'd come.

She checked her rear view mirror frequently. No one apparently followed. Did she dare return to her hotel?

She heard police sirens. Two police cars passed her in a hurry.

At her hotel, she packed a suitcase and left. She parked near the Hamburg Rail station in a public garage and took time to wipe down her car to remove fingerprints. She removed the license plates. Several blocks away, she threw them in an almost full dumpster.

The next Warsaw train left Hamburg at 7:06a.m. the next morning, arriving at Warsaw's Central Station at 2:15 p.m.

She checked into the Phoenix City Hotel, not far

from where the Pole's thugs stayed. She dreaded running into any of them, but suspected they'd already moved somewhere else.

She was given a room directly above a Wok Express 24-hour fast food restaurant, the light from its sign shining into her room. She hoped she could sleep. If not, she'd do so tomorrow on the train.

The fare to Warsaw cost 114 Euros. She'd forgotten to take money out.

She'd use an ATM inside the train station that next morning, then do another withdrawal in Warsaw, then rethought this.

Her bank account held almost 8,000 euros. Shouldn't she wait until morning to withdraw the money? No. Too risky. The police would have her identified by then, or would they?

They had no prints. They had the identity of a young blond girl in Levis with her hair pinned behind her head and wearing a red beret.

She'd leave her hair long, get rid of the Levis and the hat. She'd wear sophisticated clothes. She'd go to the bank in the morning and withdraw the money and take a later train.

She remembered Lothar, the cute assistant manager who'd helped her open an account. She'd tell the branch she visited to call Lothar. She'd get her money out and leave on the 12:39 train. It would arrive in Warsaw at 8:15 p.m. Perfect.

But what about Jürgen?

As far as she knew, he remained in the hospital wondering where she was and waiting to hear from her.

She felt awful. He needed and deserved her comfort after all he'd done for her; but not only might the police be looking for her, the Polish gangsters would searching for her as well.

Pinneburg, Germany
10:32 p.m.
Arrival

Mahmoud, Hugo, Kristoff and the authenticator, a small, nervous darkly complected man who so far had spoken not a single word, waited across the street from the train station inside a black Mercedes Sprinter Medium SR diesel panel van, Mahmoud in the driver's seat.

"He's always on time," Hugo said of the Pole. "Maybe we should wait a few more minutes."

Kristoff dialed the Pole's cell phone number and waited. Four rings and the Pole's voice could be heard requesting the caller leave a number and the time he'd called.

"We need to get going," Mahmoud said. "Everyone turn off their cell phones now!"

Everyone did except Hugo. Mahmoud glared at him. "You, too," he said.

The van left the train station and traveled down a deserted dirt road. Behind the manor house, a locked gate blocked them. Mahmoud dialed a number, there was a beep, the fence opened and they drove through.

Behind the ancient, timbered, two-manor house, an empty field stretched a quarter of a mile, edged by mature trees.

Thirty-some yards from the house, two young Asians with dyed blond hair waited. They identified themselves by code as working for the North Koreans.

"They're representatives of the sellers," Mahmoud said loudly enough for the others to hear.

Mahmoud parked his van in the shadows next to the house. He, Hugo, Kristoff, and the authenticator got out of the truck and joined the two blond men.

"What's going on?" Kristoff said.

"For now, nothing," Mahmoud said. "We wait."

"For what?" Hugo said.

"You'll soon see," Mahmoud replied.

"How long must we wait?" Hugo said.

"For as long as it takes," Mahmoud said, as if quieting a small child.

"This better be good," Hugo said.

"It will be," Mahmoud replied, but privately he worried. In his experience, nothing ever went precisely as planned.

Hamburg, Germany
11:30 p.m.
Waiting

Rebecca Forester lay fed by plastic tubes in the Acute Care section on the third floor of the Hamburg University Medical Center, located between Martinistraße and Geschwister-Scholl-Straße.

Four hours earlier, her heart stopped. She'd technically died on the operating table and was brought back to life.

Her fragile existence now depended on oxygen pumped into her mouth through a rubber tube and drugs pumped in to her veins to destroy infection and provide needed nutrients.

Her ankles and wrists had been fastened to the bed frame, its side rails raised to prevent her from falling off.

The wrist restraints kept her from trying to remove the tube from her throat, but for the moment, such restraints weren't necessary. Her were eyes shut. Only a softly beeping monitor suggested that she still had a heart beat.

Surgeons had removed two slugs from her chest, but it had been two hours since Barry and Tama, in a waiting room down the hall heard a progress report. The last one had been guarded at best.

As of eight-thirty p.m., her heartbeat had been stabilized. She'd gained color but not consciousness.

Barry and Tama were told that a few more hours were needed before she could be taken off the ventilator. If and when that happened, they'd be notified and might have a chance to visit briefly with her.

When Rebecca was shot, Tama immediately called 911 and stayed with Rebecca until medical personnel found her, then rode with her bloody body inside the ambulance to the hospital.

During the ride, ambulance personnel told Tama that her quick response had hopefully saved Rebecca's life, that another ten minutes and she'd have bled to death.

Barry, alerted by Rebecca's pressing '9' on her cell phone, had tracked Rebecca's GPS signal to the hospital but not to her.

Hospital personnel had taken Rebecca's clothes and possessions, to include her purse, which contained a loaded Glock pistol and ammunition, car keys, fake identification to include Georgia license, passport, and her cell phone.

After a frantic half hour talking to various hospital administrative personnel, Barry traced the phone to its location in a locked room.

Once he explained that he was Rebecca's husband and had traced her phone, and after several different sets of hospital officials checked his documentation, he was led to the visitors room on his wife's floor and told to wait for more information.

Entering, he discovered Tama Wu calmly reading a European edition of an old *Time Magazine*.

She did not see him enter but sensed him standing over her, looked up from her magazine and grinned.

"Well, Mr. Seymour, I presume," she said. "You now look like an old man, but I recognize the 'you' inside."

Barry nodded.

"She's your partner?" Tama said.

"Yes," Barry said.

"She'll make it, I really think that," Tama said not all that convincingly. "I was there when she got shot."

Barry sat in the vacant chair next to her and listened to her story. At its conclusion he patted her hand. "Thank you for all of that," he said.

Seldom the recipient of anyone's sincere gratitude, Tama Wu blushed.

The North Sea
11:30 p.m.
Capture

The drone long gone, the men who'd assembled and released it surrendered immediately, realizing that they had no chance to escape, throwing their weapons in a pile and anticipating their immediate execution, which did not come.

One by one, each was searched, disarmed, marched to an open area, handcuffed, manacled to the next man and left chained to the freighter's cold, wet and slippery steel floor.

"We're taking you to Hamburg," the American leading the mission said. "Then to our facilities in Frankfurt. A lot of people are anxious to talk with you."

A second commando radioed their location and asked for permission to approach the harbor.

The okay was granted, the freighter's engines started up, and the ship began to move.

Penneberg, Germany
11:30 p.m.
Delivery

Kristoff heard a soft beeping sound and tugged Mahmoud's sleeve to alert him.

Also hearing the beeping, the two blond-haired Asians separated themselves from Mahmoud, Hugo, Kristoff, and the authenticator, who still had yet to utter a word.

One of the blond Asians took out a small device

the size of a TV channel changer, and pressed a button. The device emitted a blast of light.

Several minutes later, the group gasped. A dark silhouette resembling a prehistoric flying monster emerged with a whirring and clacking over the tops of trees, hovered and seemed to take forever before finally settling gently to earth.

"Jesus Christ!" Hugo said.

Mahmoud smiled. "Great!" he said. He sounded both satisfied and relived.

The two blond Asians pointed the TV-controller device at the drone's belly and a hatch opened.

One of the Asians motioned to Mahmoud's group for help. Hugo, Kristoff and the authenticator responded.

They worked to free the boxed uranium while Mahmoud got the van and drove it to within 15 feet of the drone.

The authenticator, who until now had appeared bored, suddenly became animated. With deliberate care, he removed a six-inch-by-three-inch black plastic device from his shirt pocket and pressed a button to activate it.

The device began beeping. A small display screen at its top lit up. The authenticator bent over, held the device next to the boxed uranium, and waited.

The beeping intensified. He spoke for the first time, his voice clipped and almost a falsetto.

"A minute will be enough to get a read," he said. "This thing measures alpha, beta, gamma and x-ray...."

He stopped, glanced twice at the reading on the display screen, stood and turned it off.

"It's 235," he said. "We're good to go."

Silence. A dangerous moment. Mahmoud thought. Everyone glanced nervously at each other. Anxious minutes passed.

Mahmoud took out his cell phone and dialed a number. As if on cue, one of the two blond Asians did the same, then everyone waited.

A bong sounded on the Asian's phone. He smiled, shut his phone, shook hands with Mahmoud and said in German, "The money went through. The package is yours."

Double-checking, Mahmood took the same phone, dialed the same number and waited for the same confirmation, which came immediately. He breathed deeply and smiled broadly.

"Thanks everyone for a job well done," he said.

Wasting no time, he helped Hugo, Kristoff and the authenticator struggle to load the uranium into the van, waited for them to climb in back, and drove off.

The two blond Asians did not bother to watch them leave. One shut the drone's hatch, stepped away, pressed a series of buttons, the drone's propeller shaft re-emerged, the propellers began to turn and slowly, once again, the drone lifted straight up.

The drone rose almost straight up. He pressed a lever that would start it moving back towards the North Sea, there was a flash of light and the drone exploded in mid air.

"What the fuck?!" he said.

A loud speaker blared in German from an approaching helicopter heard not yet seen. It repeated the message in English.

"Do not move. You are surrounded and under arrest!"

Hamburg
11:30 p.m.
Visitation

The young intern entered the visitors' room and walked over to Barry and Tama.

"She's out of her coma," he said, "And the breathing tube has been removed. You can see her briefly now if you wish."

"You go alone," Tama said. "I'll wait here."

Fearful of what he'd find, and how he'd react, Barry followed the doctor through the open door and down a long corridor to a double door marked 'Intensivbehandlung.'

Through the door he could see beds, almost all occupied, divided by mobile screens. Nurses and technical personnel busied themselves. He heard the insistent beep-beeping of machines but no human sounds.

Rebecca lay in the third bed on the left at the end, her complexion pale, blue eyes blank, lips parched. She stared upwards and did not seem to recognize him.

Barry leaned awkwardly over her bed's side rails, still raised to prevent her from rolling off. She smelled of medicines and cleaning fluids. Tubes protruded from her stomach, chest and above both wrists.

"You can only stay a few moments," the doctor said softly. "We've just given her morphine so she can sleep."

"Is she going to be all right?"

"We're hopeful," the doctor said. He did not look optimistic. He lowered the railing in front of Barry, and tactfully stepped away.

Barry bent over and kissed Rebecca softly on her cheek, which felt dry and unnatural.

"Barry? She said weakly. She smiled wanly.

"Hi, Becs, it's me. How are you feeling?"

"I'm thirsty."

"Okay. Just a moment." He asked the doctor if she could have water and the doctor shook his head.

"She's been shot in the stomach. You can moisten a Kleenex and clean her lips," the doctor said.

"Just a sec, Becs," Barry said.

He walked to the front of the room, into the bathroom and returned with wet Kleenex and moistened his wife's lips.

"Better?"

"Better, Bear, Thanks."

Her voice, soft and dreamy, was difficult to hear.

"How long 'til I'm out of here?" she said. "I hate hospitals."

"A few days more," he said, not knowing, but wanting to give her hope.

If she caught his worried look she didn't register it. He held her hand, its warmth making him feel better about her chances. He watched as she shut her eyes.

"Thanks for coming, Bear," she said, the morphine drip slowly having its effect.

He released her hand and backed away.

Outside her partition, he leaned against the wall and sobbed. A young Indian female doctor tried to comfort him.

He stopped crying and looked up. Tama Wu stood next to him, staring up into his face.

"Come. Let's get a cup of coffee," she said.

"You don't have to stay with me," Barry said. Part

of him wanted to be alone, but another part appreciated and sought her attentiveness.

"I know I don't," Tama said. "But I have no children, no family. I feel connected to you and to her, and I want to help. I'm sorry for coming on to you earlier. I do a lot of stupid things. That was one of them."

"It's okay," Barry said. "Let's get a cup of coffee. Then I'll drop you off at your hotel and...."

He stopped because his cell phone rang.

"Just a moment. I need to take this," he said.

"It's early morning here," Chester' said, "and I know it's late there, but there's something you should know."

"I'm just leaving the hospital with Tama now, Chester. The Pole shot Rebecca. I've just visited her. She's under heavy sedation."

There was a pause, and then Chester said, "Oh, my, I didn't know." His voice insinuated that Barry should have told him.

"What is it you need to tell me, Chester?"

"The Pole's dead, Barry. Witnesses confirm that a young blond girl shot him early this evening outside a gas station. He's definitely dead. I've seen photographs. He was wearing some sort of armor on his chest and back, but she apparently knew this because she first shot him in the legs and then fatally in the face. Also, we got the uranium. I'll tell you more later. Call me when you feel up to it. I'm sorry about Rebecca. We'll be pulling for her here."

"Thanks, Chester."

Barry put his phone in his pocket and turned to Tama Wu.

"The Pole...some young girl killed him. That's all I know."

"He's definitely dead?" Tama looked shocked.

"Confirmed."

He watched Tama Wu's face. She seemed devastated.

"I wanted to do that myself," she said.

"Well, maybe it's best. Now we can go on with our lives," Barry said, hating his need to rely on a cliché.

"You can go back to your life with your wife," Tama said. "Me, it's not so simple."

Barry looked at her, waiting for more information that didn't come. Together they walked out of the hospital and into the moonlit Hamburg night.

July 11, 2010

Warsaw, Poland
2:45 p.m.
Rebirth

Crossing into Poland, Ania expected a surge of emotion that hadn't come. She remained wary, afraid she could be tapped on the shoulder at any moment and told, 'You're coming with us.'

Several men flirted with her during the eight-hour journey. She found it difficult to sit still, even though she'd brought German magazines to read.

Her scariest moment came a half hour before leaving Hamburg when she asked to withdraw her savings.

The process took an agonizing 20 minutes, and included calls between branches. She'd been prepared to flee at any moment, but the bank manager finally returned with her money, all in cash, as she'd requested.

He even asked her to dinner. She smiled coquettishly, for she found him attractive, but declined.

Carrying so much loose money could cause problems, so she'd asked for 100 euros in small bills and change. That way, she wouldn't have to keep taking out a large wad of money to pay for tickets, meals and whims.

The gun still in her purse, she remained alert during her long walk to the train station.

She toted a single piece of luggage, hating to leave behind much that she cherished, but she needed to feel mobile and free. Clothes and other material goods would slow and weigh on her.

She experienced another nervous moment paying cash for her ticket, still expecting to be picked up at any instant either by the Pole's goons or German police.

Once the train moved, she felt slightly more relaxed, but every stranger crossing her path set off private alarms.

Rather than stay cooped in her first class compartment with three German businessmen with bad haircuts wearing cheap suits and scuffed shoes, she spent much time in the corridors staring into space, watching fields and cities slide silently by.

She lingered in the dining car as well. She soaked up lonely passing hours drinking Pepsis and eating candy bars and bananas.

Once her train reached Poland, she relaxed again but only temporarily. Night had fallen.

She left the Warsaw railroad station pulling her wheeled suitcase, checking behind her, crossed the street, saw the lit top of a Marriott Hotel in the distance, decided to stay there, took a room on a high floor and slept.

****

In the 18 years she'd lived in Poland, she'd never visited Warsaw. So, at ten a.m. the next morning, she decided to remedy that, walking to Old Town.

Along the way, she recognized many landmarks,

to include the huge, sprawling, 43-story Palace of Culture and Science, a 30's-modernist architectural monstrosity gifted the Poles by Stalin.

Further along, she recognized and passed the Presidential Palace and inside Old town's ancient walls saw the Royal Castle.

Old Town teemed with tourists, the majority Poles from elsewhere. She loved hearing her native language and enjoyed the ancient architecture and open, adventurous, upbeat feel of the city.

For almost an hour, she stood on an old stone battlement high above the Vistula River, Old Town behind her, and watched boat traffic, filled with the joy of being home.

On her way back to the hotel, she passed several Warsaw University buildings and saw students her age lounging on the steps.

How little most of them knew of the world, she thought, and how relatively undamaged they seemed.

She thought of her parents in northeastern Poland. Should she visit them again? She'd decide later.

Back at the Marriott, she ordered a latte and took it to her room, where she sat for an hour sipping it and staring out at afternoon Warsaw.

Should she call Jürgen? Was he okay? No, she didn't dare call him. 'They' would use him to find her.

Was she, despite everything that had happened to her and everything she did, still a good person? Was she even sane?

That night, sleep came slowly. She got up once to pee and checked the bedside clock. Three a.m.

She lay across the covers, stared at the ceiling and eventually slept, wondering what she'd do tomorrow.

She still had her youth, although she'd become cynical and distrusting. She had her brains. She'd use them to make something of herself. Her parents had thrown her away. Other adults also had abused her.

To hell with them. She'd won her freedom, had money in the bank, no obligations and could become anything she wished. What would that be?

Hamburg, Germany
2:45 p.m.

Barry entered the hospital room. Rebecca was sitting up part way watching CNN. She still had tubes in her.

She turned her head and smiled. "Hi, Bear," she said.

She acted as if all was back to normal, but the covers concealed only her legs. He could see heavy bandages around her stomach and chest. Someone had combed her hair, but she wore no lipstick or other make-up.

He thought her color looked better not yet normal. He kissed her on the lips. They'd lost their parchment taste and feel.

"Whew!" he said. "I was afraid you weren't going to make it."

"So was I," she said. "Sorry I screwed up."

"You didn't. How could you have known he was wearing armor?"

"I should have figured that out when I saw the young girl shoot him in the chest and nothing happened. I should have aimed for his head

"There's something else," Barry said.

"What?"

"The Pole's dead," Barry said.

"Who's dead?"

"The Pole."

"Did Tama get him?"

"No. It was the small blond girl."

"Probably the one I saw."

"Can't be that many small blond girls trying to kill the Pole."

"True."

"So how're you feeling?"

"Okay, as long as they keep the morphine dripping. That's great stuff."

"So I've heard."

"The doctors say I'll be here another three or four days, then I'll need help for another two weeks before we can head home."

"I'll take care of you, and if you agree, I'll hire somebody to help," Barry said.

That made her smile. "As long as it's not Nurse Ratched," she said. Barry laughed.

"Chester sends his best. His people stopped the uranium from going anywhere."

"Good. What about the kids?"

"I talked with Beth last night. She doesn't like the French family she's with but does like their teenage girl, and there's some French boy she's met." Rebecca smiled.

"What about Jason?"

"He's fine. Didn't get much out of him. Kind of pissed me off." Rebecca smiled again. "At that age, they always think you're trying to run their lives."

"The timing of all this is good," Barry said. "I told

them we wouldn't be home for another two weeks. Should work out just as they're finished with their summer stuff."

"You didn't say anything about my condition?"

"Just that you sent them your love. When I called I didn't know if you were going to make it, although I suspected you would. Your color looked good and you've always been a fighter."

Rebecca smiled." Despite the corniness of that line, it makes me happy, Bear. Compliments are always nice. This whole thing was kind of a mess, wasn't it?"

"Yes, and No. We were hired to get Tama into the country without anybody knowing and protect her while she was here. We did that."

"But we didn't get our million dollars for killing the Pole."

"Maybe we'll make it up with other assignments."

"I don't think I want more assignments, Bear. I think it's time to retire. We have enough money."

"We can talk about it once you're recovered, okay?"

"Okay."

"Anything I can get you?"

"No, for now you're all I need," she said.

November 10, 2011

Savannah, Georgia
Reflections

Barry and Rebecca sat in the cozy living room of their dark red brick ranch with white wood trim. It sat on an unprepossessing lot on their less than impressive urban Savannah street.

Almost all the neighborhood houses, built in the 1950's and 60's, had been redone with original floors sanded and polished, stainless steel appliances and double-pane windows. Some had dormers added.   Even in early evening, houses around them had turned on their lights. Barry and Rebecca sat on their comfortable old sofa looking out the large living room window, drinking steaming hot cocoa, which Rebecca had just made.

The only family touches were photographs of Beth and Jason, a handsome old grandfather clock that once belonged to Rebecca's parents, and an Andy Warhol original oil of Marilyn Monroe given Barry by his mother before her death.

Their furniture, chosen by mutual agreement, had

a squared Bauhaus look, to include the couch on which they sat. Their wall art bought during trips abroad, reflected contemporary tastes as well.

They'd bought wool rugs at Ikea. These tended toward modern swirls and primary colors that got mixed with Persian carpets purchased during an assignment in Istanbul.

Already, Savannah was getting cool at night. They'd just turned on the furnace for the first time and its basement rumble could be heard.

"All that money Tama spent to find the Pole and some amateur gets the satisfaction of killing him," Rebecca said.

"Chester's people believed an escaped sex worker at one of the Pole's brothels was killing up the chain of command. That's their latest theory."

"You believe that story?"

"I have no opinion."

"Whoever she is, she's uncommonly good."

"She kind of reminds me of us."

"How?"

"She kills for morally-based reasons and never leaves a trace."

"That's interesting. You're right."

"Maybe we should try and find her."

"You think so?"

"Might be fun."

"What do we do if we do find her?"

"Nothing. We don't even have to let her know we're on to her."

Rebecca smiled. "That appeals to me. Got any leads?"

"Chester says she's Polish, and exceptionally

bright. Her boyfriend Jürgen said she was sold into sex slavery by her parents, and she was to enter a Polish university in the Fall."

"Okay."

"You think she'd return to Poland?"

"She sure as hell wouldn't stay in Germany."

"Do we know her exact age?"

"No."

"Her birthplace?"

"No."

"Her family name?"

"No."

"So where do we start?"

"With a hunch," Barry said. "Maybe Chester can help."

"No. We've told him we've retired. He'll just try to get us working again."

"I'm going to call him anyway. If my hunch is wrong, we've wasted a couple of weeks in Poland."

"It must be getting cold there now."

"Probably." He looked at Rebecca, smiled and she smiled back.

"Okay. You're on," she said.

Location(s) unknown
Mystery

When **Mahmoud, Kristoff, Hugo and the authenticator** left the farmer's field with the uranium, they were easily tracked to a deserted private airfield ten miles west of Penneberg.

As their van left the road and entered the private

airfield, the tracking satellite detected a small plane sitting on a nearby runway, its pilot either in the plane or close by.

Notified of this, the CIA team tracking the truck headed immediately for the airfield, reaching it no more than a minute before Mahmoud's van.

Two agents grabbed a portable rocket launcher from the rear of their panel truck, loaded and fired it just as the van approached.

The plane exploded, the noise deafening, parts flying in the air.

Shots struck the van from multiple directions, flattening its tires. Its engine seized and quit. Mahmoud and the others gave up without a shot.

A year later, despite multiple inquires from relatives, the whereabouts of Hugo, Kristoff, Mahmoud and the authenticator remain unknown. They were assumed to be in custody somewhere within Europe's vast system of secret prisons. Or, they could be dead.

CIA agents took custody of the uranium. Its whereabouts also remains unknown.

Shanghai, China
Despair

Tama Wu resumed her workaholic days, rising at six a.m., arriving at her offices on Pudong's outskirts by seven a.m.

She used an hour of alone time each morning to process and prioritize emails, check appointments, and isolate critical problems, then launched her official workday with meetings.

Typically, she did not arrive home at either of her houses before eight p.m.

In Germany, she'd become detached from her normal life and enjoyed being in disguise.

No one indulged her. People treated her nicely for the most part but without fear or concern for themselves. She'd forgotten how pleasant such anonymity could be.

In Shanghai, she felt isolated and feared, concluding that much of this was her fault. She had no friends in the city or anywhere in China. It had been a long time since anyone tried to get close.

She had one assistant, Zhi Gai, who made an attempt. She knew he was attracted to her. She was attracted to him as well. He was tall, beautifully educated, well spoken and young like herself.

So how had she responded? She made sexually servicing her part of his job.

She'd stand with her back to him, hands against the wall. He'd lift up her skirt, penetrate her, work her with focused intensity, ejaculate, and leave.

In the two years he worked for her, they'd never kissed. She'd treated him like a dispensable sexual slave.

Remembering mortified her. Now, like a teenager with a crush, she hesitated calling him, but finally did.

He was not home. She left a message for him to call, making an effort to sound warm, sympathetic and approachable. He didn't call back.

A week later, she drove by his townhouse in the French Concession only to learn that he'd sold the place.

An aide found his new apartment a block from his old house. She rang the doorbell and a tall, attractive young woman answered.

"Yes?" she said.

"Is Zhi Gai in?" Tama asked. "I used to be his boss and I'd like to talk with him."

The woman continued to block the entrance. She studied Tama, her expensive clothes, bag, make-up and general demeanor and concluded this was indeed the woman Zhi had called 'the dragon lady.'

"I'm not sure he wants to talk with you," she said, "But just a moment."

The woman left Tama standing on the stoop. Minutes later, Zhi Gai appeared.

He was as she remembered, the same tall, handsome man only no longer obsequious.

"Yes," he said.

"Can you step outside," Tama said.

"Sure," he said and did.

"I came to apologize to you for the way I treated you," she said. "I made a terrible mistake with you. We could have been friends, and if you'd like to try that, I hope you'll give me a call."

She looked up at him hopefully and handed him a personal card with her city address and private phone number.

Zhi Gai pretended to study the card and put it in his pocket. "I'm really surprised you stopped by," he said, then paused as if to more carefully choose his words. "But after all that happened between us, a friendship just isn't possible."

"Is it my money?"

"Yes, that's part of it," Zhi said. "I'm grateful you stopped by. You even look different."

"I do?" Tama said. She actually felt herself blush.

"Yes, you seem more approachable now. I think that's good. I sense humanity in you now."

"You do?"

Zhi Gai said nothing. He glanced uncomfortably inside the house. "I've got to go. That's Mary Chou. We're going to be married."

"Oh," Tama Wu said. She didn't offer congratulations, stepped back, held out her hand and Zhi Gai gently shook it.

"Sorry to bother you. I'm on my way," she said, gesturing to the limousine waiting for her down the street.

Just before getting into the limousine, she glanced back. Zhi Gai was watching her.

She waved, he waved back, walked back inside his apartment, and shut the door.

Hamburg, Germany
Recovery

Jürgen Hodel's sadness consumed him. His fingernail had grown back. The broken bones in his face mended and a plastic surgeon said he'd never done better work, that Jürgen looked as good as new.

There was truth in this. Unless you looked closely, Jurgen didn't look much different than before Lech and Andrzej worked on him.

The German state paid for the extensive surgery and ancillary expenses. His sympathetic employer continued his pay for the three weeks he took off work to recover and did not charge him vacation time.

After hours, he was able to resume teaching

German at the Lutheran church and had enough students for two classes he now taught at seven and nine p.m. four nights a week.

He'd even had time to get damage to his apartment fixed, much of this paid by his landlord, who had insurance.

So bones and flesh had healed. His heart was another matter.

He'd heard nothing from Ania for over three months. Was she still alive?

Her clothes remained in the closet. He often slept with them in his bed. Almost daily, he'd go through photos of her stored on his I-phone.

If she were still alive, where would she go?

He thought of traveling to Poland to look for her but could not remember the name of the village where her parents lived. Besides, he doubted she'd go there.

Travel agency employees where she'd worked said they'd not seen or heard from her, that their boss had been about to fire her because of all the time she kept taking off.

Friends advised Jürgen to see a shrink. They said he seemed obsessed with Ania to the point he could talk of nothing else.

He took their advice, but after two sessions stopped. Examining what held him together threatened to tear him apart. He felt he could not risk more introspection.

Then he received a letter from Ania postmarked Warsaw, Poland.

Dearest Jürgen, How sorry I am that it's been so long since I've contacted you. You saved my life not that long ago, gave me your love and a place to live, and I feel so inadequate because I could never equal those gifts and others you so generously gave. I've started a new life under a new identity. I do not know if this will stop people who want to do me harm from searching for me.

All I can do is hope. I've had much bad done to me, and I've done much bad in return, none of which I ever confided in you. That was to protect you. If there's a god in Heaven, you'll find the wonderful woman you deserve, as you're a good and kind man. I love and will honor your memory always.

Please forgive me,

Ania

Two friends convinced the landlord to let them enter Jürgen's apartment.

Ania's letter sat the kitchen table where Jürgen and she often ate dinner. He lay on the linoleum floor next to the table. He'd shot himself through the roof of his mouth with a revolver he'd found hidden in Ania's clothes.

Ania's weapon rested next to him, two bullets still in the chamber. He left no suicide note.

Hamburg, Germany
Revival

René Oppenheim sat in a booth staring out at the harbor, casually watching a tri-mast schooner moored there. Across from him **the Baron** studied the menu.

Around them, a prosperous group of diners, mostly male ate, drank and talked loudly as Germans in public often did.

"The Vlet's always been one of my favorite restaurants," the Baron said. "I love the brick walls and all the dark wood on the floors." He gestured at his surroundings with obvious approval.

René smiled and motioned for the waiter, who came quickly. "Have you decided?" the waiter said.

"I have," the Baron said. "A glass of the Cötes du Rhöne red, and the venison."

"Do you want a salad?" René said.

"I'll pass," the Baron said.

René ordered a glass of grappa and turned to the Baron. "What the hell is Kopfsalat in Bamberger Hörnchen ,Püree in Kartoffelravioli, bunte Bete, Salzgurkenstippe?" he asked.

The Baron laughed. "German words tend to get ungainly, and to compound matters, the menus in this particular restaurant are always fanciful, but what I suspect that means is that you'll get a lettuce salad with beets, some sort of potato ravioli, and salted sliced cucumber strips,"

"Is it enough for a meal?"

"For 23 euros it better be," the Baron said.

"Yes," the waiter said, "and the salad comes with complimentary fresh warm bread."

"At that price, it should," the Baron said.

"Okay, I'll take it," René said.

René's food came quickly and five minutes later the Baron's arrived and they ate. Neither said much for the first few minutes.

The events of the past few months, in particular the death of Lash and the Pole, then the uranium trade failure, and Mahmoud's disappearance, had left the Baron demoralized.

Why hadn't the police picked him up for questioning? Was he really that lucky? He waited for the proverbial shoe to drop but it hadn't, not yet.

In the past month, his business had vanished and he'd made almost no effort to revive it. His bank account was reaching zero. He was heavily property leveraged, and his expenses needed drastic pruning.

He still desired attractive female company, not so much for sex, but for the favorable attention it brought from other men, but at his age, attracting younger, beautiful females required lots of money.

"We have a business opportunity you might be interested in," René said over coffee after the meal. "I represent an international bank. We were helping Bernard Mannheim until his untimely death. We need a replacement and wonder if you might be interested."

The Baron's immediate impulse was to say No. He had no muscle to protect him and lacked the fraternal underworld sources to attain it.

"I'm willing to listen," the Baron said with feigned lack of enthusiasm.

"For the past few years, we've helped certain people finance a business you're already in," René said. "Some of Mr. Mannheim's sources were proprietary to him. Others were not. We could provide the others to you. That would add considerably to the business you have."

"Why me?"

"Because you're already on the ground, others

speak of your integrity, and you appear to have immunity,"

"I don't understand."

"I think you do."

"I don't."

"You managed to be involved but yet not involved in the recent transaction with a certain middle eastern restaurateur. That suggests protection of some kind, and good survival skills. My bank can provide you capital and other financial help. You're too dependent on the CIA."

The Baron did not protest.

"We're offering you a second and more generous well to draw from. You can keep right on dealing with the CIA. We don't care."

"There's a problem of muscle..."

"Yes, of course. That's always a problem, one that Mr. Mannheim thought he'd solved. We can provide you with professionals. You can interview them, try them out. Everything is negotiable."

René smiled. "Think it over. You can let me know in a few days."

The Baron said he would. He pretended to reach for the check but ultimately let René pay.

Arlington, Virginia
The end?

Chester and his wife were in their den watching the movie Gladiator, which they'd purchased from Netflicks. The telephone rang.

Chester's wife, Mary, a plump little woman with

blond hair and a permanently amused look, as a courtesy, immediately stopped the movie as Chester got up, took his cell phone out of his pocket and walked into the kitchen, where he could talk without disturbing her.

"What is it?" he said gruffly.

"It's me," Rebecca said. "Got a moment?"

"No. Mary and I are watching a movie."

"Then I'll be quick," Rebecca said. "Can you send Barry and me everything you have on that small blond Polish girl?"

"You mean the one that offed the Pole?"

"Is there another blond Polish girl we should know about?"

"No, not off the top of my head."

"Can you release the file?"

"She's not being sought by anybody. She did the world a favor."

"Good. Can you send us the file?"

"I can put something together."

"Good."

"Can I ask why?"

"Sure."

Pause.

"Why do you want such a file?"

"Because we're curious."

"Okay. Have you given any more thought to taking another assignment?"

"We have. The answer is still No. We're retired."

"If you find the Polish girl, you might let me know. She's a natural. She could make a lot of money working for me and for the agency. I'd pay you a finder's fee."

"Not interested, Chester. Get back to your movie. But before you go, how long before you can get the file to us?"

"A couple of days and no more."

"Thanks. Ta ta."

"Ta ta to you, too, Rebecca. Give Barry my best."

"I will, Chester. It's been great working with you."

"And great working with you," Chester said.

He snapped his cell phone shut. Everything has to come to an end, he thought. They were a magnificent couple and the best undercover operatives he'd ever handled.

Unlike most contract operatives, they were quitting at the right time. Nobody, except for Tama Wu, knew their true identities or where they lived.

Barry had screwed up in Montevideo and Rebecca in Hamburg. They were getting old. They should retire.

Both had lost their edge and gotten careless. They'd been lucky and must know it.

Would they stay retired? Most people who stopped clandestine work 'cold turkey' quickly got bored. Would Barry and Rebecca be an exception?

He bet he'd be hearing from them again before another year passed.

His wife looked up and restarted the movie as he returned.

"Anything important?" she said. She was used to vague responses and understood his need for secrecy, but quietly she resented his hiding so much from her.

"No, Sweets," he said. "Just old workmates touching base one last time."

"Meaning you said final Goodbyes?"

"Maybe," Chester said.

Mary nodded, no longer interested.

Tykocin, Poland
Remembrance

Ania took a weekend train from Krakow to Warsaw, then another to Olsztyn in the northeast, where she rented a car and drove even further east to Tykocin.

A week after arriving in Poland, she'd called the Jagiellonian University registrar, explaining that she'd had a severe illness, was bed-ridden, and her parents, both illiterate, had not known how to contact the university. This lie was accepted without further questions. She was invited to enroll for the fall semester.

Jagiellonian was eager to have her. Promising scholars from impoverished cities such as Tykocin were rare and prized.

Ania moved immediately from the Warsaw Marriott to Krakow, where her ability to speak German got her a job in a restaurant on Krakow's main square.

Even with tips, she made barely enough to survive. Most of her fellow waiters and waitresses still lived with parents; but to her advantage, she still had 6,000 euros saved and lived frugally.

She rented a room in an old woman's apartment down the hill from Wawel Castle, where most of Poland's ancient kings lay buried. Her landlord was friendly, not intrusive and often would invite her for afternoon tea.

Once her studies began, she juggled her waitress job around classes.

She'd concentrated on Art History with minors in English and German literature.

She made friends easily, but in general found even the nicest girls off-putting. Most came from middle- and higher income homes with working parents.

She'd learned to dress well in Hamburg, was pretty and carried herself with confidence. The richer girls assumed she was one of them and sought her out but quickly backed away.

Something about her scared them off. Her male classmates hit on her often. She turned them down.

She thought about sex constantly and missed intimacy, but told herself she'd wait until she was finished with her education, established in a career and felt free from being hunted. Then she'd allow herself to become intimate again. That was her plan.

She found nerdier, more intellectual girls fit her better, so she favored them.

To avoid attracting attention, she did not join any clubs or protest movements.

She remembered each man she'd killed. Where had she gotten the courage, hate and cunning to commit such anti-social acts?

She'd sent Jürgen a letter and afterward often felt the urge to phone him, but still feared others might be searching for her through him.

Ironically, she now lived undercover as her actual self. Every morning, she walked up ancient cobble-stoned, narrow streets and through Krakow's giant square to classes, alert and ready to flee. She hated feeling hunted but knew that in seconds she could be ripped from her life. It had already happened.

****

As she approached Tykocin's outskirts, she saw white storks perched on chimneys. They made her smile. They'd been one of her happier memories.

She spotted the Narew River to her right and remembered on a dare plunging in its cold waters with all her clothes on when she was ten.

She passed a 15th-century castle renovated when she was in her early to middle teens.

Nearing the town's small central square , she saw signs pointing to the Jewish cemetery and the town's surviving synagogue, suggesting the only visitors to this forlorn place were Jews visiting their ancestors' homes.

She drove through town, wondering if she'd see anyone she knew, and whether she'd make contact if she did.

Leaving the small city center, she headed down a rutted dirt road toward her parents' house.

She saw it, slowed and stopped the car to study it and the land around it.

She'd only been gone a year, yet the farm seemed smaller and run down, the barn closer to the house than she remembered.

She looked to see if she could spot either of her parents but did not.

She noted a new tractor sitting in the front yard. Had her abductors in some way helped her parents pay for that?

She drove slowly by, craning her neck to see if she could see anybody moving inside. Nothing stirred.

Up the road and out of sight, she turned her car around and feeling empty and sad drove back by her parents' house, through the town and on to the highway that would return to her Olsztyn, where she'd catch a train back to Krakow.

May 26, 2011

Hamburg, Germany
Updates

René and Caesar Enterprises negotiated with a Turkish syndicate to buy the brothels, which for almost six months had no oversight.

In the intervening months, girls left and managers absconded with the weekly proceeds. The police got called frequently by angry patrons, and back rents had failed to be paid.

The ending price, $250,000, irritated René, but he took it. The sale went through in December.

In March, a fire in one of the brothels destroyed it. Later, René learned that two Turkish syndicates were having a 'disagreement.'

The torching of the brothel was but one in a series of transgressions ending with building landlords kicking the Turks out, which brought further retaliation from one of the Turkish syndicates, and finally police intervention.

Dozens of Turks were deported or jailed. In the process, accusations of police kick-backs started an investigation by civil authorities, making René grateful he and his bank had uncoupled themselves in time.

****

Hugo, Mahmoud and Kristoff, after months of interrogation and torture in a Serbian prison, were quietly released. They never knew who'd held them. Had it been the CIA, or German Intelligence?

Over time, they were convinced to tell what they knew, the information disappearing into databanks somewhere for reference when needed.

One of the interrogators let slip to Hugo that the authenticator had a heart attack and died. "Nervous bugger," he said. "Found him dead in his cell. Nothing we did." He looked as if he wanted Hugo to believe this. Hugo pretended he did.

Kristoff returned to Warsaw and reconnected with a syndicate operating out of Lodz. He didn't stay free long. Picked up after a drycleaner burglary, he was sentenced to five years in prison, where he remains.

Hugo returned to find his old job at the brothels taken by a Turk. He got work in a car wash to tide him over until he found something better. As of this moment, he had not.

Mahmoud thought he got lucky. Nervously, he returned to Hamburg to run his restaurant, which had been managed by his wife and son during his absence.

His wife and son, thinking he was dead, were overjoyed by his return. A local community newspaper wanted to do an article on him, but worried about his future, he mixed that.

For several months he seldom left the back of his restaurant, did not schmooze with customers or give lavish gifts to local charities. The less others knew about where he'd been the more secure he felt.

He told Iranian contacts that he was damaged goods, that he could no longer help them. They accepted this with less than good grace, but said they understood. News of his capture and release circulated. No one came to him with smuggling requests. They assumed that whoever took him had drained him dry of information, some of which could potentially damage them. Clearly, he'd been released because he was no longer considered of value.

In late August, he was driving his car under the speed limit when he lost control, wandered out of his lane and was struck by a Volvo diesel truck. He and his car ended up in Lake Alster, the car totaled and he dead.

A routine police investigation found that his car's brakes and steering had been compromised.

Suspicions were cast on the Americans, the Germans and the Israelis, each, in turn, suspecting the others. Only the Iranians did not suspect the others, although officially they claimed they did.

****

The Baron figured that regardless of the 'special assistance' he'd provided the CIA, his involvement in the uranium deal would mean the end of him. He expected to be picked up and taken wherever they'd taken Mahmoud and the others. The tap on the shoulder never came.

"We appreciate you letting us know every step of the way," his CIA contact told him. "Without your help, we would never have busted up that uranium ring."

Regardless, he did not trust the Americans. He remained edgy and anxious to leave the armaments business he'd successfully built.

He'd had to return his million-dollar commission to the Iranians. The good news: If he did not close another deal for the rest of the year, he'd still net over $400,000 after taxes in 2010. The bad news: his expenses exceeded this by $60,000.

Yet he continued to buy art, egged on by a curator friend who told him his purchases now could be sold for considerably more money later.

His accountant, on his own time, made a list of 200 paintings the Baron's had spent $1.5 million euros to acquire. The accountant got three estimates of their auction value and determined that the Baron's collection would currently fetch approximately 750,000 euros.

Then there was his watch collection. He'd spent over 300,000 euros to acquire them. Most now sat in bank safe deposit boxes.

He'd bought bespoke suits, three at a time at an average of 2,000 euros each, and now had over 70. They filled two walk-in closets along with 60 Turnbull & Asher shirts at 200 euros each.

The Baron read his accountant's report with mounting horror. The accountant recommended liquidating all but 50 of the best paintings, all but five of the watches and all but 20 of the suits.

The Baron agreed; but when the accountant found someone who'd pay 850,000 euros for the extra suits, art and watches, the Baron stalled. He couldn't decide what to give up and what to keep.

"I'll make a decision by the end of the year," he told the accountant.

"You should," the accountant said. "That way you can declare a loss on some of what you sell, and you'll have money to pay off debts. You can start 2011 debt free."

This appealed to the Baron. He okayed the sale,

while continuing to sponsor parties for friends and business prospects at restaurants around town, hoping to impress certain women and men.

Then he met an older woman. She was several years past 40 but no one knew exactly how many because she lied about her age and other particulars.

Almost 5'8" with long arms and legs, she had delicate facial features which had undergone one or more plastic surgeries.

She exuded an oddness he liked. Her eyes told you she viewed you skeptically, as if asking who you really were. She wore designer fashion and had exquisite manners, her movements contained but always graceful.

Her level of education was unclear, but she appeared bright enough to handle most conversational topics, although she seldom stated an opinion and generally deferred to men, asking questions, listening with her head titled coquettishly.

She said she was Argentine but the Baron's detectives found no documentation for her in that country.

So, he thought, she was a mystery woman, a pretender hiding her past. Presumably through strategic marriages and divorces, she'd accumulated a lot of money.

Did she know he was an arms dealer? Likely she did. She'd probably done the same due diligence on him he'd done on her.

He'd visited her flat in Venice and her apartment in Antibes. Her tastes in art were not his. She'd chosen or had chosen for her old and established second-raters.

He suspected she bought both the Antibes and Venice places with furniture and art already there.

She'd had good work done on her face and breasts. A little flabby around the middle, he accepted this. Overall, she met his need for physical attractiveness if not youth.

He had not an ounce of fat on him. He believed that any woman or man who consorted with him should hold themselves to the same high standards. She did.

If he joined with her, he could leave his disreputable business and become an art collector and life connoisseur. He might even dally with a man on occasion, nothing serious, just recreational sex.

Everything considered, he could see his way into a new and better life with this woman. Her name was Constanza Berlioz. He could not wait for the new year to begin.

March 4, 2012

Hamburg, Germany

The Baron rehired Hugo to provide personal muscle. Hugo, intensely grateful, went out of his way to do extra tasks for the Baron, no matter how demeaning.

He picked up dry cleaning, performed chauffeur duties, even served drinks at the Baron's parties. He soon made himself indispensable.

Business was not going well. The CIA had abruptly stopped buying weapons from him. He wondered if they had another preferred supplier.

As promised, Caesar Enterprises provided muscle, two Germans the Baron did not like, so he fired them. He asked Hugo to recruit others, but so far Hugo had been unsuccessful.

His relationship with Constanza Berlioz deepened. They enjoyed parties and travel.

In the past six months, he'd sold most of his watches, gutted his art collection and purchased annuities with the 225,000 euros he netted after paying off all his debts.

Constanza heartily approved of his downsizing, which surprised him. He realized that she had plenty of her own money, was not a gold digger and had his best interests at heart.

He spent two weeks with her at her Venice apartment, then returned to Hamburg sensing that they were entering into a relationship that would last.

"Ever wonder just exactly who you are?" he asked her once.

Constanza tilted her head in typical coquettish fashion, and smiled.

"Of course," she said. "Haven't you?"

"Recently, yes," the Baron said, then he added. "I'm thinking of spending more time with you, and if I do that, the business suffers."

"Then maybe we split expenses. Would that help?"

"Are you serious?"

"Sure, why not?"

"It violates my need for control."

Constanza laughed, a high, happy trill he loved.

"I could become your house husband," the Baron said.

"I've got these lovely places," Constanza said, "and no one to share them with. We can have our accountants talk."

"That might be good," the Baron said. "I have a confession."

Constanza's face registered momentary concern, which she quickly erased. "Go ahead," she said.

"I've had you investigated."

"Well, Mr. big Baron, I've had you investigated as well," she said.

"And what did you find?"

"Nothing that I hadn't already suspected."

"What had you suspected?"

"Much that I early intuited, that you're in a business that's somewhat suspect but legal, you pay your taxes, you spend almost everything you earn...which is why I was glad to see you buy those annuities and sell off that lot of your stuff. What did you learn about me?"

"That you've had some very good people erase your previous history."

Constanza smiled but did not look happy with that.

"Which suggests you're hiding something for reasons you know but I'm unlikely ever to learn."

Constanza put her hand on top of his. "Yes, that's right," she said.

"And you know what? The Baron said, smiling.

"No, what?" Constanza said.

"Let's never talk about your and my previous identities again."

"You want to remain mystery people to each other until the end of time?" Constanza said.

"Yes."

"You realize that if we do this, each of us will continually look for clues to these previous identities you mention. It will never end."

"I suspect you're right," the Baron said.

"This is making me randy," Constanza said.

"Me, too," the Baron said.

Seconds later, he'd unzipped his pants, she'd laid back on the couch where they sat and pulled her dress up and they had quiet sex with no build up that lasted, on and off, for almost an hour, neither of them bothering to shed their clothes.

Later that evening, eating salads and drinking cheap wine at a neighborhood bistro, the Baron told Constanza that he loved her and she told him she loved him back.

He returned to Hamburg, and shut down his business, although he kept Hugo on payroll. Lastly, he notified both Chester Field in Langley, Virginia and Caesar Enterprises' René Oppenheim in the Caymans, of his decision.

Los Angeles, California
Wanderlust

For almost five months, Tama Wu traveled. She began in Macau, where she lost $6,000 gambling and decided never to gamble again.

She moved to Thailand, took a boat ride down the River Kwai and headed to Singapore, which she tired of in two days. Too sterile and business oriented, she thought.

A side trip into Malaysia also bored her. She visited Bali and the Borobudur Temple in Java, flying there in a private plane, later, concluding that attracted the wrong kind of attention and she'd not be so ostentatious again. Someone might notice and try to kidnap her.

She headed down to Melbourne, Australia, where she stayed three days. She liked the city's laid-back vibe, the beaches filled even during work days, and abundance of parks, concluding that she preferred European and American cultures because she understood them and felt free within them.

In her native China, she'd long ago become inured to top-down government interference, corruption and the legal system's capriciousness. She knew when to negotiate and when to threaten, but was tired of such constant struggle.

In Sydney, she began to tire of travel as well. She flew to Tokyo, took the bullet train to Kyoto, visited its ancient palaces and then, on impulse, entered the local Daitokuji Monastery.

She stayed a month, talking with almost no one, taking long walls within the grounds, attending 5 a.m. services, eating a vegetarian diet of soups and vegetables, sleeping on straw mats wrapped in a solitary blanket to protect against cold drafts seeping through ancient walls.

She left with renewed purpose. She'd sell Dragon Motors but would not leave commerce.

Her financial advisors told her that she'd net as much as 250 million dollars, once taxes and other expenses were settled.

She'd keep her Shanghai house and sell the opulent one outside town, move to Los Angeles and produce movies. That would be fun.

Southern California's sunny climate appealed to her. She had a Stanford Business degree and money. That would give her entrée. She'd take her time. She'd start a new life as a new person.

Ford and Volkswagen immediately authorized the lawyers to launch their tedious negotiations, remaining in contact through cell phone and the Internet.

She found a house in Hollywood Hills with a killer view of Los Angeles she could rent for $15,000 a month while Dragon Motors remained in play.

In the interim, she hired a recently retired Toyota senior vice president to run the company and handle all but final negotiations for her.

    She called Rebecca to give her the news.

    "You'll have to visit us here in Savannah when you have time," Rebecca said.

    Tama said she would and extended an invitation to visit Los Angeles any time.

    "You'll always have a place to stay here," Tama said.

    The Dragon Motors negotiations dragged. In February, Tama flew from Shanghai to Los Angeles and moved into her new rental.

    She had Citibank's wealth management group, arrange meetings for her with agents and studios.

    Imagine me, a Hollywood producer! She told herself. What a wonderful life I now have!

Krakow, Poland

Found

Rebecca watched Ania's gait, a purposeful, straight-ahead stride that said get out of my way, not a typical way for a young woman to move.

    "There she goes," Rebecca said.

    Both she and Barry sat at an outdoor table in front of the Bonerowski Palace, where they'd been staying the past three days, a portable heater behind them not needed as the weather hovered in the mid 60's.

    They watched her, head held high, full book bag on her back, wearing Levis, blue parka, tennis shoes, and a gray sweat shirt, long blond hair to her shoulders.

    She moved purposefully across the cobble-stoned market square towards a an open gate in the western wall. Her eyes occasionally darted left and right. She'd occasionally stop, pull up a sock and glance behind her.

'She's still wary," Rebecca said.

They knew her routine. She'd catch a bus outside the walls of the old city to her intensive English language course, which began at 9 a.m.

****

Barry and Rebecca had only recently focused on finding Ania. Officially retired, both struggled to fill their days, Barry in particular.

Rebecca had shopping, tennis matches, gym workouts and firing pistols and rifles at a nearby range to occupy her.

Barry went to the rifle range, and played golf or tennis occasionally. He thought about going back for a doctorate but knew they'd have to move to Atlanta for him to do that.

So, while he told himself he waited for the rest of his life to begin, he turned to finding Ania, reading and thinking about the material in the file Chester sent, the majority of it exhaustive interviews with Jürgen Hodel.

From the transcripts, Barry learned that Ania had grown up in a small town somewhere in northeastern Poland, name unknown, the child of semi-literate farmers who'd inherited the land from the wife's father's parents.

Barry tried to imagine how that experience influenced her. Initially, it would have given her a provincial outlook, he thought, but maybe also the desire to escape.

She'd told Jürgen that she'd been accepted to a prestigious Polish university, one where girls from small, impoverished farming towns seldom gained admittance. Jürgen said that she took enormous pride in that accomplishment.

Jürgen commented several times on her facility with languages and her extensive work learning to read, write and speak German.

He mentioned that she'd been auditing art history courses at Hamburg University and had expressed an urgent need to learn English, and planned to do that in the next year.

When asked if he knew about her sex-slave past, Jürgen said that he did; but when confronted with questions about her killing two men at the brothel where she worked, he appeared shocked, denying any knowledge.

Her sex-slave past might make her angry towards men, Barry thought.

The detectives had asked about this. Jürgen said that No, she was a loving companion, entered into sex joyfully and did not have a mean bone in her body.

He said that she remained constantly fearful that thugs from the brothels would try to hunt her down, which happened.

Asked if she had a weapon, Jürgen admitted that she carried one, that he was himself anti-gun but understood her reasons.

He confessed to helping her get fake identification and a German driver's license. Asked where he thought she might flee, he said he didn't know, that she could go anywhere. She learned languages quickly and clearly knew how to survive in foreign environments on her own.

He said he doubted she'd return to Poland. When asked why, he said Ania had called the local police station to learn that her parents never reported her missing.

She believed they needed money and sold her into slavery to get it. Based on this, Barry assumed she would not return to her hometown or contact her parents again. Rebecca remained unconvinced.

"Regardless, I think she's in Poland," Barry said. "Polish is her native language. The country's got almost 40 million people. Easy enough to hide there."

"What if she did try to contact her parents?" Rebecca said.

"We could always bring along an interpreter and ask them," Barry said.

"Would the parents be cooperative?"

"Likely not."

"Agreed," Rebecca said, "The parents have their iniquity to conceal."

"Iniquity?"

"Yes, Smartie. They sold their own daughter into slavery, remember? I think she's gone back to school."

"Okay. Why?"

"Because Chester's report found that she had almost 8,000 euros in a bank account."

"I read that. She's got enough to survive for awhile."

"Plus, she'd likely get a job working in a store or waiting tables," Rebecca said. "She speaks German as well as Polish, and maybe by now a little English. That would make her attractive to tourist businesses."

"That's a hell of a lot of money to save in less than a year."

"Stolen from her victims, probably. Also, she worked awhile for that travel agency."

"Did Jürgen know she had all that money?" Barry said.

"Don't think so."

"So she was concealing it from him because…"

"Because she was planning on leaving him."

"That sounds harsh," Rebecca said.

"I'm just reporting what seems likely. You know what I think?"

"No."

"I think she'd go back to school?"

"Good assumption. She's bright, wants to learn English and has an interest in art history. School can provide that, and she'd be back among her peers."

"Imagine how naïve people her age must seem to her now," Barry said. He laughed.

"True. The next question is, where would she go. The University of Warsaw?"

"Maybe," Barry said. "We can check there; but I did my Google due diligence. Warsaw University is like the University of Michigan or Berkeley, a big, prestigious public university, but not like Jagiellonian University in Krakow. It's a combination of Harvard and Amherst, much more exclusive, heavy into the liberal arts and other deliberately impractical stuff. The previous Pope graduated from there. So did that Polish female poet who won the Nobel Prize. I'll bet that's where Ania got accepted and where she'd go."

"Nice assumptions, Bear."

"Thanks. Want to take a brief vacation in Poland?"

"Sure." She suggested they stop off in Villefranche-sur-mer, where they kept a second house high on a hill overlooking the harbor.

"The new garage is almost done, although there's still concrete to lay. I got pix yesterday from Maurice the contractor, Barry said.

"He didn't send me any."

"I've been the one dealing with him," Barry said. "I'll email them to you."

"Okay. I'll get us a flight and hotels," Rebecca said. "We can start in Warsaw."

"Naw. Let's go straight to Krakow and start here," Barry said. "I hear Warsaw's drab and uninteresting. Plus, Jagiellonian U. is in Krakow. Outside Krakow, we can go water rafting in the mountains bordering Slovakia, and hike. We haven't been anywhere since Hamburg." "Okay," Barry said. "We'll leave early next week."

****

Finding Ania took two days. They gave money to a clerk in Jagiellonian's student center to get a list of all freshmen and their home towns.

They found an Ania Olinska from Tykocin, Poland, parents deceased. The clerk's list included her address, an apartment block down the hill from town center two blocks from the Wisla River.

They headed there the next morning. Either Rebecca or Barry would walk the area while the other watched the apartment building.

They singled out six young people, presumably students identifiable by their book bags and casual dress who rented rooms from pensioners in that one apartment building.

Four were girls, and three of these were real or bottle blonds, but only one was 5'2" and walked with the purposeful gait Rebecca remembered.

Today was decision time. Would they confront her or let her be?

"Chester will pay us to tell him where she is," Barry said. "He thinks she'd make a great agent, that she has the same skills that he identified in us back when we were in Sentari."

"I feel the same way," Rebecca said. "What do you want to do?"

"You really want my opinion?"

"I do."

"I say to hell with Chester. We should let her live out her life and not interfere."

"I knew you'd say that," Rebecca said, pleased.

"No, you didn't."

"Yes, I did."

"We've had a great life," Barry said.

"But I almost died," Rebecca said.

"Yes, there's that."

"And you almost got offed by the Pole back in Montevideo."

"Escaped with an inconvenient bullet in my heel."

"And I rescued you."

"You did."

"So we have an agreement?"

"We do. We let her go."

"Oh, Barry," Rebecca said. "You make me hot. Let's go back up to the room and rut like sows."

"I shall pleasure you as you've never been pleasured before," Barry said. He left a 50 Zloty on the table, hurried through the hotel entrance, they climbed the stairs, two steps at a time, and rushed hurriedly into their room.

Coming in January, 2013.....

Death in LA

A Barry and Rebecca Forester Adventure

By John J. Barnes

Beautiful young Lori Adams moves from Michigan to LA to become an actress, only to find herself six months later raped and left for dead in Malibu. Also in LA, highly sexed Chinese entrepreneur and wannabe movie producer Tama Wu finds herself targeted by a vicious criminal Mexican crime syndicate. The killings begin. Barry and Rebecca fly to LA to help Tama, only to become targets themselves.

Here's a sample chapter from John J. Barnes' upcoming **Death in LA**...

Pasadena, California

10 p.m.

René Openheim, one of three Caesar Enterprises senior vice presidents, sat uncomfortably in a dark restaurant down the street from his corporate apartment.

Across from him, issuing occasional grunts of pleasure, Boris Ling greedily consumed his steak, the sharp sounds of his silverware constantly striking the plate.

René watched with annoyance. He'd come to LA to solicit clients for his new private bank chartered in Bern, Switzerland.

He now enjoyed the company of beautifully educated, successful, convivial men, meeting them in their offices, at the downtown-LA Jonathan and California Clubs, and at their grand estates in nearby San Marino and West Side enclaves Beverley Hills, Holmby Hills, Pacific Palisades, and Malibu.

Representing a legitimate enterprise and dealing with legitimate prospects made René reflect without pleasure on his previous life dealing with low lifes typified by the man who sat across from him now in the near dark of this windowless restaurant.

Boris Ling looked like a low-level wise guy and in no way the titular head of a giant criminal enterprise.

A half-breed Chinese, his Russian mother contributed his light brown hair, eyebrows and thick lips. His father gifted him with a typically small (5'6") lithe, sinewy Asian body and eyes.

Boris lacked his predecessor's Black Tong tattoo. He'd been brought in from Hong Kong to run the Tong and take over from his disgraced predecessor, Raphael Leong.

Leong was ignominiously killed in Montevideo during a botched kidnapping attempt he'd organized.

His bungling made the Black Tong a laughing stock in the worldwide criminal community. Boris Ling's job was to quickly restore the syndicate's once fearsome reputation and expand its influence.

"So what exactly is this new bank you're starting?" Boris asked. He slurped his wine and patted his lips with an already soiled napkin.

In his 40's, he wore a LA Dodgers baseball cap on backwards, his hair sticking out around its edges, and a neatly pressed, short-sleeve shirt that said 'Stanford' on the breast pocket.

The guy is a sports nut. Probably has UCLA tattooed on his ass, René thought.

Despite his small size, Boris' small dark eyes radiated menace. Even his shrugs and the way he shifted his buttocks on his chair suggested he might any moment lunge for your throat.

"We invest for high net worth individuals," René said glibly, "Generally those with assets, liquid or otherwise, exceeding $50 million."

Boris nodded. "Does this mean you won't be

handling my account any longer?" He spoke as if delivering a threat.

"I've been taken off your account, but we haven't decided who'll take over from me," René said. "Do you have anyone in mind you'd like to work with?" '

"You're still handling my problems until the new guy shows up, right?"

"Yes, I suppose so," René said, betraying little enthusiasm.

"I've got a new source south of the border," Boris said. "He needs capital to secure a route into the U.S. I can vouch for him. I told him I'd talk with you."

"You'd co-sign for him?"

Boris thought about that. "We're talking $18 million."

"Can't you handle that internally?"

"Yes," Boris said, "But we prefer not to. We're being watched."

"You want my bank to meet with this subcontractor of yours in Mexico?"

"Yes. You've provided such services before. You're not under surveillance. We'll of course pay you for your trouble, but there shouldn't be any. A lunch at a nice hotel, a drop-off arranged. Your bank has done this more than I have, I'm sure."

Boris' 'being watched' reference made René start to sweat under the arms, a common problem when stressed. He'd changed to a stronger deodorant and it helped but seemed to be failing its mission now.

Of course Boris and his friends were being watched, he thought. They're criminals, and I'm still associating with them and presumed complicit if spotted.

"We can do what you ask," René said. "But we need to do our own due diligence on your Mexican contact, which will take awhile?"

"You stalling me?" Boris said.

"No," René said nervously. "I'm just telling you how we operate. Ask anyone in your organization."

Boris considered that. "Okay. I will. Are you available to meet in two or three days?"

René wanted more than anything never to see Boris again, but he saw that he had no choice.

"Yes, of course, although it could be awkward. I'm spending most of my time on the West side."

"Then perhaps we can meet over there," Boris said.

"Rather keep it here," René said. "I've been coming to Pasadena longer and know the area."

"As you wish," Boris said, clearly suspicious and annoyed. "Something else. I need money moved directly to Mexico. Can you also handle this for us?"

René again felt his underarms moisten. Boris for his own unshared reasons, wanted Caesar Enterprises to start several initiatives for him in Mexico, where the bank did not operate, although Boris likely didn't know this. Would his board go for that?

"Something might be arranged," René said. "Our headquarters people will consider this. It's not up to me.

I'll have to get back with you."

Boris did not receive this well. "I need an answer on this soon, like at our next meeting," Boris said. "Or…"

He did not finish his sentence. René got the point. Either Caesar Enterprises did as asked or Boris was prepared to take his business elsewhere.

"Okay," René said. "Now, as we agreed, I'm going to leave by the back door. I'll let our Cayman Headquarters know what you need and get back."

"I want you personally to handle all of this," Boris said. "I don't want you handing this off to some flunky. Fuck your new private bank. You work for me until I say you don't, understand?"

René felt like screaming, but kept his cool. Boris had recently renamed Black Tong Associates 'West Associates,' believing the WASP name gave him and his syndicate more 'class.'

West Associates annually moved 15 to 20 million dollars into and out of Caesar Enterprises. Lose such a client and the Management Committee might take away my enjoyable new assignment, René thought.

Handling Boris carefully now became a priority. René's chance for a clean and fully legitimate new life with few if any ties to Caesar Enterprises, and no more dealing with criminals like Boris, depended on this.

****

René moved quickly out the restaurant's back door, through a half filled parking lot and into the hot sun.

Further down Lake Avenue, he ducked into a

flower shop, brought a mix of roses and peonies for his apartment, headed over two streets and back to the apartment. He did not appear to be followed.

Caesar Enterprises had purchased a corporate one-bedroom, second-floor place on Green Street near Lake Avenue, not far from where he'd lunched with Boris and close to what most people considered Pasadena's de facto retail business core.

René spent as many as 200 nights a year in hotel rooms all over the world, most not corporate owned. He liked the Pasadena arrangements best. He could park his rental car in his own guaranteed basement spot, walk to restaurants and stores, and be in downtown LA in 20 minutes.

But now that he also sought rich clients on the West Side, he was reconsidering. The Pasadena place was as much as an hour's drive from the majority of his likely new clients.

Meanwhile, Boris scared him. The man was like a leach. He'd suspected he'd keep inventing new assignments to keep René close.

Awful. He also didn't like adding Mexico. He knew no one and wasn't comfortable in Mexico City. Somebody else could handle that country.

René knew that the CIA and FBI were aware of his connection to Caesar Enterprises, but so far, according to 'inside' sources, neither organization had incriminating photographs or other materials linking him with anything unsavory.

He had the chance to escape the money laundering businesses for good. Only Boris prevented this. If he had to kill the man, if it came to that, he would.

As of last week, others had taken over his clients in Miami, Seattle, Hamburg, Germany, Moscow, Russia and Rome, Italy. He could not have been happier.

Governments were developing increasingly more sophisticated and devious ways to identify criminal enterprises and track the money they generated across borders and time zones. He believed he was exiting Caesar Enterprises in time.

René's new bank in Bern, Switzerland, seeded with $300 million in fresh capital, and named Phoenix New Century Enterprises, would start clean but at a disadvantage.

A multitude of established private banks, some hundreds of years old, already existed. So did wealth management divisions of German, French, Swiss and American banks.

Phoenix New Century needed to separate itself from the others without seeming too risky.

René, with his Harvard MBA, extensive experience finding places to pot and grow money, impeccable manners and unflappable personality was the obvious choice to head up Phoenix.

Just turned 48, he'd already developed ties with Citibank executive vice president, Perry Welbin, who'd suggested Tama Wu as a likely interested high-worth individual. She'd be René's next target.

****

An agitated Boris Ling phoned Carl, his Number Two man. "Weird lunch," he said. "The fucker stuck me with the bill. Put a tail on him, okay?"

"Done. We know where he lives. No problem."

"He's starting a new bank. I sense he wants to distance himself from us. We can't have that. Get his likely customers' names. We'll threaten to harm them if he doesn't cooperate."

"Good plan, Boss."

"Thanks."

Nobody disrespects me, Boris thought. I need René close. Once I've got from him what I need, he's dead.

To read more, order 'Death in LA' on Amazon or Kindle, available in March, 2013.

Made in the USA
Las Vegas, NV
23 December 2023